Christmas Candy

By

DARIE McCOY

Frost Family Series Book Three

Edited by: All That's Wright

Cover Art/Design: A.S. McCoy

*For all the Candy's out there. You are **the** Rock Star, Baby!*

I have learned not to worry about love, but to honor its coming with all my heart.

— ALICE WALKER

Prologue

Candy opened the door leading from the garage directly into the kitchen at her Aunt and Uncle's house. The rich aroma of baked beans and grilled meat permeated the area causing her stomach to grumble.

"Hey, Aunt Bee. Hey, McKenna." She called out in greeting as she ushered her oldest nephew in behind her. Hands full at the stove and bar top respectively, her aunt and cousin smiled returning the greeting.

"Auntie, where do you want Kaden to put these drinks?"

"Kaden baby, take those drinks outside to AJ. He knows which coolers still need to be filled." Aunt Bonita tilted her head toward the glass doors leading onto the deck to indicate the direction Kaden should go.

"Yes, ma'am." He replied as he used the edge of the counter to rebalance the two cases of sodas before heading outside.

Meeting him at the door, Candy opened it and waited for him to exit before closing it behind him. Turning back into the kitchen, she pasted a hopeful smile on her face.

"Hey, Auntie. Do y'all need any help? I can do something if you need me to."

Before her aunt even opened her mouth, Candy knew the answer would be 'no'. It was always no. Yet, she asked each and every time.

"Thank you, but I think we've got it. I appreciate the offer though."

"Oh...Ok." It was a no, but not as harsh a no as she expected. Aunt Bonita was getting soft. Either that, or she was in an uber good mood today. Dejected, Candy looked around, contemplated going out to sit by the pool, then decided to park herself on a barstool to watch.

When she'd hitched one hip up to take her seat on the tall chair, McKenna slid a large rectangular container in front of her. Candy's eyes flew up to meet her cousin's amber gaze. McKenna smirked before winking.

"You can't sit in the kitchen and just watch. You have to do something." She smiled at Candy, her eyes twinkling with mischief.

"But Auntie said—"

"Don't worry about Auntie. Come wash your hands, then cut these veggies for the salad." McKenna winked then shooed Candy off the stool.

Happy to be allowed to do anything, Candy hopped from the stool and hurried around the corner of the countertop to the sink on the other side. Internally, she shook her head. It was a damn shame that being entrusted with the small task of cutting vegetables for a salad made her feel like she'd won first place in an intense competition.

In Aunt Bonita's kitchen, small victories mattered. The only other people she normally allowed near her stove were McKenna and Safara. Mostly McKenna. Safara, only occasionally.

Spending extra time at the sink making sure her hands were pristinely clean, Candy watched as McKenna placed a cutting board, knife and the pre-washed selection of vegetables on the countertop where Candy could reach them.

Ignoring the heated stare from her aunt, and the silent conversation between the two women, she dried her hands then went to stand at her new station. Nervous butterflies fluttered in her belly now that she'd actually been given a task after asking for so long. She was well aware of her aunt's belief that she and her sisters couldn't boil water.

The belief was based partially in truth. Candy could cook breakfast foods, and make a hell of a sandwich, but she wasn't good with dinner —especially not on the scale required for a cookout.

Now that she was older, she wished she'd been more insistent on staying to learn when her mom put her out of the kitchen while she was growing up. Sherilyn Hampton didn't like anyone in her kitchen. She normally showed up at the cookout with whatever dish she was assigned and didn't linger in Aunt B's kitchen.

Candy on the other hand, was a glutton for punishment. She showed up with drinks, chips or paper goods, then still asked if she could help on the off chance Aunt B actually said yes.

Tentatively, she picked up the knife and placed a cucumber on the cutting board. She'd cut cucumbers before. This was by far not the first time, but being given a cooking adjacent responsibility at a family gathering made her more than a bit anxious. She hovered over it so long, McKenna bumped her side.

"You're overthinking it. Just slice it."

Biting her lower lip, she looked over at her cousin. "Like this?" She said with uncertainty as she sliced the end off, being careful not to slice it too thickly.

"I don't have to peel it or take out the seeds?" She asked.

"No need. I had Driscoll get the kind that doesn't have big seeds and without bitter skin." McKenna smiled while patting Candy's arm. "Relax. You'll be fine."

"Thank you." Candy whispered.

As if McKenna had talked him up, Driscoll walked in from the deck with an empty metal pan in one hand and a squirming little duplicate of himself tucked under his other arm.

"Driscoll, shouldn't there be meat in that pan?" Aunt Bonita questioned as she took the empty container from him.

"Yes, ma'am. I was trying to do my duty when this one turned into Usain Bolt heading for the pool. I dropped the pan to catch him."

Driscoll made grumbling noises while nuzzling the toddler's belly causing him to erupt in a fit of giggles.

Candy watched the scene with a warm feeling. Aunt Bonita went to the larger sink to wash the pan while McKenna turned to her husband and child. They were so cute; the sweetness was toothache inducing.

"DJ, daddy gets plenty of exercise. You don't have to get his heart rate up like that." McKenna joked as she reached out to take him from Driscoll's arms.

"No." Driscoll said as he turned, moving the child just out of McKenna's reach. The move surprised Candy; so, she stopped slicing and gave them her full attention.

"What do you mean no?" A frown wrinkled McKenna's brow.

"We talked about this. He's too heavy."

Blowing out an exasperated breath, she rolled her eyes. "He's not. He's my baby. I can hold him if I want."

"He's well over thirty pounds and your limit is fifteen."

"First of all, the doctor said up to twenty-five pounds was fine. Secondly, she wasn't talking about me holding my child."

"Fifteen, twenty-five, either way, he's over the limit. So, no picking him up. If you want to hold him, go sit. I'll put him in your lap."

"I'm not a kid. I don't need to sit to hold the baby."

"Love..." Driscoll drew out the word in a warning tone.

"Wait...Are you pregnant?" Candy asked the scowling McKenna. She normally wouldn't put herself in their conversation, but the thought hit her brain seconds before the question flew from her mouth.

"Yes. I am." McKenna turned away from Driscoll pouting. Pointing over her shoulder at her husband, she continued.

"He hears whatever he wants to hear and thinks the orders from the doctor to not engage in tasks that are too strenuous or lifting anything too heavy means I can't even do normal stuff—like pick up my own child when he wants to be held."

Driscoll's expression darkened, then he started to speak but was interrupted by the doorbell. The sound garnered everyone's attention, causing them to look at the door leading to the garage. On the other side of the double-paned glass stood a smiling Kenneth Holmes.

Aunt Bonita beckoned him inside with the wave of a hand and he stepped through the doorway looking like sex on a stick. Quickly averting her eyes, Candy went back to her salad prep duties trying to ignore his lean, but muscular frame encased in a polo shirt and cargo shorts.

Kenneth didn't allow her to completely ignore him though. He walked in greeting everyone by name. Including her.

"Hello, Candace."

"Hello, Kenneth."

She'd almost swear he put extra emphasis on the first part of her name and drew out the second part as some sort of tease. But, when she looked into his face, his expression was placid. Devoid of teasing or mischief of any kind. It was more a look of expectancy, but she had no idea what to do with that, so she dropped her gaze back to the cutting board.

"What do you have there Kenneth? I told you that you didn't have to bring anything." Aunt Bonita asked as she moved around the counter to open the box Kenneth placed on the bar top.

Lifting the lid, she let out a squeal startling Candy, almost making her cut her finger. Warmth wrapped around her hand holding the knife and the chatter in the room faded away.

"Careful."

Kenneth's piercing light grey eyes probed hers until she gave him a nod of acknowledgement. Once she did, he removed his hand then straightened from the counter separating them. Aunt Bonita's voice cut through the fog and Candy tuned back in to the conversation.

"Is this a Sock It To Me cake?"

"Yes, ma'am it is." Kenneth's lips stretched into a blinding smile.

"Thank you, Kenneth. You didn't have to bring anything, but I appreciate it." Aunt Bonita gushed.

Candy watched incredulously. Kenneth was allowed to bring something edible to their family gathering while she was relegated to drinks and paper goods? *On Juneteenth! What in the actual fuck? That's all kinds of wrong.*

Frustration, mixed with a tinge of hurt colored her expression as she observed Aunt Bonita gush over Kenneth before he exited the patio doors with Driscoll holding his wiggling son while Kenneth carried the newly washed metal pan.

Resentment bubbled up and pushed words from Candy's mouth. It's the only thing she could blame for her uncharacteristic outburst.

"Why does he get to bring something and I can't?" She heard the whine in her voice, but couldn't control it. Her feelings were hurt. He wasn't even family.

"Do you really want me to answer that?" Aunt Bonita asked with a quirk of her eyebrow.

"Mama, stop it." McKenna grabbed the box and tipped it forward for Candy to see the bakery sticker affixed to the top.

"He bought this cake, girl." She said tapping the logo.

"Oh."

Chagrined, Candy dipped her head then grabbed the hard-boiled eggs McKenna had already peeled. She spent the next few minutes trying to figure out the dicer she was given to make cutting the eggs easier.

Once she finished the eggs, McKenna took over the task of putting the salad together. By that time, other family members had arrived. So, Candy went outside to sit by the pool and watch the kids splash around.

Try as she might, she couldn't stop her eyes from wandering to Kenneth standing under the deck with AJ, Driscoll, and Uncle Drew. He seemed at ease in the group, engaging in the conversation while laughing along at whatever they discussed.

She visually inspected him from the top of his perfectly coiffed blond hair to the tips of the boater shoes covering his feet. She absolutely didn't look at the size of his feet. Nor did she note how long his fingers were as they wrapped around the drink in his hand. She for sure didn't study the area between his hips trying to figure out if everything was to scale.

Splashing and giggles pulled her out of her trance. She looked away from Kenneth with his male perfection. Seconds later, her gaze was drawn back only to find his eyes waiting for hers. Lifting the dark brown bottle, he tipped it in her direction, winked and pulled his sunglasses from the top of his head. Placing them over his eyes, he gave her a knowing smirk before re-engaging in his conversation with the other men.

Mortified that she'd been caught ogling him, Candy stood moving to a seat without a clear view of the shaded area under the deck. She didn't want to give Kenneth the wrong idea. She wasn't in to him or anything. She just enjoyed looking at a nice piece of man candy. He was the only non-relative present; so, of course he was an easy target.

Her bestie/cousin Kari dropped into the seat next to her garnering her attention and giving her the perfect distraction. Grateful for the diversion, Candy fell into their normal banter, catching up even though they talked daily. She was able to completely block Kenneth's presence from her mind. Almost.

Chapter One

IS THIS PIE?

Kenneth swiped his badge and walked into the air-conditioned office space. It was barely eight a.m.; yet, it was already ninety degrees outside. Nodding to his co-workers already seated at their cubical desks as he walked through, he made his way to his office to the left side of Driscoll's.

One of the perks of sharing the number two position in the unit was not having to contend with office noise when he needed to concentrate. Opening the door, he placed his leather case down and dug into his thermal cooler to pull out the clear plastic containers.

Setting the containers on the table beside his coffee machine, he rounded his desk then lifted the lid of his laptop. Before he could get logged into the system, Scott poked his head in the open doorway.

"Is this pie?" His eyes gleamed as he stepped inside picking up one of the containers.

"Yes. Have a slice." Kenneth said drily.

Scott hadn't waited for an offer. He'd already popped the container open and grabbed a plastic fork from the caddy on the same table which housed the coffee maker.

"Thanks. Don't mind if I do." Scott grinned before shoving a huge bite into his mouth.

"Mmmm. So good." He shut his eyes savoring the flavor of the treat. Closing the lid and placing the dessert back on the table, he lied to himself about saving the rest for later. Kenneth was certain he was lying because Scott had a horrible sweet tooth. Anytime anything sweet crossed the threshold of the office, Scott sniffed it out in seconds. Granted, he didn't eat just anyone's food. He'd still investigate to see if it was safe to indulge.

Kenneth could relate to his friend's reluctance to participate in pot lucks and the like. Being raised by an uncle who was a chef, he'd had kitchen cleanliness drilled into his head from a young age. Everyone didn't subscribe to that level of care, so he didn't blame Scott for being cautious.

Dropping into one of the chairs in front of Kenneth's desk, Scott started their usual morning routine. Depending on which of them arrived first, they would go to the other's office to discuss plans for the day and any new assignments they needed to review with Driscoll.

Once they'd finished going over the schedules and assignments, they moved on to personal conversation.

"What did you get up to this weekend?" Scott asked as he reached for his pie. The pieces were generously cut, so there was still plenty left in the container.

"Not a whole lot. Uncle Ray came to town for a visit. So, I hung out with him."

"Oh yeah? If he'd come last week, y'all could've celebrated the holiday together." Scott made the comment with a sly smile on his face as if the thought of two Caucasian men celebrating a holiday centered around the freedom of African Americans was comical.

"You forget who my Uncle Ray is, man. We were celebrating June-teenth in the park long before it was a national holiday. I'm from Brooklyn. It's a cultural melting pot. Uncle Ray and I participated in just about everything—especially if it involved food."

"Yeah... Aight. Your uncle is cool people. So, I give you that. You could have taken him with you to Driscoll's in-laws. He could have charmed the aunties."

Chuckling, Kenneth shook his head. "He'd charm the aunties

alright. He'd go through their social media letting them know which of their friends' significant others would swing his way."

Kenneth and Scott were laughing at the imagined antics of his favorite uncle when Driscoll walked past his glass wall. Lifting his free hand, Driscoll waved, but kept walking. A few moments later, he came back to lean against the doorframe.

"What has the two of you in here cackling like two hens?" He asked before taking a sip from his thermal mug.

"Your boy was just telling me how Uncle Ray would have no problem hipping your wife's aunties to which of their friends' husbands would swing his way."

Frowning over the top of his cup, Driscoll pierced Kenneth with a stern look.

"Never. Ever. Let your uncle get together with my mother-in-law and her sisters-in-law. They're enough on their own. They'd have him into things he's never heard of, trust me. You don't want that."

"Don't talk about Miss Bonita, Miss Sherilyn and Miss Tami like that. They're sweet ladies." Kenneth said with a grin.

Driscoll scoffed. "Yeah. That's what they want you to think. Those three are hell on wheels when they get together. And don't let Mama Bee's sisters come into town."

He puffed his cheeks mimicking the sound of an explosion. "Like. Big."

Laughing at Driscoll's exaggerated expression, the three moved on to discuss work topics. Scott and Kenneth reviewed the information they'd already discussed to get his final approval before they each branched off to officially start their day.

Kenneth continued with his day as usual until he received a text from Carolyn, the Director of Operations at *Gentle Hands*. He volunteered there a few times a month and went over on an *as needed* basis in emergency situations.

She texted to confirm his visit later to help them finish the update to their security system. Even as a trusted volunteer, he couldn't simply drop into the facility unannounced. It was a shelter for battered and abused spouses and domestic partners which accepted all genders. The inclusivity of the facility was one of the primary reasons he chose to volunteer there.

The other reason he felt compelled to volunteer was his experience growing up with his Uncle Ray. Against the wishes of a few of his family members, his parents had chosen Uncle Ray as his guardian in the event of their deaths. They didn't expect that they would be taken so young nor at the same time, but as law enforcement, they planned for the eventuality.

Kenneth sat back in the chair at his desk as the memories washed over him of being a ten-year-old boy who'd just lost his parents. His uncle was in his mid-twenties and living with his partner as well as working for him at his restaurant.

Turning his chair toward the window, Kenneth allowed himself to be transported to the past.

Kenneth startled awake at the hand on his shoulder shaking him from his slumber. Eyes wide, he peered into the shadowy face of his Uncle Ray hovering over his twin bed.

"Come on, KG. Time to get dressed. We have to go."

Uncle Ray whispered to Kenneth. Shushing his complaints about being awakened at such a late hour, he rushed Kenneth through the process of slipping pants and a sweater on over his pajamas then bundling him up.

In minutes, they descended the seldom used back stairs of their building with heavily stuffed backpacks strapped to their backs and two duffle bags filled to capacity. After his initial confusion, Kenneth silently followed his uncle's instructions.

His heart raced anxiously wondering if they would make it out of the building before Horatio returned. Uncle Ray told him Horatio received a call. He went to check on a problem at the restaurant. The restaurant closed at ten p.m.; so, Kenneth's young mind couldn't fathom what reason would warrant a phone call and require him to leave at such a late hour.

Stepping out of the building, a brisk wind whipped through Kenneth's already disheveled blond hair, briefly blowing it into his face. He didn't complain. Especially not once they stepped under the illumination of the streetlight and he saw the swelling around his uncle's left eye along with the red marks beneath his chin.

This wasn't the first time his uncle's face and body showed the evidence of Horatio's anger. When he'd first come to live with them almost a year ago, Horatio had been kind and welcoming to Kenneth. It wasn't until a few months had passed that Kenneth started to see glimpses of the real man.

Horatio never went so far as to lash out at Kenneth, but he'd seen him do things to Uncle Ray which made Kenneth wish he was bigger and stronger to stop the older man. When Horatio went into his rages, Kenneth was usually sent to his room—no matter what time of day it was.

"This way."

His uncle nudged him to the right, in the direction of the subway and away from the parking garage where Horatio kept his coveted Mercedes 500E. He barely let either of them ride in the vehicle he ordered special from the dealership so he could have it as soon as it became available.

Kenneth hated that shiny black car. Almost as much as he hated Horatio. The older man used the car as a status symbol to lord over them the kind of life he provided for them to enjoy. Except Kenneth couldn't tell where he was doing more than allowing them to live in his Manhattan apartment which sat right on the edge of the higher-end condos.

"Where are we going, Uncle Ray?"

He didn't want to be a bother, but his young brain wouldn't stop firing off questions to which he had no answers himself. Still somewhat groggy from sleep, he really wanted to crawl back into his warm bed.

"We're going to visit Aunt Chrissy for a few days."

His uncle hustled him through the turnstile sticking coins in the slot. Knowing his destination quieted at least one of the questions in Kenneth's mind. Aunt Chrissy had two kids around Kenneth's age, but she had a large apartment in the Bronx with an extra bedroom.

Even though he wanted to, Kenneth didn't ask his uncle why they were leaving in the dead of night. He only hoped they never had to come back to live with Horatio. They'd left one time before and stayed with one of Uncle Ray's friends, but Horatio was there early the next morning to pick them up. Uncle Ray never talked about his friend after that.

Arriving at Aunt Chrissy's an hour later, Kenneth drowned out the sounds of his uncle and aunt's conversation as he trudged to the spare room, stripped off the top layer of his clothing, and slipped beneath the heavy quilt on the guest room bed.

Sleep took him quickly; he didn't wake until mid-morning. Opening his eyes, he surveyed the room. The teal-colored walls with the floral border reminded him of his location. The smell of food triggered rumbling in his belly and he hopped out of bed in anticipation. Quickly washing up in the hall bathroom, he put on his jeans and sweater then wandered into the living room just in time to hear his aunt and uncle in a heated discussion in the eat-in kitchen.

"No, Chrissy! Absolutely not! Will and Linda wanted him with me. I'm not leaving him here." Uncle Ray said in a harsh whisper.

"Why not, Ray? It's not like you can take care of him right now. Look at you. You have a black eye, with bruises all over your body. You showed up on my doorstep with nothing but a couple of backpacks and duffle bags to your name. How can you take care of him like this?"

"I'll figure it out. I won't abandon him."

"Ray...Be reasonable. The boy would be better off here with me and Bradley. We could put him in the same school the boys go to; he would have built-in friends in his cousins."

"I said no, Chrissy. I'm done talking about it."

"Well, I'm not done. I don't know what William and Linda were thinking when they designated you as guardian. You're too young for this type of responsibility. You're barely twenty-five. Besides, living the lifestyle you live isn't good for an impressionable child."

"Excuse me?"

"You heard what I said. I look over a lot because you're my baby brother, but I can't sit back and watch you ruin this child's life. I'll take you to court if I have to. I've already discussed it with Bradley."

"I knew I shouldn't have come here."

Kenneth heard scrapping noises, then his rounded the corner to see him frozen in the middle of the living room, his eyes wide with fear. Unable to control it, Kenneth's lower lip began to tremble. His Uncle Ray to gathered him into his arms, hugging him tightly. The embrace broke the dam of Kenneth's emotions and tears streamed down his face.

"Shhh...It's okay. No one is going to take you from me. We're going to be ok. I promise."

"You shouldn't lie to the boy." His aunt's biting comment caused Kenneth to grab onto his uncle's shirt, sobbing even harder.

The past year had been rough for him. Losing both parents at once to gun violence, then he was thrust into an entirely new environment. Just when he'd begun to adjust, the real Horatio appeared bringing chaos and anxiety that he'd never had to deal with before.

Now, his aunt wanted to tear him away from the only constant in his life. Even before his parent's death, his Uncle Ray was a big part of Kenneth's life. He saw him at least twice a month. He'd only seen his Aunt Chrissy around the holidays. The instant friends she'd mentioned were two bullies who happened to be related to him.

To the background of his aunt's protests and threats, his uncle gathered Kenneth and their belongings. They left the apartment in search of other shelter. Unaware of his uncle's inner turmoil, Kenneth happily left his aunt's home without eating so much as one bite of the food she'd prepared.

Knocking against the metal doorframe pulled Kenneth from his memories. Rotating toward the door, he discovered Scott leaning into his office once again.

"Hey. It's almost time to knock off. Wanna grab dinner and a drink?" Scott asked with a hopeful expression.

Shaking his head, Kenneth went about locking his workstation and stuffing his leather messenger bag. "Can't today. Gotta go to the shelter. I told them I'd help with the security upgrade."

"Ah. Ok."

"Aren't you going to be tied up with your coaching duties?" Scott normally practiced with his junior football players on Mondays; so, Kenneth was surprised he offered.

"Nah. I don't do summer league. My league doesn't start up again until August. I have a few weeks before I have to shape young athletes."

"Oh. Ok. Well, if I hadn't already promised to go by the *Gentle Hands*, I'd definitely take you up on the offer."

"No worries man. I'll see you tomorrow." Scott waved and walked away, nodding to their co-workers on his way out.

Kenneth was happy for the interruption. Exiting the building, he got into his car, pressed the ignition button then pointed the vehicle in the direction of the shelter, with thoughts of he and his uncle's situation all those years ago still on his mind. Had Scott not pulled him away, one could only guess how long he would've been trapped inside his remembrances.

The following four to six months after they left Horatio's condo had been difficult to say the least. Word had spread in the restaurant community and his Uncle Ray was ostracized. He couldn't even find a job as a line cook, despite being a graduate of the prestigious Culinary Academy of New York.

His money soon ran out, so they had to leave their hotel, but finding a shelter to take the two of them was nearly impossible. His uncle didn't want to risk someone calling children's services, so he tried domestic abuse shelters all over, but none accepted men. Let alone men with children. By a stroke of luck, his Uncle Ray reconnected with a classmate from culinary school. Someone he knew before he got involved with Horatio.

Miss Toni had been a literal life saver. She had a tiny apartment in Brooklyn, but she welcomed them with open arms and even helped his uncle find a job away from Horatio's toxic reach. It took another six months for his uncle to get promoted earning a salary which would allow them to move out of Miss Toni's apartment into a home of their own.

Neither he nor his uncle ever forgot Miss Toni's kindness. She and Uncle Ray were now the best of friends. Kenneth considered her his aunt. Despite her having a family with children of her own, he regularly touched base to make sure everything was okay in her world. Just as he would his biological aunt—if he still spoke to her.

Not many people knew about that part of his life. It wasn't because he was ashamed, but he'd realized everyone couldn't be trusted to know everything. He learned that lesson the hard way.

Reaching his destination, he pressed the trunk release and exited the vehicle. He closed the hatch, after he gathered what he needed, then walked up the sidewalk leading to the non-descript building with mirrored glass obscuring the inside from view. Standing on the mat, he didn't need to request entry.

Since they expected him, Miss Carolyn had obviously had someone on the lookout. There was a buzzing noise, then the door unlocked allowing him entry. He'd have to talk to them about automatically opening the door for people. Including him. Security should verify the person was who they said they were and they hadn't been compromised.

He entered the building making a beeline to Miss Carolyn's office. After he mentioned the lapse in security protocol they discussed what remained of the system upgrade. Once again, he assured her the people coming in had been thoroughly vetted. As they completed their conversation, the crew in question arrived and he focused his mind on the task at hand.

Chapter Two

DEAR GOD NO

"I'm just saying, they act like I'm completely without skill in the kitchen. I got so freaking nervous, I forgot how to do simple shit." Candy complained to Kari as she entered the tiny mudroom and took off her shoes.

"I don't know why you let Auntie get to you. I know I can cook. She knows I can cook, but I don't say boo about her not asking me to bring anything for the cookout. I like being able to show up, eat and go home."

"You said the operative words. Both of you know you *can* cook, so you see it as less work for you that she never asks. Whenever you do decide to show up with something, it doesn't mysteriously disappear like the time Natalie showed up with an unrequested side dish."

Once she mentioned it, even she had to chuckle at their aunt's antics that day. Kari's giggles weren't far behind as they both remembered the look on their aunt's face when Natalie came to the gathering with stuff she claimed was broccoli casserole.

Even Candy admitted the concoction didn't look appetizing. But the frozen grin on Aunt Bee's face as she accepted the container was a disturbing mix of horror poorly camouflaged by a smile. In her defense,

Aunt Bee really did try to be nice about it. She deflected quite craftily every time Natalie asked what happened to it.

First, she said it must have been in the fridge. The next time Natalie asked, she replied that she could have sworn it was out on the table. Still her cousin wouldn't let up. So, Aunt Bee pointed to an empty container and said it looked like it was all gone. Finally, she got tired of Natalie asking and told her nobody wanted to eat the mayonnaise filled jumble of indeterminate vegetables.

Giggling to the point of cackling, Kari laughed harder than Candy at the shared memory. "Why couldn't she just let it go? Oh Lawd! I won't ever forget that. Aunt Bee is a whole mess, but she was right about Natalie's salad, casserole, whatever it was. It looked nasty. Natalie knew better. But you know her lil feelings were hurt so Uncle Drew made Auntie apologize even though she was one hundred percent correct."

"I'm with you when you're right." Candy's amusement tapered off as she walked into her small kitchen looking around trying to decide what she wanted for dinner.

Wishing she'd stopped to pick up take out, she washed her hands, then went to the fridge and started pulling out deli meats and cheeses to make a sandwich. Once she decided which meat she wanted to use, she reached into the breadbox taking out a small rounded loaf of challah covered in black and white sesame seeds.

"I hear banging around. What are you doing?" Kari asked.

"Making a sandwich."

"Ooo... I love your sandwiches! What kind?"

"Nothing fancy, just hot pastrami on Challah bread with pickled onions and Swiss cheese." Putting away the items she didn't plan to use, she pulled out two types of sandwich spread.

"See...This is what I'm saying. It's not that you lack skill in the kitchen. You just don't use your skills to make the kinds of things people are used to at large gatherings."

"Girl, it's a sandwich. Don't get me wrong. I make delicious sandwiches, but it's hard to mess it up."

"The hell you preach. I've had plenty of sandwiches that I regret wasting calories on. Your version of a sandwich has my mouth watering just thinking about having a bite. I'd willingly run suicides to burn off however many calories are in those things."

Blushing at the compliment, Candy ducked her head even though Kari couldn't see her. She was comfortable issuing praise, but not great at receiving it. Re-focusing on her dinner, she kept her hands busy slicing the bread and prepping the meat.

"While I appreciate the compliment, no matter how bomb my sandwiches are, making a sandwich isn't real cooking."

"Lies."

"It's true."

"Ok. Fine, if that's what you believe, and you're tired of feeling like you're at a disadvantage in the cooking department, carve out some time to learn. That's what I'm doing."

"Since when? And why do you need lessons?"

"A few months now. I wanted to cook traditional Japanese meals, but I couldn't get the hang of it from videos on the internet. So, I asked Daisuke's mom; she's been teaching me some of her families' recipes.

It's actually brought us closer together. I mean, she's always been friendly, but I think me actively trying to preserve part of their culture makes her happy. It's a win-win. You should try it."

"With who? You don't have time to come to my house showing me things I should already know. I wouldn't want to infringe on you and Daisuke's time by coming to your place too often. Same goes for McKenna.

Not Aunt Bee, because... reasons. And as much as I love my mama, she's not very patient with other people in her kitchen. Besides, I don't want to hear her mouth about waiting until I'm damn near forty to learn to cook."

"First of all, thirty-four isn't forty. Second, you don't have to deal with your mama; there are other options. You could take a class at the culinary academy."

"I have no desire to be a chef, Queenie."

"For your information, they offer adult cooking classes as part of a community outreach program. There's a fee, but it's not a lot."

"How do you know?"

"Google is free. I looked it up just now while you were ranting about your lack of options to learn."

Candy's phone buzzed on the counter and she wiped her hands before swiping the screen to look at the message.

"I just sent you the link. Why don't you look at the times they offer the class and see what works with your schedule? Since you mostly work for yourself, I'm sure you can manage to carve out at least a couple of nights a week.

It looks like they have three class levels, each lasting for eight weeks. If you like the first one, then you can pick up the others."

Biting her lip in thought, Candy scrolled through the options. "I don't know, Queenie. I'll look into it though."

"I can't ask for anything more."

After a few more minutes of general conversation, they ended the call. By that time, Candy's dinner was ready to place in the toaster oven for the final step. Turning the dial, she slid the halved, open-faced pieces onto the rack and closed the door.

While she waited for the cheese to melt, she picked up her phone. She perused the course offerings with more intent than she did when Kari first made the suggestion. Maybe it wasn't such a bad idea. They offered more than the one-night events she'd heard about in the past. Not much could be learned in one night unless a person already had a good foundation.

Candy sat in her vehicle gripping the steering wheel trying to decide whether to go inside or go home and consider the fee she paid as a donation to the school. It wasn't fear of the unknown which had her butt glued to the seat with her fingers locked in place around the steering wheel. It was the uncertainty.

She was confident in her skills as a make-up artist, because she knew she wasn't just kick-ass at beating faces, she could also make monsters look so realistic digital effects weren't needed. The steps she went through to learn her craft weren't easy, but the skills came to her naturally.

This...This she wasn't sure was an innate skill she possessed. Truthfully, cooking on the scale some people in her family did it hadn't interested her very much. But, if you put her in a deli, she could rattle off which meats were the saltiest, which broke down best in heat and which ones should only be served hot. That's why sandwiches were her jam.

Her phone dinged. She took one hand off the steering wheel to slide a finger across the screen to read the message.

Kari: Get out of the car and go inside.

Candy: What makes you think I'm still in the car?

Kari: Are you saying you aren't still sitting in your car staring at the building?

Candy gritted her teeth in frustration. This is what she gets for telling Kari she'd signed up for the level one class offered on Tuesdays and Thursdays at seven p.m. Looking at the time on her phone, she saw that she had ten minutes to make it across the parking lot, into the facility and find the right classroom.

Candy: Ugh! Fine! I'm going.

Kari: Great! Call me after.

Candy: Mhmm

Slipping the device into her purse, she zipped the pocket, draped the strap across her chest and exited the vehicle. Even though the sun still shone brightly, she'd planned for darkness at the end of the class by parking under a light not too far from the entrance.

Nodding to the few people coming and going along the same walkway, she made her way through the doors. After a brief discussion with the security guard at the front desk, she was on her way to her first session.

Her senses were assailed by the smells emanating from the classrooms, making her mouth water as she traversed the corridor. It probably wasn't the best idea for her to work through lunch, but it was the only way to guarantee she'd be done with her client in time to make it out of the city to get to class without being late.

Checking the numbers on the placards outside each room, she finally reached the correct one. The slight buzz of conversation drifted through the open doorway. Stepping inside, her gaze roamed over the classroom set up. As this was her first time in such a setting, she was surprised to see the stations were arranged in a semi-circle with the largest station—presumably for the instructor—placed at the top center of the arrangement.

The way the ten cooking areas were set up gave each student an unobstructed view of the instructor and the other students. There'd be no complaints from anyone about someone taller preventing them from seeing everything that happened anywhere in the room. Six of the ten stations were already taken.

So, Candy walked to the first available station farthest from the door. She didn't want the distraction of seeing or hearing what happened in the hallway any time someone wandered by. At least, that's what she thought.

Just as she placed her purse into an open cubby at her station and stood up, a figure appeared in the open doorway. *Well...Fuck..* It was Kenneth. As in Kenneth Holmes, her new cousin's co-worker. What was he doing here? He had a messenger bag slung over his shoulder making her wonder if he was a student or simply in the wrong place.

Scanning the room with those captivating grey eyes of his, he stopped when he reached her shocked face. One side of his lips tipped upwards in a crooked half-grin and he gave her a quick nod before stepping fully into the room then walking directly to the larger cook top in the center of the semi-circle.

Dear God no. Candy prayed internally that she wasn't really seeing what she was seeing. She wasn't ashamed of trying to learn new skills, but she also wasn't broadcasting the information. Now, she stood behind a countertop looking at the man who made her insides perform acrobatics and who was close enough to her family to receive cookout invitations.

"Good evening, class." Kenneth's deep voice flowed like honey from, what she considered, his entirely too perfect face.

"My name is Kenneth Holmes. This is Introduction to Cooking – Level I. I'll be your instructor for the next eight weeks, during which time we'll cover topics from spices to flavor combinations, ending with each of you preparing a basic meal from start to finish. How does that sound?"

Blinding everyone with his bright, toothy smile, he walked to the front of the instructor's post and leaned back against the counter.

"Before we get started, let's go around the room to allow me to put names to the faces on the roster. How about we start over here?" He asked pointing to the forty-ish looking man with the salt and pepper beard closest to the door.

Starting on the other side of the room, meant Candy would be last. She gripped the edge of the counter, mentally preparing herself for what she hoped was a very brief moment in the spotlight. The guy with the beard was Clive. Next to him was a blonde with a pixie cut named Kelsey.

By the time Wynter, Penny, Rachel and Jack introduced themselves, her palms had begun to sweat. It wasn't fear, it was proximity. Something about Kenneth made her nervous. That's why the few times she'd been in his presence she'd made sure to put distance between them. Unfortunately, unless she ditched the rest of the sessions, she'd see him up close and personal for the next eight weeks.

"And last, but not least..." Kenneth smirked as he prompted Candy to tell everyone her name.

"Hello everyone. My name is Candace Hampton."

Avoiding Kenneth's probing stare, she made brief eye contact with her potential classmates. Potential, because the verdict was still out on whether she'd come back for the remaining classes.

"Thank you all for indulging me in that little exercise. If I can press my luck a bit more, I need to get an idea of everyone's comfort level in the kitchen environment."

Reaching into the leather bag, he pulled out a short stack of papers and a handful of ink pens. Starting with Clive, he gave each person a piece of paper then a pen.

"Don't worry. This isn't a test. It's a short survey. It'll help me to understand how much or little help each of you will need in the coming weeks to assist you in meeting your goal. There are no right or wrong answers. So, please be as honest as possible."

By the time he'd finished his explanation, he stood in front of Candace. When she reached for the paper, he held onto it for the slightest bit longer than required before releasing it and offering her a pen.

The ensuing tug-of-war with the pen almost made her reach into her purse for her own. Letting go under the heat of her glare, Kenneth smirked again before strolling back to the instructor's area.

"The survey is relatively short; so, it shouldn't take long to fill it out. I'll give you five minutes, starting now."

Tapping the face of his watch, Candy figured he started a timer when she heard the beeping noise. Affixing her eyes to the page in front of her, she read the questions and checked the appropriate boxes answering honestly as requested. Even if she wasn't sure she'd be back, it didn't cross her mind to pencil whip the form to hurry through the process.

Three sharp beeps broke the silence, indicating the end of the five minutes.

"Okay. Time. Everyone, please pass your papers to the left. Feel free to keep the pens."

Once all of the surveys were placed in front of Candy, Kenneth strode over. Actually, it was more of a prowl. Not that she was looking very closely. Stacking them neatly, she slid the papers to the edge of the counter and pulled her hands back before he stopped in front of her.

"Thank you, Miss Hampton. I appreciate it."

His words weren't out of line. Neither was his tone, but something about his eyes made her catch her breath and look away. He really, really, needed to take his fine ass back to the other side of the island doubling as the teacher's desk.

Chuckling, he picked up the papers granting Candy her wish. He went back to his work area, clipped the sheets together then dropped them next to his messenger bag.

"Ok. Next we'll have a tour of the kitchen which will become your second home for the next eight weeks. While I don't expect you to learn everything there is to know during such a short timeframe, be warned...I will challenge and push to pull out the very best in each and every one of you."

A shiver raced down Candy's spine at the emphasis he placed on the handful of words at the end. Against her will, her mind dropped into the various ways that statement could be taken. She didn't dare look at him, but she felt the heat of his gaze as she stared blankly at the empty marble surface in front of her.

Moving behind his work station, he instructed each of them to pull open the corresponding drawers and cabinets in their areas while explaining the importance of putting things back in their proper place in the kitchen.

"I've discovered that a large part of the nervousness people feel related to cooking stems from them not being comfortable in the space. It comes from not orienting their tools in a way that is logical for how they will be used and in places those tools will be needed."

He made his statement while pointing out why the cutting and chopping knives were located near the cutting board which was strategically placed between the sink and the cooktop. He moved on from the utensils and cookware to the refrigerators lining the back of the room to store the perishable food items that the school supplied for each class.

The only exception to what the school supplied would be in regards to the class where they'd select their own meal and bring the necessary materials.

He ended the visual tour by walking to a door flanked by a refrigerator on either side. Motioning for them to follow him, he led them into a vast pantry area. Every available piece of wall space was utilized for shelving with the things inside divided into logical sections depending on the item and its potential use.

Once he was done explaining the contents of the space, they filed back into the classroom returning to their workstations. He spent the remainder of their allotted time performing a demonstration at his work area while firing questions at the group getting them to participate in the process so they weren't simply watching as he cooked what he called a simple meal of alfredo pasta with grilled chicken.

At the close of the class, Candy grabbed her purse and hightailed it out of the classroom quickly leaving the building. Once she was in her car, she considered texting Kari, but decided against it. Starting the vehicle, she pulled away from the parking space with her mind made up.

She couldn't come back. Nope. That man was dangerous enough to look at without adding in how utterly sexy it was to listen to him discuss food as if it were the key to life. She'd figure out later what to tell her bestie. Maybe she could switch to another section. For the sake of her sanity and starving libido, she needed a plan.

Chapter Three

THESE ARE NOT SPICES

Striding down the corridor the following Thursday, Kenneth approached the classroom for the Level I Adult cooking class. Most people had no clue about this part of his life. Those closest to him knew of his degree in the Culinary Arts, but even they weren't aware he'd taken up teaching at the Logan City Culinary Academy.

That's why when he saw Candace's name on the roster, he knew she was in for a shock. He wondered if she would come back for the second class. He hoped she did. They'd met enough times to be acquainted, but she always appeared a bit skittish around him.

He'd contemplated asking her out, but thought maybe she wasn't into him the same way. Their interaction at the cookout caused him to revise his line of thinking. When she almost cut herself and he touched her hand, he felt the way her pulse quickened. He saw the flush creep into her cheeks beneath her golden-brown skin.

Then, he caught her staring at him while she sat beside the pool. Yeah… Candace Hampton, at a minimum, found him attractive. Having her show up in his classroom was like Christmas came six months early. It took everything in him not to show all thirty-two of his teeth when he crossed the threshold and saw her perched primly on the stool at her workstation.

Even with the counter and range top blocking his view of her lower half, his eyes greedily scanned the parts of her luscious frame he could see. The memory of her curvaceous body outfitted in a simple crimson red polo with black slacks made him groan. The monogram initials CH overlaid with a two brushes sat just above her left breast, drawing his eyes to the rounded globes.

Despite the raging of his hormones, he remained professional during their first class. Mostly... He couldn't resist testing the limits just a little. He didn't go too far, at least he didn't think he had. However, the way she sped out of the classroom at the end of the night was the reason he considered that she may not come back.

For her sake, he hoped she got up her nerve and came back. It would be a bad look for him to run her name to get her info then track her down. There may or may not be rules and regulations saying he wasn't allowed to do such things, but he would if she tried to bolt.

On the outside looking in, it would seem he was taking things too far. But, he didn't think so. Atlanta and the surrounding area had a plethora of beautiful women, but it had been a while since he was drawn to anyone the way he was to Candace. Sure, he'd had some thought-provoking conversations, but the intellectual stimulation hadn't carried over physically.

Something told him, it wouldn't be that way with her. She had a brain behind her beautiful face and gorgeous body. She hid it behind her skill with make-up brushes and color palettes, but it was there. Brains, beauty and a banging body. Possibly dangerous, but he didn't care.

Stepping into the empty classroom, he quickly unloaded his ever-present messenger bag then began setting up his station for the night's lesson. His review of the surveys informed him everyone had at least turned on the stove before. Their issues primarily dealt with lack of success with anything which wasn't pre-packaged with clear instructions.

They all expressed low confidence in their ability to cook anything from base ingredients alone. That was a decent starting point. It allowed him to shape this first lesson to actually get them learning. They only had eight weeks, so they needed to jump right in.

As the students started trickling into the classroom taking up the same work areas they'd claimed the previous class, he greeted them then swung his gaze back to the open doorway. Each time someone entered and it wasn't Candace, he got more and more irritated.

Was she really going to not come back simply because he was the instructor? Her name was still on his roster, so she hadn't changed to a different class. He'd checked with the office to be certain. It had only been a couple of days. Sometimes the school administrators were a little slow updating schedule changes.

From his spot at the center of the semi-circle, he leaned back against the countertop and made small talk with his students. He never allowed the school to put more than ten people in his classes to ensure he'd be able to give each student individual attention.

Kenneth wasn't one to waste people's time, so when the clock rolled to seven p.m. without Candace gracing the doorway, he clenched his jaw, swallowed his disappointment and clapped his hands to get everyone's attention.

"Ok, everyone. Let's get started."

Reaching out a hand, he picked up two clear shakers and held them in front of himself. He was just about to ask for a volunteer to describe the contents of the shakers when the patter of footsteps coming to an abrupt halt drew his attention to the open doorway. His eyes raked over a flushed Candace as she attempted to slip quietly into the room.

"Pardon me. I apologize." She pushed out in a barely audible huff as she walked around the back of the room to reach her station.

Watching her intently, he waited until she'd reached the work area, stowed her purse and perched on the stool.

"Now that everyone's here. Let's try this again." Temporarily releasing her from his gaze, he held up the shakers again.

"Who can tell me what these are?"

"Salt and pepper?" The unsure response came from Wynter. Her brow crinkled as if she was confused as to why he'd ask such a question.

"Yes, Wynter. It's salt and pepper. But what else? What do many people think salt and pepper actually are; what do they use them for?"

"To season food?" Clive responded with the same confused expression as Wynter.

Kenneth ignored the giggle poorly disguised as a cough coming from Candace's station.

"Wrong. These..." He shook the items in his hands. "are condiments. Forget what you heard. You season food with herbs and spices— before and during the cooking cycle.

Spices are used to enhance the flavor of whatever you're cooking. And these..." He shook the shakers again.

"... are *not* spices. If you searched for spices on the internet, you wouldn't find these two listed. If you do see them, they won't be in the form you put in a shaker and sprinkle over your food. They'll be listed as an ingredient in a spice blend. We'll get to those later."

Walking to the other side of his station, he pulled out a tray containing a small selection of basic spices in labeled tins. Taking off the tops, starting with Clive, he carried the items to each station allowing each person to smell the spices individually.

When he reached Kelsey, she leaned over as if she expected him to wave each container under her nose instead of picking them up herself. He leaned away lifting one eyebrow. His silent message hit it's mark. A red flush crept up her cheeks. She ducked her head and picked up the spices going through the same routine he'd just completed with Clive.

While he stood before each student, he discussed the various properties of the spices and dried herbs, describing the ways they enhanced the flavor of particular meats and vegetables. He encouraged them to shake out small amounts to taste each one. Once he reached Candace, he continued his spiel.

"Now, most people think paprika doesn't add anything. They think it's just for color and as a garnish to finish off the dish. Something pretty to look at which doesn't contribute much."

Staring into her eyes, he continued to extol the virtues of paprika even though she hadn't yet made it to that particular spice on the tray. Despite the mundane nature of the topic, his voice took on a husky quality. It was as if he was talking about her inherent qualities and abilities instead of the red powdery substance in the metal container.

She was indeed beautiful. He'd argue with anyone that she was far more than her pleasing exterior let on. Her gaze dropped to the tray as she lifted the tin with the paprika label. Waving it under her nose, she inhaled the aroma of the spice.

"It's more than simply a pretty red spice you use to give your food a pop of color to finish it off. Depending on the variety, it adds a sweet and smokey quality to the dish as well. It's a finishing touch which could mean the difference between a bland dish and one that makes you want seconds or thirds."

Her hand froze in midair. She inhaled sharply before quickly lowering the spice. Once she put the tin back on the tray, he continued. "Don't sleep on paprika. There's a reason it's considered a spice, and plain white salt doesn't make the list."

Winking, he picked up the tray and took it back to his area where he affixed the lids to the open containers. Turning back to the class, he clapped his hands.

"Now it's time to cook!" He smiled broadly even though his students wore varying expressions, from discomfort to downright terror.

"Stop it with the looks people. I read your answers to my survey questions. You aren't completely inept in the kitchen. You only lack confidence and maybe some basic cooking principles.

I'm here to provide that. Don't worry; we're starting out small. I'll be right here to guide you through each step."

Indicating the refrigerators and the door to the pantry, he explained the items they would prepare for the night.

"Tonight, you're going to take what you just learned regarding spices and apply it to a simple meal of roasted chicken with potatoes. First, you'll need to set your oven to 400 degrees so it can begin to heat.

There are chicken breasts and leg quarters in the refrigerators. Your choice as to which you make. They're individually wrapped so you don't have to worry about repackaging anything.

The potatoes are stored in a bin in the pantry. That's also where you'll find industrial-sized versions of the spices we just reviewed as well as others we didn't get to yet. I'd advise taking a handful of the small bowls from the cabinet at your station to pour your selections into a separate container.

Everything else you need is at your station. I'm going to cook the same meal here on my range, but keep in mind you don't have to do exactly what I do. I want you to branch out a little and try the blends to suit your tastes."

While they reluctantly went about gathering their selections, Kenneth pulled his supplies from the smaller refrigerator built into his larger work area. He took a few minutes pulling out the food items, herbs, spices and cooking utensils he needed before stopping to check on their status.

Calling out encouragement to those looking at their assembled materials with skepticism, he went back to organizing before washing the potatoes. He'd already taken care of properly cleaning the chicken breast.

Even knowing the recommendations from supposed experts said not to wash meat, he still couldn't simply remove meat from the package and cook it. He shuddered at the thought. Not to mention, his Aunt Toni might hop on a plane just to pop him good for even considering it.

Once he placed the newly scrubbed potatoes and a knife on the cutting board, he looked around seeing that everyone was at their counters working except Candace. Frowning, his gaze swept the room before settling on the open pantry door. It shouldn't take very long to pour a few spices into bowls and grab some potatoes.

Making a quick walking tour to nudge individual students in the right direction, he made his way to the pantry. Inside Candace stood with her back to the door with her phone in one hand and one of the industrial sized spice containers in the other.

He knocked against the doorframe to get her attention, but she didn't move a muscle. Strolling closer, he stepped behind her looking over her shoulder at the container of dried oregano she held.

"Need some help?" He asked, speaking directly into her ear.

At the sound of his voice, she gave a startled jerk. Her phone went flying one way and the plastic container landed at her feet at an odd angle causing the contents to spill.

"Shit! You can't sneak up on people like that!" She whisper-screamed at him while clutching her hand to her chest.

"I didn't sneak. I made noise at the door, but I guess you were concentrating so hard, you didn't hear me." Certain she didn't find this situation half as amusing has he did, he worked to suppress his smile.

Her phone buzzed reminding both of them it was no longer in her hand. Looking around, he spied it peeking from beneath the shelf on the opposite wall. He went to retrieve it for her while she stooped to pick up the container of oregano.

It took him two steps to reach the other side of the room, however when he turned back around, he was gifted with the sight of her rounded backside clad in curve hugging jeans. Despite years of lessons on being respectful to women and the wealth of self-control he prided himself in having, he stood stock still staring at the delectable bottom.

As he stared, a series of scenarios ran through his mind. His shaft hardened, straining against his zipper painfully quick and he shifted attempting to subtly relieve the ache. Her phone buzzed again in his hand. She turned around catching him frozen between ogling her plush cheeks and looking at the display to glimpse the message on the screen.

Candace's eyes pinged between his face and the phone in his hand prompting him to look at the device. He couldn't miss the preview of the message displayed there. *She was cheating!*

Technically, the assignment wasn't a test. But, they'd been asked to use their own instincts to select the herbs and seasonings they would use. Instead of doing that, she'd been in the pantry messaging someone. Said person was replying with suggestions.

Lifting his gaze from the phone, he raised an eyebrow and held it up where she could see the message preview as well.

"Explain."

She had the audacity to flush prettily and turn her head, avoiding the phone as well as his gaze. Kenneth wasn't having it. Stepping into her space, he grasped her chin and turned her face to his. Once again, he held the phone up, only this time it put it to her face unlocking the device.

"What are you doing?" Her brow creased in a frown as she reached for it. "Give me my phone please."

"No. You've lost phone privileges."

"Excuse me?"

"You heard me. You've lost phone privileges. The assignment was to select items on your own. I can see you don't care to follow instructions; so, I'll just hold on to this until class is over."

Her jaw dropped: she sputtered as if she couldn't decide which insult to hurl at him. While she fumed, he tapped the message and called the sender.

"Are you serious right now?" She said through clenched teeth then furtively looked over her shoulder into the classroom.

"One hundred percent." He stared at her as he listened for the call to connect.

"Hello?" A woman's voice answered.

"Hello, Kari. This is Kenneth."

"Kenneth?"

"Yes."

"Kenneth Holmes?"

"One in the same."

"Okay...Kenneth, why are you calling me from Candy's phone?"

"I'm calling to ask you a favor."

"Okay..."

"I'm trying to teach Candace to trust her instincts, but she's being somewhat...resistant."

"Okay...What does that have to do with me?"

*"She's apparently trying to get you to do her work for her by asking for suggestions. Could you show support and help her by **not** providing ingredients and recipes while she's in class?"*

"Is this what Candy wants?"

"Candace wants to learn to cook. I am here to teach her." He wouldn't lie and tell her Candace was on board with his request, but he had to ensure Kari knew where he stood on the matter.

"Mmhmm." Kenneth heard a male voice in the background before Kari put the call on mute. A few moments later, she came back on the line.

"Okay, fine. I won't help Candy while she's in class, but I draw the line there. If she asks me for help while she's on her own time, I won't turn her away."

"That's all I can ask. Thank you. Have a nice evening."

"Mhmm. You do the same."

Pressing the icon to end the call, he slipped the phone into his pocket. He looked at Candace as she stood there with the oregano container in one hand and a crumpled paper towel in the other.

Over the course of his conversation with Kari, Candace's face transitioned from shock to a mask of anger. The way her brow dipped and her nose crinkled was cute as hell, but he wouldn't tell her that.

It'd probably piss her off more and make her think he took pleasure in angering her. He wasn't pleased about it. No matter how cute her little scrunched up face looked.

"Can I have my phone please?" Although her tone was even when she asked, he heard the quiver of irritation.

"No."

"You can't just take my property. That's not how this works."

"This works, however I say it works. You failed to follow instructions. Actions have consequences."

"You never said we couldn't use our phones to ask for help."

"You really want to go there? I didn't say you couldn't use your phone, but what part of, *'I'm here to guide you'*, didn't you understand?"

The mutinous set of her chin was all the answer he required. Chuckling, he took a step closer and she took a step back. Holding her gaze, he advanced until her back was pressed against the shelf behind her. Although he stood just shy of six foot four, he didn't exactly tower over her.

He liked that too. The way she was tall to go with the thickness of her curvy body. The package made his hands itch to touch her. He didn't. He had more self-control than to tempt himself with a classroom full of people on the other side of the open door.

"Mr. Holmes?" Kelsey interrupted their stare-off.

Turning to the door, he looked at her. "Kenneth." He corrected her reference to him as Mr. Holmes.

"Okay, Kenneth. I have a question and wondered if you could help me over here?" She pointed over her shoulder fidgeting in the doorway.

"Sure. I'll be right there." He waited until she walked away to look at Candace again.

"We'll discuss this later. For now, go with your gut, pick something, then come out and join the group."

Patting his pocket, he smirked then walked out of the little room leaving her standing inside silently fuming. He didn't bother to look back. He'd left her to fend for herself, so he expected her to take a few extra minutes.

Striding between the cooking stations, he stopped in front of Kelsey as she stood before her cutting board affecting the demeanor of a little girl lost. He really, really didn't like the coy games some women played. She'd made no secret about her attraction to him. Unfortunately for her, it wasn't mutual.

"Okay, Kelsey. What questions do you have?"

"I picked out some spices and stuff, but I'm not sure what to do from here." She waved a hand limply over the small bowls she'd filled much too full with her selections of seasonings.

Placing both hands on the edge of the counter, she leaned forward. The move drew attention to her large breast being squeezed by the position of her arms. Ignoring the obvious invitation, he offered suggestions before moving on to Clive who was struggling with cutting his potatoes.

In his peripheral vision, he saw Kelsey's pout, but made zero acknowledgement of it as he helped Clive. While he was busy with Clive, Candace appeared in the doorway of the pantry, shot him a withering glance and sullenly approached her cooking area with her bowls of seasonings.

Chuckling internally, he methodically made his way around the room trying to give everyone equal attention. He brushed it off when Candace refused his offer of assistance and went back to his cooktop to finish his prep then get his dish in the oven.

Chapter Four

EASY WAY OR HARD WAY?

You can do this. You can do this. Candy chanted to herself as she stood before the raw chicken and whole red potatoes which still needed chopping. She hadn't hung around her mother's kitchen much, but there's no way she spent as much time around Kari and Aunt Tami to not at least pick up the basics. *Right?*

It brought her some degree of comfort to see her classmates were all struggling in one form or another. Except Kelsey. Normally, Candy didn't bother with women like Kelsey. In her line of work, watching a young woman throw herself at an older man was common place. Except in their case, they were trying to land a role in the film industry that wasn't linked to porn.

Nothing against porn, but she didn't work with many women in that industry. The one's she knew didn't try nearly as hard for male attention as Kelsey was trying with Kenneth. Candy would've had secondhand embarrassment for the woman were it not for the sly glances Kelsey shot in her direction.

She'd hazard a guess Kelsey was confused at the attention Kenneth was showing her. The little jabs he normally reserved for when they saw one another at gatherings had morphed somewhat. She didn't recognize the man who pressed her back to the shelving in the pantry.

If Kelsey hadn't interrupted, Candy wasn't sure how far he would've taken their interaction. Just thinking of the way he looked at her when he backed her into the shelving, made her stomach flutter and her core clench. Despite being livid with him about him confiscating her phone, she couldn't deny how his confident swagger affected her.

If the shoe were on the other foot, she might be as salty as Kelsey about him paying such close attention to another woman. To Kelsey, it was probably a foreign experience, especially considering their physical differences. Where Kelsey was blonde with a petite little body attached to breasts that were a tad large for a person having such a small frame, Candy was five foot ten inches tall in her socks with abundant plus-sized curves.

Women like Kelsey tended to assume a man wouldn't be interested in a woman like Candy unless they couldn't have the petite blond with the big tits. Women like Candy were supposed to get the leftovers, not be the first choice.

Joke's on her. Curves were in and Candy had the thirsty men in her social media DM's to prove it. Not that she took them up on their offers, but the offers were made. *Regularly.*

Surreptitiously, she watched Kenneth as he sprinkled seasonings on the chicken breast before drizzling olive oil over it, then rubbing the seasonings and oil on the meat. Mimicking his actions, she ignored how strong his fingers looked massaging the innocent little breast.

She absolutely didn't notice the way the veins in his hands looked or the way those veins traveled up his exposed forearm. Instead of his business casual attire he'd worn during the previous class, he sported a short-sleeved chef's coat with coordinating loose fitting trousers. They did nothing to mask his appeal, if anything, it ratcheted up a notch.

While she matched his movements, she did take a small piece of his advice selecting a spice blend which looked and smelled like the Cajun seasoning that graced the cabinets in most of her family member's homes. Concerned about over doing it, she sprinkled it lightly before doing the same with the onion powder, garlic powder and ground thyme. Following his process, she rubbed the spices and olive oil to coat her own chicken breast.

By the time she'd finished he'd inserted the meat in a small roasting bag, placed it in a baking dish and slid it into the oven. Then, he moved on to the potatoes. Luckily for her and the rest of her classmates, he'd prompted them to preheat their ovens to the required temperature before they selected their ingredients. So, she didn't have to ask him what to do on that front.

Noting that after he chopped the potatoes into large cubes, he then followed the same basic procedure of sprinkling herbs, spices and coating them with olive oil, she followed suit with her own small collection of spuds. If she was learning nothing else, she was acquiring the skill of cooking for one.

"The skills you're utilizing tonight can be transferred to cooking in larger portions. We'll build on them each class until you're comfortable cooking larger meals." Kenneth interrupted her thoughts as if he were reading her mind.

"Don't forget to write down what seasonings you used tonight. If you like the combination, you'll want a record so you can duplicate it at another date."

He placed a second covered baking dish into the oven then closed the door. Afterwards, he started walking around the room checking on each of their progress. For a change, he started on her side of the room and worked his way to the right.

"Try not to cube the potatoes quite so small. If they're too small, they'll cook more like home fries than roasting." He murmured to her.

He stood quietly in front of her watching as she adjusted the knife to cut larger pieces of potato. Steeling her nerves, she was determined to not show any outward sign of how she quivered on the inside from his close scrutiny. Eventually he moved on to Jack offering him tips before repeating the process with Rachel and the others.

Once everyone was ready to put their dishes in the oven, he instructed them on setting the timer using the one built into the stove. He also mentioned they could use their smart watches and cellphones to set reminders as well. When he mentioned cellphones, she scoffed, the sound much louder than she intended.

His piercing gaze informed her he'd heard the noise. Remembering his words from the pantry, she focused her attention on the buttons on her stove. Suppressing the shiver snaking down her spine, she pretended to be unaffected by his penetrating stare.

"Actions have consequences." That's what he told her earlier. His gaze telegraphed a clear reminder of those words. Giving herself an internal pep talk, Candy reminded herself she was a grown woman. He wasn't in control of her.

Okay, the scoffing might've been the tiniest bit rude, but it wasn't like she intended it to be so loud. The room was abnormally quiet at the time. It's the only reason he even heard her from where he stood in front of Clive's cooking area.

Still, he wasn't the boss of her. She didn't even understand how he came to be the instructor for a class like this. McKenna and Driscoll had never mentioned him doing anything other than working with Driscoll at the Treasury Department.

With her items in the oven and her timer set, she cleaned up her station which allowed her mind to wander. Looking around the room, everyone else was doing the same, cleaning their stations and putting things away.

While their food cooked, Kenneth passed out sheets of paper with names and descriptions of various herbs and spices as well as a chart showing which combinations paired best with particular meats, seafood and vegetables. It was actually very informative. In addition to the take-home sheets, he instructed them to pull two square saucers from the cabinets. They would use them for plating.

He also went over how to know when certain meats were cooked completely. He mentioned using meat thermometers to check internal temperatures until they gained enough experience to know how long and at what temperatures the item required for it to cook completely. He highlighted which meats could be served at varying stages of doneness while cautioning them about the ones which absolutely must be cooked completely well done for food safety purposes.

Grudgingly, she admitted he was pretty good at the whole instructor thing. Not counting the totally overbearing way he forced her to rely on herself. She knew she could've asked him questions, but stubbornness kept her lips sealed. It didn't keep her eyes and ears closed, but she didn't directly ask him for assistance. Eavesdropping while he helped someone else didn't count.

After roughly twenty minutes, Kenneth instructed them to remove the covering from the potatoes and cut the roasting bag from the chicken then put both back into the oven for the remainder of the cook-time. With a little less than thirty minutes remaining in the class, beeps erupted into the room in a cacophony of noise when all the timers went off in quick succession. Silencing the alert from her stove, Candy pressed the button to end the baking cycle, grabbed the pot holders and removed the food from the oven.

"Now we find out how much you all learned tonight." Kenneth's lips stretched to reveal a toothy grin.

He'd already removed his chicken and potatoes then plated them quite artistically on rectangular plates. Rubbing his hands together, he walked around the semi-circle commenting and complimenting everyone's efforts.

Poor Jack's chicken looked like it had a case of the measles. Candy wasn't sure what he'd done to it for it to look like that, so she averted her eyes to her own culinary results. It didn't look as succulent and pretty as the food on Kenneth's plates, but in her opinion, it didn't appear completely inedible.

Carefully, she plated them on the individual plates as instructed then waited for everyone else to finish that step. Once they were done plating, Kenneth picked up his chicken. He described the herbs and spices he'd used.

Next, he did something Candy didn't expect. He cut the meat into eight equal portions and walked toward her. He speared a piece with a fork and she had a brief moment of panic when she thought he was going to try to feed it to her.

"Each of you, please get out another plate." Relief along with a tinge of embarrassment flooded her. She quickly retrieved a plate from the cupboard.

The small knowing smirk was her only indicator he'd read her body language and keyed in on her thought as he placed the chicken on her plate. He didn't linger in front of her, he moved on to Jack repeating the process until everyone had a small portion.

"Ok. Taste it and see if you can detect the different flavors influenced by the spices I used."

"Mmmm! It's so good!" Kelsey moaned.

Candy rolled her eyes then popped the sample into her mouth. Flavors burst on her tongue and she chewed slowly savoring the succulent piece of meat. Kenneth wasn't all talk. The meat wasn't overly seasoned, but still flavorful. It was good, but not good enough for the theatrics Skipper was performing down there.

"I think I taste a bit of the garlic." Kelsey gushed, holding a hand to her chest and licking her lips.

"Thank you, Kelsey. But it's not necessary to tell me what notes you pick up. I want you all to get comfortable recognizing the different elements each spice or herb brings to a dish."

It was petty, but Candy didn't care. She got the slightest thrill when he shot Kelsey down. Chick gave off mean girl vibes. Candy wasn't a fan of mean girls. She'd dealt with that crap enough with some of the spoiled wanna-be starlets she'd worked with when she was first starting out as a make-up artist.

Since she had years in the industry and a stellar reputation, she didn't put up with that high school behavior from anyone—even if they were paying her. In the beginning, she established clear boundaries and let her work speak for itself.

"Okay, everyone has tasted my meat, it's time to share your masterpieces with the class. If you would, take out some additional plates."

A completely juvenile giggle bubbled in Candy's throat when he said, 'tasted my meat'. Her immediate thought was about the double meaning for *his meat* and how knock-off Barbie would be more than happy to taste *his meat.*

Quickly coughing to cover her faux pas, she bent to get the small plates from the cupboard. With her head virtually inside the cabinet, she silently got out the last of her adolescent laughter under the guise of following instructions.

"Is everything okay, Candace?"

Startled, Candy knocked her head against the cabinet when she jerked at his question.

"Ouch!" Standing with one hand filled with plates and the other rubbing the top of her head, she frowned before immediately wiping the expression from her face.

"I'm fine. Thank you." She responded primly.

"Are you sure? You seem a little jumpy tonight."

He was goading her. She knew it from the smile hovering at the corner of his mouth. Not taking the bait, she gave him a stiff nod.

"I'm positive. Just getting plates to follow your instructions."

She put extra emphasis on the word instructions. It was a dig at him for what he'd said in the pantry about her not following them earlier. The glimmer of a smile slid from his face and his eyes hardened the slightest bit.

"It's good to see you're learning." He murmured. Not loud enough for everyone to hear, but she heard him.

After placing tent cards on her station, he moved away allowing her to breathe a little more easily. She had no idea why they pushed each other's buttons.

"I'm placing the tent cards at each station so that you can write your name on a card when you leave a plate at your classmate's station letting them know which dish came from whom.

This isn't something we'll do each class, but since you all used different ingredients I think it's a great exercise in seeing how the different flavors marry together. You should grab a drink from the fridge. Preferably water so the drink doesn't overpower the food."

Ducking her head to hide her expression, Candy focused on her task. She had a hard and fast rule about not eating just any old body's food. Her stomach tensed with anxiety just thinking of participating in the activity. Only knowing that Kenneth was watching over everyone making sure they observed good food safety eased her mind.

Once everyone had dished out portions for the rest of the class and the collection of plates with tent cards were lined across each person's station, it looked like a competition. Grabbing a bottle of water, she stood looking at the selection starting to feel like a judge on one of those cooking shows.

"Okay, we're all set. I suggest everyone start tasting before the food gets cold. We want to get the full effect." Kenneth encouraged them and picked up a fork spearing a potato on the plate closest to him at the instructor's counter.

Taking a deep breath, Candy started from the left taking one bite of potato and one bite of chicken from each plate. Everyone didn't miss the mark, but not everyone hit it either. The tastes ranged from cardboard bland to overly salty with only a couple landing close to a happy medium. Including her own.

She didn't consider her dish a complete failure. Her chicken wasn't dry, but in her quest not to over season, she hadn't put enough of the spices to really get the job done. She made a note of it on the paper next to where she'd written her ingredients.

The potatoes she'd chopped too small were crispy just as Kenneth said they would be, so she couldn't gauge the roasted quality because she'd put the larger pieces on her classmates plates to save face.

Thankfully, Kenneth didn't ask for them to verbally assess one another's meals. Once the tasting was over, he passed each of them note sheets with his observations of their efforts, asked that they load the plates and utensils in the dishwashers then dismissed the class.

Everyone cleaned their stations, said their goodbyes and left the classroom. Everyone except Candy who stood with her arms folded across her chest staring at Kenneth expectantly.

Kenneth hummed to himself as he re-stacked papers, slipped them into a folder and placed the folder into his messenger bag. Sliding the strap over his head, he stopped humming and looked at Candy as if he was surprised she was still there.

"Oh. Candace. Did you have a question?" He asked as if there couldn't possibly be any other reason she'd stayed behind.

"You still have my phone."

"Oh!" He patted the pocket of his pants before reaching inside, pulling out the device and walked toward her holding it out.

"Here you go."

With the cooking station separating them, she stretched her arm across it to pluck the phone from his fingers. Without comment, she slipped it into a slot on the side of her purse.

"What? No thank you?" It sounded as if he was teasing, but she couldn't be sure.

"Thank you? Why would I thank you? For taking my property?" She asked walking around the edge of the counter putting her farther away from him and closer to the door

Moving the bag from his side to drape behind him, he reached her in one large step clasping his long fingers around her wrist.

"You're still salty about me taking the phone, so you can't see how I helped you by removing a crutch."

"What crutch? I asked one person for advice and suddenly I'm using a crutch?"

"Easy way or hard way?"

"What? What are you talking about? The easy way or hard way for what?" Her brow crinkled in confusion at the abrupt change of subject.

"Are you going to admit there's a spark between us or are you going to keep pretending and make me show you?" Using the hand on her wrist, he drew her closer.

Tugging at her limb she attempted to pull away. "Okay, now I'm really lost. We went from talking about you taking my property to you saying I was using a crutch, now you're talking about sparks. Can we stick to one subject please?"

"We both know you're attracted to me."

His eyes bore into hers even as she turned her head to avoid looking directly at him. Gently grasping her chin with his other hand, he tipped her head to bring her gaze back to his face.

"Hey, no reason to be embarrassed. Number one, we're adults. Number two and most important, the attraction is mutual."

The tip of his tongue peeked out and she couldn't stop her eyes from tracking its movement as it swiped across his lips. The action and his nearness caused havoc to her senses. Clearing her throat, she pulled herself together.

"I, uh...I fail to see how any of what you just said pertains to the original topic of you taking away my phone like I'm some wayward teenager."

"It makes perfect sense to me. If you weren't pretending you weren't attracted to me, you would have asked me questions about your assignment. Instead, you hid in the pantry to text your cousin to ask her to help you.

Your avoidance of our chemistry led you to lean on Kari like a crutch in the place of, I don't know, asking your instructor to point you in a direction."

"Wow...You really think a lot of yourself. I have no problem expressing myself when I find a man attractive. You're mista—" Candy's words were swallowed as Kenneth's lips covered hers in a scorching kiss.

Swiping his tongue into her mouth he captured her moan, and added his own. She inhaled sharply when his fingers wrapped around the side of her face fisting in the hair at the nape of her neck, tugging just hard enough to sting, but not really hurt.

Candy's thoughts ceased. She was caught up in the way he consumed her so completely. One arm snaked around her waist and pulled her body flush to his allowing her to feel the hard lines of his muscular frame. Her hands clutched at the sides of his shirt, holding on, feeling as if she were drowning in the sensations and he was her anchor.

Being pressed against him that way was a heady experience, especially while he devoured her with his mouth demonstrating the skills of his talented tongue. Her core clenched without being touched; another pleading moan escaped her lips and was imprisoned by his kiss.

The kiss tapered off to gentle pecks while they tugged one another's lips. They stood in the middle of the classroom wrapped in one another's arms, pressed together from forehead to toes, breathing heavily. The fingers of his left hand were still tangled in her hair, while his thumb stroked her jaw. Entrapped in the moment, the outside world was of no consequence. So, neither of them heard the click-clack of footsteps until the very last moment.

Kelsey emitted a strangled squeak drawing their attention to where she stood at the doorway like a deer caught in headlights. Realizing she was still in Kenneth's arms, Candy attempted to extricate herself from his embrace. His arm tightened around her waist holding her in place.

"Stay." The one-word command was given with a stern expression before he turned his gaze back to Kelsey.

"Did you forget something Kelsey?" He asked her while holding Candy firmly in his arms.

"Um. Well. I was going to ask you a question…" Her facial expression shifted displaying the range of emotions she couldn't contain. There was shock, anger, disbelief and hurt. Her bottom lip quivered. Candy knew what was coming next.

Whether she was genuinely hurt or using a ploy to make herself Kenneth's primary focus, didn't matter. What mattered was the way he responded to knock-off Barbie's emotional display.

"A question about what?" He responded with an even tone. It held no indication he was remotely moved by the tears now welling in Kelsey's eyes.

"Don't worry about it." She swiped at the lone tear dripping down her cheek and averted her eyes.

"Are you sure? It must have been important, if you came back to ask." He was saying all of the appropriate things as an instructor, but he hadn't moved away from Candy. Not one millimeter.

Sniffing, Kelsey swiped her face again as redness creeped up her neck into her cheeks.

"I'm sure. I'll write it down and ask it on Tuesday." Mumbling an indistinct goodbye, she turned and fled the room.

"I think you hurt her feelings." Candy said once the sound of Kelsey's retreating footsteps faded.

"I'm not here to spare her feelings. I'm here to teach her to cook."

"True. But, it's obvious she's crushing on you. You hurt her feelings being all cold."

"I didn't hurt her feelings. She hurt her own feelings. It's very obvious I'm not interested in her in the slightest. I haven't given her any encouragement. So, if her feelings are hurt, she only has herself to blame."

"That's cold."

"That's honest. It's the only way I operate." Dropping another lingering peck on her lips, he pulled away.

"Come on. I'll walk you to your car. It's dark out."

Releasing her from his hold, he put a hand at the small of her back and ushered her from the room. They didn't speak until they reached the driver's side door of her SUV.

"Are we just not going to talk about what happened back there?" She held her keys in her hand, but made no move to get into the vehicle.

"Which thing? We talked about my lack of interest in Kelsey and I was pretty clear about my interest in you. Are you saying you aren't interested?"

"No that's not what I'm saying, but you are being a little high handed. Wherever it is you think we are, we aren't there yet."

Stepping closer to her, he placed a finger under her chin tipping her face up to maintain eye contact.

"Where I think we are is at the beginning but not the start."

Her eyebrows drew together. "The start is the beginning."

"Not for us. We started two years ago when we met at Driscoll and McKenna's wedding. We've had a friendly acquaintance where we were polite when we encountered each other, but didn't go further."

Cupping her face in his hands, his fingertips slid into the hair at her nape.

"Now, we're at the beginning. The beginning of getting to know each other in different ways and on a different level."

"What if that's not what I want?"

His hands fell away and he stepped back. She immediately felt the loss.

"If it's not what you want, then I'll back off and we'll go back to the start."

Illuminated by the overhead lights, shadows danced across his face making his stoic expression look harsher. Candy wasn't one for games. But, she did like to see where a man's head was and how he responded to not getting what he wanted.

Closing the distance between them, she placed a hand on his chest covering the Culinary Academy patch located above his heart on his shirt.

"I didn't say it's not what I wanted. I asked what if."

Sliding his hands around her waist, he tugged her forward until they were flush again. "Don't play games with me, Candace."

"I'm not playing games. I asked a question. You answered."

Gliding her fingers upward, she continued until she reached the almost buzzed strands at his nape. Prickly and soft at the same time, she curved her fingers to gently scratch at his scalp. A low feral growl was her only warning as Kenneth backed her against the SUV engulfing her in another all-consuming kiss.

Somehow, they managed to get themselves under control and separate. Her hair was held away from her face with a headband yet he smoothed the coily curls back as if they were blocking his view. His eyes said he wanted more, but he dropped his hands. Plucking her keys from loose fingers, he pressed the unlock button, shifted her to the side and opened the door.

"Go home, Candace. Call me when you get there to let me know you made it safely." He said, then closed the door, shutting her inside.

"Okay..." In a daze, she dragged the seatbelt across her body and pressed the ignition button.

He stood at a safe distance while she backed out of the space. Once she cleared the parking spot, she tooted the horn before driving away. Her mind raced with everything that had taken place.

Wait. He said to call him. She didn't have his number; so, how was she supposed to honor his request? By the time she made it to the stop signal at the edge of the parking lot, her phone buzzed. Checking the display on the center console, she looked at the four-word message.

Lock me in. Kenneth

Instead of following his directive, she selected the voice activation button on her steering wheel and instructed the automated voice to call Kari. She had to tell somebody about what just happened. Besides, she owed her supposed best friend a few words for selling her out in less than twenty seconds.

Kari answered the phone on the second ring. Not giving her a chance to do more than say hello, Candy started spilling.

"Girrrrl... You are *not* going to believe what just happened to me!"

Candy spent the drive recounting the events of the evening right up to the point where Kenneth put her in the car. By the time she made it home, she wasn't as keyed up, but still carried a mildly giddy feeling in her stomach.

Wrapping up her call with her bestie, she took out her phone to send Kenneth a text informing him that she was safely at home. His response came over a few minutes later as she was walking into her bedroom.

"So, you do know how to follow instructions. Good girl."

If asked, she wouldn't be able to articulate why the first sentence disappeared after she read the second sentence. She had no idea why those too little words sent heat directly to her center. Putting the phone down, she walked straight into the ensuite bathroom. She needed a shower. A cold one.

Chapter Five

THAT'S PETTY

Kenneth sat behind the desk in the tiny security office at the shelter reviewing the report from the previous shift. The room was just big enough for the array of flat screen monitors mounted to the longest wall.

He didn't normally work this shift or monitor the camera feeds when he volunteered, but it was a favor to Carolyn. Their previous security officer took another job. She had a replacement, but the person couldn't start until Tuesday.

It was Sunday. Other than finishing his lesson plan for the week, he had nothing going on. Much to his disappointment, he didn't have a date with Candace. It wasn't for lack of trying. He didn't think she was brushing him off, but her weekend was booked working on a movie set.

He had no idea how demanding it was for make-up artists until he started trying to connect with her. She was self-employed, which normally meant she set her own hours. To a degree that was true, but it also meant she couldn't turn down too many clients in a row if she wanted to stay in business.

He hadn't realized the sacrifice she made to even have Tuesday and Thursday evenings available to attend his class. He didn't call her that Thursday night, instead he sent her a few text messages on Friday checking on her throughout the day arranging a time for them to actually talk once he understood having a face-to-face date was out of the question on such short notice.

He'd never really thought about the fact that movies and some television shows which shot on-site would have to shoot some scenes at night which would require the crew from the grips to the make-up artists to remain available until the director called an end to filming for the day. She had a couple of clients shooting a movie on a set right outside of Atlanta.

Her work schedule squashed any hopes he had of seeing her since she'd adjusted her sleep routine in order to be available during the night. He wasn't a selfish prick who'd try to manipulate her into agreeing to get less rest just so he could see her. He'd waited this long; he could wait a couple more days.

After all, she was committed to the class. So, there were at least two days during the upcoming week where he was guaranteed to see her— even though he'd be forced to keep a professional distance for the first two hours.

Looking up from the papers in front of him, he scanned the monitors. Instead of a few monitors that rotated between images from the different cameras, each monitor displayed the feed from two cameras. Kenneth set them up so the screen was split in lieu of alternating between the two attached devices.

Reviewing the image from the camera directed toward the hallway outside the security office, he saw a figure pacing back and forth. Tapping a few keys on the keyboard, he transferred the image to a closer screen so he could see the person better.

Standing, he leaned over and opened the door. Poking his head out, he called out to the young woman.

"What's up La-La? Why are you wearing a hole in the carpet?"

Coming to an immediate stop, the young woman turned around to face him, but didn't move closer. Widening the opening, Kenneth stood in the doorway and waited for La-La to find her words. The nineteen-year-old was one of the young ladies who'd come into the shelter on a special dispensation a year prior after he and a few friends had discovered her along with six others being held captive by a human trafficker.

"I got in." Eyes rounded with fear and uncertainty stared at Kenneth.

"You got in? That's a good thing. Right?"

Dropping her gaze, she tugged at the hem of her oversized t-shirt and twisted it between her fingers.

"I think so."

"You think so?" He relaxed his stance, leaning against the door jamb waiting for her to talk her way through it.

LaShun, or La-La, had been through a lot in her young life. It led her to have very little trust in people in general and even less trust in men in particular. The first time she spoke to him directly was a shock, but little by little he'd proven he could be trusted.

One of the ways he did that was not pushing her to talk and never, ever crowding her space. The irony of how he broke his second rule with Candy wasn't lost on him. He'd repeatedly crowded her space and wasn't likely to stop any time soon.

"Yeah, it's a good thing." La-La broke the silence. Leaning with her back to the wall opposite from the security office, she turned her face back toward him.

"So, why the long face?" He had an idea, but he wanted her to say it aloud.

The therapist on staff coached them on the basic components of her methods so they could reinforce the teachings with the residents if and when a resident trusted them enough to come to them with an issue. She didn't want anyone's healing to get derailed by a staff member going off script.

Most of the of the people in the shelter were temporary and weren't addicts, but they had years of learned behavior to unlearn. Many of them had confidence and self-worth issues to work through. Hence the onsite therapist coupled with mandatory sessions.

"Am I ready for that step?" She asked quietly. Sliding down the wall, she sat with her legs crossed and her hands folded in her lap.

Glancing over his shoulder to the monitors, Kenneth mirrored her position in the doorway.

"What makes you think you aren't ready?"

"It's a long way from here. I won't be able to work at the shelter anymore. I won't know anyone. I'll have to start all over and find a new job because I only got a partial scholarship."

"So, it's not that you don't think you're ready, you're afraid of leaving the safety of this place and the people."

"No! Well...Maybe?"

"You know it's okay to feel apprehensive about new things, right? It's perfectly natural."

"I know...But what if Miss Carolyn is wrong about me? What if I'm not smart enough?"

"You. Not smart enough? The girl who breezed through her GED course and two semesters of Community college in less than a year while holding down a full-time job?"

Kenneth kept his tone light as he tried to convey how impressed he was at her accomplishments. La-La worked really hard, but it appeared imposter syndrome had her in a choke hold.

"That was the GED and community college. This is a four-year university. It's not the same."

Leveling a piercing stare at her, he replied. "I'm not sure what you've heard, but it's not easy to pass the GED test. I know more than a few people who had to take the classes and the test more than once. It's very comprehensive.

Besides, the courses you took at Community College were advanced math and science courses. Those professors didn't give you those top scores. You earned them."

At his praise, she ducked her head. She'd come a long way, but she was still visibly unsure of how to respond to a genuine compliment. He understood.

Years of living in a world where a compliment from a man was typically followed by some unseemly request, meant all such gestures caused discomfort and suspicion. The number of men were only nice to women when they wanted something from them sexually didn't help matters. It was a bad look, but they continued to follow the pattern.

"It's not a big city like Atlanta, but it's still large. What if I get lost there?"

Now they were getting to the real reason she was apprehensive. Getting lost was how she referred to the way she ended up being held in what was essentially a harem of under-aged girls by Vincente Renfro, a human trafficker who masqueraded as a legitimate business owner.

"La-La...There are no guarantees in life, but I do know you're not the same girl you were six years ago. You're not even the same girl you were eight months ago.

You have all the tools you need to make a good life for yourself. But, first you have to learn to trust yourself and your decisions."

"That's hard." Plucking at the ripped spot at the knee of her jeans, she kept her eyes downcast.

"I know, but you've already made great progress. We both know Miss Carolyn wouldn't have encouraged you to fill out those applications and helped you hunt for scholarships if she didn't believe you were ready to leave this place. I damn sure wouldn't have written recommendation letters if I thought you didn't have the tools to go out there and kick ass. You've got this."

Holding out his arm, he leaned forward slightly. "Don't leave me hanging."

A wry grin started at the corner of La-La's mouth, then she stretched out her arm to bump fists with him.

"Thanks, KG."

"Anytime, kid. Now get outta here. I've got work to do." Grinning, they stood and said their bantering goodbyes. She walked through the door leading to the staff quarters. He went back into the security office, closing the door behind him.

After a few more hours, Kenneth was contemplating eating the light meal he brought with him or calling the kitchen and asking for a plate of whatever they were cooking today. While he considered his options, his cellphone buzzed on the desk.

Kenneth's face split into a huge smile when he saw the message from Candace. She'd obviously received the gift he'd sent her.

Candace: OMG! Thank you! You didn't have to do that!

Kenneth: You're welcome. I hope they didn't wake you.

Candace: They didn't. I got in around two this morning. I've been up for a few hours now. I was just about to grab something from the fridge when they rang the bell.

Kenneth: Good. I was hoping they would get there while you were awake.
Candace: Are you at the shelter?
Kenneth: Yes
Candace: Are you where you can talk? I'd rather talk than text.
Kenneth: Sure thing. Give me a sec.

Candace's request to talk solved his dilemma on what to do about his meal. He'd take even a few minutes talking to her over eating the food from the kitchen. He'd make do with what he'd packed in his thermal lunch bag after their talk.

Tapping the phone display, he initiated the call. She answered almost immediately. Once they'd exchanged pleasantries, they moved smoothly into conversation.

"So, do you like it?" Kenneth asked since she hadn't brought the gift up other than to thank him for sending it.

"I do. It was very thoughtful of you. Like I said, I was getting ready to scrounge up a meal, so this was right on time. How did you know this was one of my favorite places to eat?"

"I didn't. I like it and I thought you might enjoy it as well."

"Whenever I'm on the west side of town at lunch or dinner time, I have to stop at Chelle's place." She told him.

"My selection was a happy accident. I know how it is getting in late after working through the night. So, I wanted to make sure you had something available and didn't have to expend too much energy—especially when you have another long night ahead of you."

"Aw...That's really sweet of you."

The line fell silent after her declaration. Kenneth listened to the sounds of her opening containers and moving around in the background.

"Hey, Kenneth?"

"Yeah?"

"Do you wanna have lunch with me?"

"Sure. When?"

Swinging his eyes away from the monitors, he sat up straighter in the chair and stared at the phone in disbelief. He'd planned to ask her out for cocktails or coffee after their next class, but if she wanted to see him sooner, he was all for it.

"Right now."

"I'm a little busy right now."

"I know. You're at the shelter. Did you pack a lunch?"

"Yeah..."

"Ok. So, grab your lunch. We'll switch this call to a video chat and have lunch together." The smile he heard in her voice put one on his face as well.

Not wanting to keep her waiting too long, he quickly dug the container from the thermal bag and popped it in the microwave in the corner of the small office. Just as the notification dinged alerting him to the end of the warming cycle, his phone pinged with the request to video chat.

Grabbing it, he propped it upright on the desk and selected 'accept'. He couldn't contain his grin when her face appeared on the screen. Her wide smile exposed the dimple in her right cheek and her eyes sparkled.

Her hair was pulled up into a poofy bun held together by a bright yellow headwrap which seemed to make her skin glow. For a person who made her living using make-up to beautify others, he rarely saw her with more than a light gloss or color on her lips. He guessed when a person had skin as perfect as hers, it wasn't a concern.

"Hey there!" She beamed, wiggling her fingers in time with the greeting.

"Hey yourself, beautiful. You look amazing for a person who's been pulling long overnight hours."

Blushing prettily at the compliment, she dipped her head slightly before responding.

"Thank you. I feel like I could probably sleep another six hours, but then I'd really throw my sleep cycle off."

Confusion furrowed his brow. "Don't you have to be there again tonight? Maybe your body is telling you to get more sleep so you'll be alert enough to not poke an eye out putting on your client's mascara."

Chuckling, she shook her head and speared a bit of the veggies with her fork. "Lucky for me, I don't have to be on set tonight."

She popped the food into her mouth, chewing happily and dancing a little in her seat.

"Oh yeah?"

"Nope. They shot all the scenes my client wanted me for on Friday and Saturday night, so no more nights on set for me. At least for that movie."

"Is that a good thing? Does it affect your fee? I don't want to get in your finances, I've just never been personally acquainted with someone in your profession." He wasn't sure how it worked and was genuinely curious.

"You haven't? I'd think working on Secret Service details you would've come in contact with people like me regularly; especially since folks who need security details tend to be in front of the camera a lot, whether it's giving interviews or attending events where they need to look their absolute best."

"I was only on protective detail for a short amount of time. I've mainly worked on the Treasury side for the majority of my time with the Service."

"Oh. Well as far as how I deal with my clients, it depends on what type of contract we draw up. I'm sometimes contracted by a studio or other times by individuals. In this case, I'm more or less on retainer.

No matter how little they need me, I'll get my fee. If they exceed our agreed upon time commitment, then there's an additional fee worked out."

"Like an attorney." He interjected.

"Mhmm. Just not one of those, *I don't get paid until you get paid,* types. I'm not about that life. I require a deposit and installments over the course of the contract period."

They both chuckled, then the conversation lapsed into a comfortable silence while each of them ate their meal. Ideally, he would've preferred to physically be in her presence, but this wasn't a bad substitute.

"Question." Her expression was so serious, he wasn't sure what to expect, so he put his utensils down and leaned forward.

"Shoot."

"How does a Secret Service agent end up teaching a cooking class for adults? Also, why do you let people think you're buying the things you bring to gatherings? Because you didn't buy the cake you brought to the Juneteenth cookout did you?"

Chortling lightly, he took a quick swallow of his drink. He knew she'd eventually get around to asking. He was surprised it had taken as long as it did.

"Fair questions. I'll start with the last ones and work my way back to the one that'll take longer to answer. How about that?"

Waving her hand in an encouraging gesture, she agreed. "Whatever works for you." Grinning, she picked up her own drink to take a sip.

"Yes, I did make the cake I brought to the cookout. I don't buy things I can make if I have the time and inclination. I never told them I bought it.

After the first time I brought something, I didn't realize they'd made that assumption until much later. The event was long over. It happens a lot because most people don't expect men to know their way around the kitchen other than grabbing a beer from the fridge."

"But you never corrected them." She probed him with one eyebrow lifted in suspicion.

"No...I didn't. I could've, but since they haven't said anything to me directly, I was waiting to see how long it took for someone to ask."

"That's petty."

"What's your point?" He wiggled his eyebrows playfully. "Anyway, on to the next part of my response. I was raised by my Uncle Ray with the help of his close friend Toni, both of whom are chefs. Aunt Toni owns one of the best soul food restaurants in Brooklyn with a few more along the east coast. My uncle has a modern cuisine restaurant in Manhattan and a couple of others in the area.

I was always underfoot with them when they were building their brands working as executive chefs in other people's restaurants before finally getting their own. I loved the environment and thought it was what I wanted. So, I went to culinary school immediately after high school.

As it turned out, no matter how much I loved perfecting my craft as a chef, I was actually running from following in my parent's footsteps."

Her face scrunched at his last statement, so he knew what was coming. "Why wouldn't you want to follow in your parent's footsteps? No judgement. I'm way off from what my parents do, but their professions don't interest me at all. Why were you against doing the same thing as your parents?"

Slowly releasing a pent-up breath, he answered. "Both of my parents were in law enforcement. Detectives with NYPD. They rarely ever worked cases together, but they did on occasion."

He watched as the realization washed over her. He tracked the exact moment she put two and two together, but he finished speaking in spite of her already knowing the conclusion.

"I still don't know all of the details, but they were killed in the line of duty working a case. The people who did it were eventually captured and are currently serving the second of two life sentences in prison."

"Oh my God! I'm so sorry."

"Thank you, but I'm okay. It's been thirty years, so I'm good now." Dropping his gaze back to his food, Kenneth continued hoping his words didn't ring as false to her ears as they did to his. Despite the time passed, it was still difficult for him to discuss the death of his parents.

"I had a good life with Uncle Ray. We had a bit of a rough start, but we worked it out and he was a great parent.

Anyway, after I realized I couldn't run from what was in my blood, I enrolled in criminal justice classes. I used my culinary degree to work my way through college, then law school before embarking on my career with the federal government.

I still enjoy cooking and helping others discover their culinary gifts, which is how I ended up teaching at the academy."

"Wow. You've had an interesting journey."

"That's one way to say see it." He smiled ruefully. "Let's just say it hasn't been dull."

They chatted for another half hour before he reluctantly brought an end to their lunch date. He had to physically make his rounds at the facility.

However, he did secure a second date for the next day. Once he discovered she'd left Monday open thinking she'd have to work Sunday night, he saw it as the perfect opportunity for them to have a low-pressure outing.

It also gave him an opportunity to see her before their class on Tuesday. He ended the conversation with a feeling of anticipation. He couldn't remember the last time he was as excited to spend time with a woman.

His elation lasted well into the day. When he spoke to his Uncle Ray later in the evening, his uncle commented on how downright cheerful he sounded. He asked Kenneth point blank if he'd gotten laid and was still riding the orgasmic high.

Laughing at his uncle's candor, he admitted to having met someone, but assured him they were nowhere near that stage. To himself, he acknowledged to not having made it there only because the opening had yet to present itself. He most definitely wanted Candace. In any and every way she would allow.

Chapter Six

I'M NOT A JEALOUS MAN

Candy stood up straight from the woman seated in front of her, stepping away so the up-and-coming starlet could see her image in the mirror. This wasn't one of Candy's favorite actors to work with, but she kept it professional. Her contract was with the studio, not the actress.

Bliss Meadows always stopped just shy of saying or doing something which would have Candy tell the studio not to put the twenty-one-year-old back in her chair. It was like she knew she only had so much rope before she'd have to test the theory of who was more important to the producers.

Candy never flexed. With anyone. It wasn't bragging to say she was exceptional at her job. She had the awards and accolades to show for her skills. Because of that, she was highly sought after. If she didn't want to work with someone, if they were rude or repugnant, she didn't work with them. Period.

She set clear expectations for her professional relationships. Usually there weren't issues, because she could work with just about anyone with ease. Show business people were a special breed and most were more emotionally fragile than people would ever believe. Bliss always seemed on the edge of some sort of hissy fit.

Her nose scrunched as she regarded her reflection. Her face was flawless. Candy knew it. Bliss knew it. The stylist asked for a look which would come off as a natural glow under the harsh studio lighting. Candy followed those instructions to the letter.

Yet, instead of getting up from the chair and going to wardrobe to finish getting dressed, Bliss sat there staring at her reflection. Tired of watching Bliss's dissatisfied expressions, Candy asked one of the assistants to get the stylist.

When she called out to the PA, Bliss looked at her, but she made no comment. Instead, she tapped away at the phone in her hand. It was like that thing was glued to her fingertips. It was a wonder it didn't take Candy even longer to finish her face considering she had to ask Bliss to lift her head or close her eyes numerous times because the girl kept trying to text during the process.

It took considerably longer than it should have to complete such a simple look because Candy was tasked with repairing the damage Bliss had done to her face in tanning beds and whatever else she did in her quest to attain the perfect golden-brown coloring. Her skin was already an even honey color. Candy didn't get her obsession with being darker. Before she could even start applying make-up, Candy had to pull out her special bag to take Bliss through a quick skin treatment.

It added time, but she had to allow a gap between the completion of the treatment and the application of the make-up. Candy was serious about skin care; so, she didn't half-ass it when it came to dealing with the sensitive skin on the face. No matter how irritating the owner of the face might be.

The stylist approached with a producer hot on her heels. Candy checked her watch. If her part of this shoot went on much longer, she was going to be late for class. Things had been going really well with the class as well as with Kenneth. She didn't want to be late or possibly miss due to a pissing match between a creative and a money manager.

"What's the problem?" Jerricka, the head stylist asked.

"There's a problem?" Candy asked. "I didn't think there was a problem. I'm done with Bliss for the next part of the shoot. I think this is what you asked for to go with the wardrobe and scene. Am I correct?"

Candy had learned early on to be the first to speak. The person who spoke first shaped the narrative. If she wanted to make certain the conversation stayed on track, she had to assert herself immediately.

Fletcher, the producer, stood by with an expression which spelled trouble, but Candy was hoping the situation could be diffused before there was an explosion of tears from Bliss. Candy hadn't asked for Fletcher. There was no reason for him to be in the trailer. His presence was Bliss's doing. That's who she was messaging. Candy was certain of it.

Jerricka inspected Bliss's face with a skilled eye before turning back to Candy. "This is perfect. Exactly what I asked for. Great job as usual."

Judging from the wrinkle in Bliss's un-botoxed brow, she wasn't happy the stylist approved.

"Thank you. Is there anything else you need from me? I've taken care of Eric and Deanna already, but I can touch them up if necessary." Candy checked her watch again. "I have another hour here before I need to head out."

Shaking her head, Jerricka responded. "No. I don't think there's anything else. Once we see how everything looks under the lights we should be good. I know today is your early day; so, I'm sure Taylor can handle any light touch ups to gloss or anything like that."

"Jerricka, can I speak to you a moment?" Fletcher extended his arm toward the trailer door. The two exited closing the door behind them.

Internally rolling her eyes, Candy started cleaning her soft brushes and airbrush system to set the make-up station to rights. Bliss sat in the chair tapping away at the cellphone while bouncing her leg.

"Bliss, Jerricka approved the look; so, you can go to wardrobe."

Bliss finally stood from the chair and moved away, but she didn't leave the trailer. Candy's patience was wearing thin. She felt the shit storm coming, but she still fought against getting dragged into it. In less than five minutes, raised voices reached her ears despite the closed door.

Candy was laying her first batch of clean brushes on a drying towel when Jerricka and Fletcher stepped back into the trailer. One look at Jerricka's face told Candy who'd won the argument. Fletcher directed puppy dog eyes at Bliss who promptly teared up. *What in the entire hell was going on?*

Looking around the trailer, she saw the other two make-up artists avidly watching the entire scene. They were quiet as church mice with their eyes and ears tuned into everything happening at Candy's station. As soon as they had a free moment, she knew they would shoot out of the trailer hunting down the gossip.

"Bliss, do you have an issue with your styling?" Not mincing words, Jerricka got straight to the point.

"Jerr, it's like I told you outside, it's not an issue with styling per se. It's more of the wardrobe and make-up doesn't fit Bliss's vision of the character." Fletcher spoke instead of allowing Bliss to take the brunt of Jerricka's ire.

"Is your name Bliss?" Jerricka shot Fletcher a withering glance. "Bliss's vision of the character isn't relevant unless Neal says it is. You remember Neal right? The director?

Until Neal says differently, my job is to ensure her wardrobe and make-up match *his* vision of the character. If the two of you have a problem with that, take it up with him."

When Jerricka pointed between Fletcher and Bliss, the flood gates opened. Tears poured down the young woman's perfectly made-up face. *Shit.* Candy thought. Even with the fixative she used to set the make-up, Bliss was ruining her work.

She might not have gotten her way on getting styled the way she wanted, but the actress had dropped a wrench into Candy's plans for the evening. For the next thirty minutes the little make-up trailer was bursting at the seams with people all working in one way or another to smooth over the situation or gawk at the circus. Candy continued her tasks as if they weren't there until a resolution had been reached amongst them.

She'd already decided today would be the last time she put a brush to the face of Bliss Meadows. The wanna-be starlet had gotten a whiff of being a star and was already starting shit. When Jerricka came over to apologize as well as ask Candy to repair the damage Bliss had done with her snotting and crying all over the place, Candy pierced her with a pointed expression.

"Yeah... I know." Jerricka said with a knowing look.

"Just so we're clear." Candy replied.

She and the head stylist had a great working relationship they'd cultivated over years of working together on films and television shows. Jerricka knew without Candy telling her that Bliss was on Candy's shit list. Therefore, she'd have to find someone else to service her in the future.

Without another word, Candy returned to the chair where Bliss sat mutely pouting. Working with efficiency, she removed then reapplied the make-up. Due to the type of look Jerricka requested, she couldn't just touch up what was already there. She had to start over.

While taking care to do a good job, she worked quickly. Once she was done, she politely informed Bliss, then stepped away. Wordlessly, she began cleaning her tools again. Fletcher had hung around in the background. So, when Candy turned away to gather her things, he swooped in and led Bliss from the trailer.

Candy still didn't know what the hell was at the bottom of Bliss's little tantrum. Honestly, she didn't care. She'd started the day with a smile and anticipation. Studio mess had put a damper on her good mood so she wasn't looking forward to another two hours on her feet— even if it was spent doing something she was starting to love.

Candy's calf-length skirt flapped around her legs as she hurried down the corridor. She was twenty minutes late to class. She hated being late. Combined with her day at the studio, she probably should've skipped this one. But, she couldn't do it.

Her phone had already dinged twice with notifications from Kenneth. Initially, it was concern. Once she floated the possibility of not coming to class at all, the tone of the messages changed, which in turn pissed her off.

Who did he think he was to demand she follow through with her obligations like she was a child who asked for dessert and couldn't finish it once it came? They'd had a really great date on Monday, followed by another on Tuesday after class, but they hadn't seen one another since.

They'd existed on text messages and phone calls for the past two days. It wasn't like she didn't want to see him. She didn't want to people any more for the day. In that state, she normally went straight home, ordered in then took a long bath to decompress.

Rounding the edge of the doorway, she entered the classroom to see the lesson was well underway. Mumbling an apology, she skirted the back of the room to her station. She pulled up in surprise when she noticed Clive had relocated to her immediate left instead of being in his original spot closest to the door. He looked up from the veggies on his cutting board to smile at her, then went back to what he was doing.

Placing her purse in the cubby below the counter, she stood and found herself trapped by Kenneth's penetrating gaze. Instead of making a snarky remark as he'd done the previous time she'd been late to class, he pointed to the white board behind him.

"The ingredients you need for tonight's lesson are written on the board. Please collect your materials and try to catch up." His voice was flat as his eyes remained locked on her.

Brushing off his cool demeanor, she checked the list then moved around gathering her items. To save time, she grabbed entire containers from the pantry instead of measuring things out in the ingredient bowls. When she got back from the pantry, a cutting board and knife had been placed next to the sink for her. Clive was walking back to his station.

"Thank you." She murmured.

"No problem." He replied as he returned to dicing his veggies.

Apparently, the session for the night was instructor guided. The class was following along with Kenneth as he went through the stages of prepping the meal. Despite being so late, she was still able to almost catch up due to some of her classmates still not being very proficient with the chopping and dicing portion of food prep. She was slightly behind, but not so much that it hindered the group.

The class passed without much incident. Kelsey smelled blood in the water, so she once again started circling Kenneth trying to make a play. When he shot her down, yet again, Candy heard a low snicker from Clive. When she glanced at him, he quickly ducked his head covering the noise with a cough.

Smiling in understanding, she returned her focus to following along with Kenneth to complete her meal. As usual, once they'd finished cooking, they performed a taste test. Some people tasted their creations then immediately boxed them up. Others ate a few bites before they did the same.

Candy opted to taste, followed immediately by boxing. Since she was playing catch up, she didn't have the time her classmates had to clean between steps, so by the time she'd loaded the dishwasher, the classroom was empty of everyone except her and Kenneth.

He was still playing the quiet game, so she grabbed up the containers she'd removed from the pantry walking into the oversized closet to return them to the shelves. The snick of the door closing and click of the lock caused her to pause. She whirled around to see Kenneth standing with his back pressed against the door.

His expression was unreadable, but his posture spoke volumes. He was not a happy camper. She'd gauged that much from his last text message, but this looked different. It felt different. Unsure how to address it, she turned back to the shelving.

When she heard the door, she'd stopped what she was doing. She'd placed the last container only partially in place. It perched precariously on the edge; so, she pushed it the remainder of the way into position.

The air stirred behind her and she felt the warmth of Kenneth's body in her personal space. It brought back the memory of the first interaction they'd had last week. Only this time, she knew how his body felt pressed against hers as well as how his lips felt when they captured her own.

Rotating slowly, she faced him bumping his chest with her shoulder as she made the transition. He didn't move to give her more space and she didn't request it. Once they were face to face, she broke the silence.

"Are you going to talk to me or just stare?"

"Both."

"Ok...So talk."

Initially he stayed silent. Releasing an exasperated breath, she shifted to the side preparing to leave, but his arm shot out blocking her escape.

"Kenneth..."

"You know...I had a kind of shitty day today, but I pushed through because I knew coming here would make me feel better." Trailing his fingers up her bare arms, he drew small circles as he talked.

"This class is normally a satisfying experience, but with you here, it became the highlight of my day. I really needed that. So, when you said you weren't coming, I'll admit I had a moment. I actually intended to apologize for my behavior when class was over, but now I have questions."

His digits stopped their trek at her shoulders where he toyed with the wide straps of her shirt resting there—slipping beneath the straps he touched the skin.

"Questions, such as?"

"Why are you leading your little friend on?"

"What?" Candy's brow furrowed in genuine confusion. "What little friend?"

"Clive."

"I sincerely have no idea what you're talking about."

Abandoning the straps, he wrapped his fingers around the back of her neck lifting her chin with his thumbs. Lowering his head, he invaded her space even more.

Why her core picked that moment to clench, she couldn't say, but between the sound of his voice and the way he touched her, the walls of her center slickened in arousal. This wasn't sexy. *Was it?*

"I'm not a jealous man. Not normally, but I have eyes. I see the way he looks at you."

Leaning closer, he spoke the words directly into her ear, tickling her lobe. Pulling her head back as far as his hold allowed, she locked eyes with him.

"Do you also see the way I'm *not* looking at him? I've said exactly two words to the man since the first day of class, which was also the first day I recall ever meeting him."

"So, the smiles and giggles were my imagination?"

"Seriously? This is what we're doing? If it is, maybe we should just stop whatever this is right now."

"It's that easy for you? You can just turn it off?" His voice deepened to nearly a growl.

She thought there wasn't any space between them, but he shifted his frame closer to hers blocking her vision of anything but him. With her back against the open shelving, there was nowhere for her to go.

"No." She replied breathily. "It's not easy for me, but if you're already accusing me of things, maybe this isn't what we should be doing."

"Is that what you think?" He asked, but he didn't really want an answer because his lips snatched her response before her words reached the air.

His kiss wiped her mind of any thought which didn't include the feelings he awakened in her. The hands that were previously hanging limply at her sides, grasped onto his shirt eager to feel his hard body beneath her fingers.

Shoving one hand into the hair at her nape, he used the other to skim down her body, stopping along the way to tease her curves. A moan escaped her when he slipped his fingers into the bodice of her fitted top and tweaked her nipple. Instinctively, she clamped her thighs together in response to the bolt of pleasure shooting through her channel.

"You like that?" Kenneth delivered the words in a husky chuckle. "If you like that, you'll love this."

His words were followed by his fingers shoving her panties to the side, unerringly finding her clit then providing a pinch with just the right amount of pressure. So caught up in the kissing, she hadn't even realized he lifted her skirt.

Kenneth's fingers squeezing the little bundle of nerves was a shock of pleasure causing her to cry out. Lost in the moment, she gave no thought to her location as she allowed herself to dip her hands beneath his shirt to feel the warmth of his skin and the hardness of his body. Curving her fingers, her short nails scraped against his back drawing a hiss from him.

Lifting his head, he speared her with a heated look before grabbing her hands removing them from inside his shirt. Her confused expression was met with a cryptic half smile as he reached out, grasped the straps at her shoulders and forcefully tugged them down her arms exposing her breast to his hungry eyes.

Chapter Seven

MY OWN PERSONAL CANDY

He should stop. He knew he should, but he couldn't. This wasn't the place, but his body wouldn't listen to reason. She tried to break things off. Kenneth couldn't allow the idea to take root. Stopping now wasn't an option. Maybe that first night, before he tasted her sweet lips, he could've let her walk away.

Not now though. Now, she was in his system. Just the thought of not having her tipped his mind into a space he would normally consider unhinged, but currently seemed perfectly legitimate.

Once the air hit her bountiful breast, her nipples puckered calling out to him like a siren's song. Cupping the generous globes, he licked her sand dollar sized areola before capturing a turgid peak between his teeth nibbling with alternately firm and gentle bites. Candy's gasping moans were his guide to applying the right amount of force to bring her the most pleasure.

Her fingers dove into his close-cropped hair; her nails scraped across his scalp sending a pleasurable zing straight to his already throbbing cock. He really should stop. But, he didn't. His logical mind was safely tucked away in the corner behind a steel door where he could barely hear the sage advice being offered.

Not that he was listening for it. The feel of her silky-smooth skin made him wish for more time to explore, but their need had grown urgent. All he could think about was sinking inside her heated channel.

Moving from one breast to give the other equal attention, he simultaneously sought out the edge of her skirt lifting it until his fingertips encountered her thick thighs. He couldn't wait to feel them wrapped around him as he drove into her sweet depths. He'd yet to taste her, but he was certain he'd become addicted with the first lick.

The whimpering sound she emitted when he made contact with her thighs prompted him to once again seek out the treasure at the apex of her legs. Reluctantly releasing her nipple, he gave her breast a parting kiss then dropped to his knees before her.

To clear the path to his goal, he tucked the edge of her skirt into the waistband and jerked her panties down to her ankles. Tapping her left calf then her right, he instructed her to lift her feet to completely remove the garment. Stuffing them into a pocket he finally allowed himself to look at the object of his current obsession.

She kept the area neatly trimmed, but not bare. Just the way he liked it. He was in favor of a well-maintained garden, but he didn't care for a completely bare landscape. Leaning forward he inhaled her fragrance. Her scent washed over him.

With a low growl, he lifted her left leg, tossed it over his shoulder and dove face first into her delicious smelling pussy. Her flavor burst on his tongue. It was impossible for him to suppress his delight in her taste.

"Mmmm...So sweet. My own personal Candy." He murmured before diving back into her depths.

His shaft thickened in his trousers, but he couldn't tear himself away from her slick folds to relieve the ache. It was just as he thought. One sample and he was addicted.

Gliding one then two fingers into her channel, he delighted in sucking her clit while lapping at the sweet cream dripping from her passage. Her whimpers of enjoyment quickly became his favorite soundtrack.

As much as he relished in the noises, his throbbing cock demanded to feel the gripping warmth his fingers enjoyed. Crooking his digits, he located that special spot and applied pressure while tugging on her clit.

"Oh, oh, oh shit! I'm gonna... Oh!" Candy's voice trailed off with a keening wail as she reached her climax.

Not wanting one drop to go to waste, Kenneth quickly withdrew his fingers from her sheath replacing them with his tongue. He lapped at her fountain of ambrosia until her tremors subsided to intermittent gasps and jerks.

Planting one last kiss on his new favorite treat, he shifted her leg from his shoulder then stood. Admiring the flush beneath the surface of her beautiful golden-brown skin, he took pride in her disheveled state. Her body leaned against the shelving as if it were the only thing holding her upright.

Wrapping his arms around her, he allowed her to feel the stiffness of his length pressed into her belly. Starting at her shoulder, he kissed a trail across her collar bone and up her neck.

"You're so beautiful when you come, baby. Do you want to show me again? Hmm?"

Peppering kisses along her jaw, he recaptured her lips swallowing her moans. Releasing their pillowy softness, he stared into her face. Heightened arousal held her eyelids at half-mast as she released shallow pants.

"Tell me, baby. Tell me you want to feel me inside you, that you want me to see how good you look when you take all of me."

The gravelly quality in his voice was foreign to him, but he didn't dwell on it. He needed the words so he could bury himself inside her velvety center.

"Yes. Please, Kenneth. Let me feel you."

Nimble fingers reached beneath his shirt skimming his abdomen before landing at the top of his pants and tugging. Jerking his hips back, he grasped her hands pinning them above her head.

"Stay."

The one-word command was issued with a piercing look before he removed his hands then released his throbbing shaft from the confines of his trousers.

Her desire filled eyes followed his movements as he rubbed himself while staring at the decadent picture she presented. Later, he'd reflect on how fucking perfect she was in that moment, but not now. Now, he had to get inside of her before he lost what little control he had left.

"Open." Tapping her inner thighs, he issued another directive to which she immediately complied.

"Good girl." He murmured smiling at her sharp intake of breath following his praise.

Spreading her thick legs made him groan at the lusty thoughts flooding his brain.

Planting a scorching kiss on her slightly parted lips, he bent at the knees, slipped an arm under each thigh and stood lifting her from the floor. Using the shelving to his advantage, he balanced her against the surface as he guided his eager cock into her silken walls.

Her startled gasp, followed by a gratified moan was music to his ears as he pressed into her. The way she clamped down on his length almost pulled his seed straight from his shaft on the first thrust. As eager as he was to find release, he wanted to experience her orgasm while he was deep inside her. That wouldn't happen if he blew his load within the first minute.

Unconcerned about anything aside from pleasing her, he began his crusade to bring her to completion with shallow thrusts ending in the circular movement of his hips to press his pelvis against her clit. The added pressure against the little bundle of nerves caused her to release another gush of warmth bathing his turgid length, making him stiffen even harder inside her.

He wasn't going to last, but he had to see her fall over the cliff into bliss with him. Beginning a driving rhythm, he watched her face listening to her sounds of enjoyment allowing them to guide him to the place he needed to be to tip her into nirvana.

When her head dropped back on her shoulders and her pants transitioned from incoherent words becoming a jumble of noises, he knew she was almost there. Dipping his head, he traced the column of her throat with his lips before latching onto the stiff peak of her nipple.

The combination of breast play, clitoral stimulation and his hard length shuttling in and out of her slick pussy pushed her exactly where he wanted her. Her teeth imprisoned her bottom lip then her eyes squeezed shut as she tumbled into oblivion once more.

The sight of her achieving her release catapulted him over the edge with her. His smooth thrusts became jerky pounding until he went ramrod straight, embedded to the hilt in her clasping walls. His seed spurted from him in a surprising torrent. He was sure he'd never come so hard in his life.

Kissing her lips, peppering her face, neck and shoulders with affection, he praised her for her responsiveness to his touch, how well she accepted him taking his full length into her sweet depths. The hitch in her breathing followed by the tightening of her walls on his shaft alerted him to the resurgence of her arousal.

The scent of their lovemaking hung thickly in the air, but it didn't obscure the combined aroma of the herbs, spices and other ingredients housed in the over-sized closet. Knowing they couldn't stay as they were, he pulled out of the warmth of her snug channel setting her on her feet.

It was much later before either of them acknowledged nothing separated them during that key moment. In real time, they took a few minutes to come down from their orgasmic pinnacle—staring into one another's eyes allowing reality to seep into their bubble.

With one more kiss, he stepped back and helped her straighten her clothing before tucking his semi-hardened length back into his pants. It hadn't been five minutes since he was inside her and his dick was already gearing up for another round.

Regardless if that would happen tonight, it didn't need to happen again where they currently stood. Gently guiding her from the room, he nudged her toward her station to grab her purse suggesting she go across the hall to the ladies room to freshen up. As she walked away, he turned back to the pantry to see how much, if any, damage they'd done.

By the time she returned, he'd finished in the pantry. The damage had been pretty contained, but he did toss some of the items from the shelves. He made notes to have them replaced. It was bad form to fuck his woman in the pantry of the classroom, but he couldn't bring himself to regret a single second of it.

Gathering his things, he wrapped an arm around her waist and they left the room. Their night was far from over, but a change of venue was in order.

At eight a.m. on a Saturday morning, Kenneth stood on the porch of the craftsman style house waiting patiently for Candy to answer the door. He no longer thought of her as Candace, even in his thoughts. However, his reason for calling her Candy was different from everyone else's.

Once he tasted the sweet flavor of her essence in that pantry, he could only think of her as his own personal candy source. While not a part of the Dom-Sub community, he'd been told more than once he exhibited the tendencies of a Pleasure Dom. Giving her pleasure and taking her to the brink time after time had become his addiction. He had no desire to be cured.

The door opened to reveal a fresh-faced Candy dressed in a bright yellow tank top paired with neutral-colored capris he was certain hugged the curve of her voluptuous ass perfectly. He'd instructed her to dress comfortably. She had followed his directive from her outfit, to the way she swept her hair up in a coily puff atop her head.

Slipping one arm around her waist, he pulled her to him and planted a kiss on her lips while simultaneously closing the door. Tapering the kiss to gentle pecks before he put them completely off track, he pulled away to look into her face.

"Well, hello to you too." She smiled showing off the cute little dimple in her right cheek. Patting his chest, she extracted herself from his arms.

"You look beautiful. Are you all set to go?" He asked, watching the sway of her hips as she walked away from him.

"Yup. Just let me grab my purse." She tossed over her shoulder.

Following her deeper into the house, he forced himself to look at the artwork on the walls. If he didn't, they'd never make it to any of the activities he had planned for them. He'd been looking forward to this all week.

Between their schedules, they had to make a concerted effort to see one another. This was the first Saturday she wasn't working and he wasn't volunteering. As much as he'd love to spend endless hours making her delirious from continuous orgasms, there had to be more to their relationship than amazing sex. He was determined to show her his interest in her extended beyond the sexual.

Once she retrieved her brown leather crossbody purse, he snagged her hand, led her out to his vehicle and they began their journey to Piedmont park. Because she lived in Logan City, it would take them roughly forty-five minutes to reach their destination. By the time they arrived and found parking, the Fresh Market would be open.

They kept up a light banter on the way, but didn't delve into any deep discussions. The moments where they lapsed into silence were comfortable and unstrained. That was one of the things he enjoyed about spending time with her outside of the bedroom. They didn't have to fill every second with chatter.

They could simply exist contentedly in the same space. It was something he hadn't experienced often in his previous attempts at dating. Due to his career, some women seemed to think they had to prove themselves to be extra interesting in order to hold his attention.

It was completely unnecessary, but no amount of reassurance from him worked to squash such behavior. With Candy, it was never an issue. She was completely comfortable in her skin. If she had a question about something, she asked. If he asked her something, she answered. She didn't feel the need to spout her achievements and accolades to him, even though he knew she had plenty to brag about if she chose to do so.

"Is this why you told me to wear comfortable clothes and shoes?" Candy asked while staring at the sign announcing their entrance into the park.

"Yes, it is. I'm sure you've been here before and are familiar with how far parking is from most of the events."

"I'm aware." She continued staring out of the window. "I didn't know they had anything going on over here this early in the day though."

"Well, it seems you're going to learn many new things today." He smiled as he maneuvered the SUV into a space near an easily recognizable landmark. It would help them locate it when it was time to leave.

"It would seem so." She murmured releasing her seat belt when he put the car in park.

Before they got out of the car, he produced a tube of sunscreen encouraging her to apply it to her exposed skin. He slathered the protective lotion on his legs and arms before volunteering to do her hard-to-reach areas.

With laser focus, he concentrated on smoothing the cream on her shoulders and the part of her back exposed by the dip in her tank top. It would do him zero good to get caught up in how soft her skin felt under his fingers. Their day was all mapped out; his intention was for them to enjoy every minute of it.

Once he was done helping her with the sunscreen, he shut off the vehicle and hopped out. He rounded the car, pleased she'd unlatched her safety belt, but hadn't attempted to open the door to get out. He lifted the hatch to retrieve his produce bags from the trunk before continuing around to her side. Opening the door, he extended a hand to help her out.

"I see one of your lessons has already taken root," he murmured into her ear before dropping a quick kiss to her cheek. "Good girl."

Smirking devilishly, he observed her trying to hide the effect those two words had on her. She could try all she wanted, but he'd figured her out. A well placed, *'Good girl'* from him was a quick way to jump start her arousal.

Even though it would be hours before he'd actually do anything to relieve the ache his words elicited, he smiled in anticipation of keeping her at a low throb. He held an internal debate on how long she could withstand it before she folded.

Leading her to the row of bicycles, he stopped at the sign and scanned the QR code to open the app. He rented two bikes from the ones available. From one of their previous conversations, he'd learned she knew how to ride—even if it had been a while since she'd done it. Riding a bike was one of those things which was etched into one's muscle memory. Once a person learned, it was easy to get re-acclimated to the activity.

"Where are you taking me that we need bikes? I'm not sure I'm dressed for biking trails. I'm dressed for comfort not for exercise."

Selecting a bike with the most comfortable looking seat from the rack, he rolled it towards her. "Don't worry. The bikes are to make it easier for us to get from place to place inside the park a little more quickly. No trail riding. I promise." Tipping the bike handle closer to her, he encouraged her to take it.

Once she had it securely, he went back and pulled another from the rack for himself. Placing the produce bags in the basket attached to the front of the bike, he swung a leg over to mount it. Looking at her expectantly, he waited for her to do the same.

"Are you good?"

"I'm okay."

Despite his confidence she could handle it, he felt compelled to check on her well-being before they set off on the path. Keeping the pace on the moderately low side, they made it to the farmer's market to see vendors already set up ready to sell their fresh produce. Swinging off his temporary transportation, Kenneth motioned for Candy to follow suit.

Pushing their bikes alongside them, they approached the first tent on the right side of the path. It was large with the opening big enough for them to roll the bikes inside. Candy hesitated, but Kenneth waved a hand for her to bring it along. Grinning broadly, he greeted the older man with deeply tanned skin and short dark hair shot through with gray.

"Buenos Dias, Emiliano! Como estas?"

"Estoy bien, mi amigo."

Shaking hands with his friend, Kenneth turned to introduce Candy. Lightly grazing his fingers along her arm, he nudged her forward.

"Emiliano, this beautiful lady is Candace Hampton. Sweetheart, this is my good friend Emiliano. He has some of the best organic produce you'll find at this market."

Candy's eyes widened slightly at the endearment, but she recovered quickly. Extending a hand, she accepted Emiliano's handshake, murmuring the normal pleasantries.

They exchanged small talk for a few moments before Kenneth asked if they could park their bikes behind Emiliano's tent to keep them from being rented by someone else while they shopped at the market. As expected, his friend agreed with a wave of his hand.

Kenneth met Emiliano during his first visit to the Green Market not long after he moved to the city. Kenneth was exploring weekend activities online when he stumbled across the event schedule for Piedmont Park noticing that they had a farmer's market starting in early spring extending to the beginning of winter.

New to the city, he had no plans, so he struck out early one Saturday to check it out. It quickly became his favorite place to get produce, fresh bread, jam along with a multitude of other items he used for his personal cooking and sometimes in the classes he taught.

After stashing their bikes alongside the bins behind the tent, they came back inside where Kenneth took Candy around to the neatly arranged crates. With their dinner plans in mind, he began selecting vegetables.

His strategy for their date was to start at the Green Market, next go over to the Ice Cream Festival that was scheduled to begin in a couple of hours, then head to his place where they'd put some of the items they bought to use. If everything went as he planned, the day would be enjoyable and end with a great meal they prepared together.

Chapter Eight
WHAT DID THAT SAY ABOUT HER?

Candy wasn't sure what to expect when Kenneth asked her to spend the day with him. They'd been seeing one another as regularly as they could for a few weeks. Things were moving quicker than she usually allowed, but she couldn't seem to stop the momentum. Honestly, she really didn't want to.

There were no hard and fast rules to restrict them from doing whatever they wanted as consenting adults. She was approaching her mid-thirties and Kenneth was over forty. They weren't little kids experimenting. They enjoyed each other's company. There was nothing wrong with that.

Observing him, she marveled at his enthusiasm for tasks others may consider mundane. She'd noticed it in class as well. For a man with such a fit body, he had a genuine love affair with food. Even when they weren't together in the teacher-student environment, meals or snacks were a component of their activities.

At the moment, he was browsing the crates of vegetables in Emiliano's tent—picking up various legumes. From what she could see, Emiliano primarily had varieties of tomatoes, but there were crates of onions and peppers as well. Kenneth turned the tomatoes over in his hands, sniffed then lightly weighed them before either placing them back in the crate or in the produce bag dangling from his fingers.

"The key to picking good tomatoes is looking for vibrant coloring, feeling it for firmness and smelling it right here." He pointed to the green stem tipping it closer to Candy's nose, inviting her to take a whiff of the fruit most people treated as a vegetable.

"Do you smell that? Smells kind of earthy and sweet, right? That's how you know you have a good one." He smiled showing even white teeth.

His enthusiasm was contagious and she returned the gesture. It was nice to see him so excited about a task. His face took on a boyish quality when he explained things of interest to him. Spotting a viable candidate, she picked it up then went through the process he demonstrated before raising it for his inspection.

"I think this is a good one." She said holding up her plump, red, offering.

Wrapping his fingers around hers, he lifted it closer to his nose, sniffed it then pulled it back for further examination. Nodding, he displayed another of those knee-buckling grins.

"Good job, Babe." Gliding his fingers around her nape, he tugged her forward and pressed a quick kiss to her upturned lips before going back to the perusing the crates as if he hadn't just caused a flood of moisture in her panties.

Taking a second to give her girlie bits a stern talking to, she eventually returned to the great tomato search as well. "Do you have a particular amount of these you want? I think I might get one or two for sandwiches."

"Hmm... Of this kind, I think we need five for what I have planned. If you want a tomato for sandwiches, you should get this kind." He pointed to the larger tomatoes in the next bin labeled, Brandywine.

"They slice well and have a great flavor."

"I usually get the beefy ones from the grocery store, but I'll try these out."

"Those work too, but I like these better." He shifted to allow her easier access to the container.

Stepping closer to the section with Roma and Cherry tomatoes, he started his selection process over, picking up bundles then evaluating them before either placing them in the bag or back in the crate. Tearing herself from watching him make ordinary tasks look sexy, she made her choices and joined him.

Once they had what they needed from Emiliano's tent, they paid for their purchases. He allowed them to tuck their purchases in a secure location to keep their hands free as they walked around the market. Neither of them had eaten breakfast, so they grabbed pastries along with juice from a kiosk near the entrance.

As they made their way through the maze of tents, stands and kiosks, it didn't surprise her that Kenneth knew someone at almost each place they stopped. He had a magnetism about him which drew people to him.

Whether it was his good looks or his abilities as a social chameleon, but the vendors were all smiles when he approached their booths. Well, most of them were all smiles. A few of the women's expressions turned sour when they saw him holding her hand or deferring to her in conversation. Kenneth was either oblivious or unbothered, so Candy followed his lead in how she interacted with them.

She did get the chance to impress him with her knowledge of bread varieties when they stopped at a vendor selling artisan breads. She'd eaten the last of her focaccia a couple of days earlier, so she selected the size best suited for making one sandwich and declined the offer of croissants from the seller.

"No thank you. I'm planning to make sandwiches and I typically have croissants with breakfast."

"Are you sure?" Kenneth asked. "It doesn't have to be either or, you can get both. These croissants are the perfect size for sandwiches." He held a money clip in one hand prepared to pay for her selection.

"I'm sure. I don't care for the way the croissant flakes sometimes. It makes for a messy eating experience. I know the focaccia crumbles a bit, but not to the degree that a croissant does."

"If you're sure..." He held the statement out as he added a baguette to their purchase then accepted the cloth bag from the young lady selling the baked goods.

Time flew by as they worked their way through the extensive market filled with just about every type of garden-fresh item one could imagine. It wasn't a conventional outing for a date, but she was glad he'd brought her there. She sincerely enjoyed it and planned to come back in the future.

With Kenneth's hands filled with their purchases, they wound their way through the booths to reach the shelter of Emiliano's tent. Once they'd retrieved their bags, they went around to the back and loaded the items into the baskets on the bikes with him taking the bulk of them while placing the breads and other, lightweight items, in her basket.

When they were done loading up, they said their goodbyes to Emiliano and biked back to Kenneth's vehicle. The sun was higher in the sky, causing a rise in the temperature. So, the breeze generated by riding felt amazing as it whipped through the blousy tank top she wore.

After they unloaded the items into the expensive Snow Beast cooler in Kenneth's trunk, they wheeled the bikes in the direction of the racks. She veered left to load her bike onto the rack not noticing that he was no longer beside her.

"Babe? What are you doing?" He called out to her. Turning, she realized he was pointed in the opposite direction of the rack.

"I'm putting my bike away. Aren't we done?"

"Not yet. We have one more place to go before we grab lunch." Suspicious of his mischievous grin, she slowly rolled in his direction.

"Don't look so worried. You're going to love it."

Swinging a leg over to mount his bike, he motioned for her to do the same. Giving him half-hearted side-eye, she climbed on and followed him as he took a different path than the one that led them to the market. She exercised regularly, but she hadn't ridden in years. She was certain her quads were going to make her pay later.

Riding alongside him, she figured out where they were going before they got to their destination. As they drew closer, the sounds of music and people reached her ears. Then, she saw bright colored inflatable air dancers waving their floppy arms as they wiggled in the wind.

A bright smile took over her face when the event banner came into view. He'd brought her to the Ice Cream Festival! The excitement coursing through her was reminiscent of the joy she felt attending similar events as a child. She'd brought her niece and nephews to this event last year, but she'd forgotten this was the weekend for the festivities.

They slowed to a stop, then located a rack to park their bikes. She waited while Kenneth fiddled with the app ending the rental. They'd rented the type that could be left at any rack and picked up by someone else, but she hoped the two they had would still be there when they returned.

Initially, they went from stand to stand getting samples before she finally tried a variety that made her want a whole scoop. Getting a different flavor for himself, Kenneth got her a waffle cone with a scoop and a half of the rich creamy goodness. She didn't even know it was possible to purchase a half scoop, but she went along with it.

Dipping her spoon into the decadent combination of vanilla bean ice cream with salted caramel, almonds and chocolate mousse chips, Candy's mouth watered in anticipation. The first spoonful hit her tongue, making her head drop back on her shoulder. Her eyes closed as she savored the sweet, salty goodness.

"Mmm... It's so good!" Her moan of enjoyment couldn't be contained; she hummed pleasurably as the cool, sweet treat, trickled down her throat.

When she lifted her lids, Kenneth's heated stare captured her gaze almost making her forget the ice cream in her hand. The look projected many things having nothing to do with the dessert and promised things that were best done in private. Only when he looked down at his own portion was she able to resume eating the delicious concoction.

He'd selected lemon cake ice cream for himself. It was a lemon-flavored ice cream with chunks of lemon pound cake inside. Candy wrinkled her nose at his offer for her to try it.

"No thank you."

"Are you sure? You keep staring at it. I don't mind sharing."

The way his voice dropped an octave when he offered to share brought forth thoughts which had zero to do with ice cream, but she managed to stay on topic with her response.

"I'm sure. It seems like the cake would be soggy. Cookies barely hold up to being in ice cream without going soft."

"The cake isn't soggy and the ice cream is quite delicious. Here. Try a little taste." Scooping a small portion of ice cream with some cake on the edge of the spoon, he held it to her lips.

Skepticism colored her expression as she eyed the offering. Kenneth advancing the utensil while making choo-choo noises broke her. She parted her lips to accept it with a giggle at his antics.

"Mmm!" She exclaimed, surprised at the taste and texture of the cake with ice cream combination.

Tapping her nose with the back of the spoon, then planting a quick kiss there, he grinned at her amazement.

"What did I tell you? Good, right?"

Swallowing, she nodded in agreement, then went back to eating her own sweet. They moved along, walking while enjoying their ice cream, people watching and chatting about the festivities. At one point, she could have sworn she saw her youngest nephew, Bryson.

However, the kid was there and gone so quickly, she couldn't be sure. It probably wasn't him anyway. Her parents had the kids this weekend. Candy wouldn't have seen Bryson without at least one of them being with him. They barely let Kaden go places without them, it was highly unlikely seven-year-old Bryson was out unsupervised.

She had such a good time with Kenneth, she almost pouted when he suggested it was time to go.

"Don't give me that face." He wrapped his fingers around her forearm and tugged her closer to him.

"We've had enough carnival food. Besides, we didn't think to put on more sunscreen. Your shoulders are getting a little red. It looks like you're getting sunburned. Time to call it a day, Baby."

His fingers lightly grazed the top of her shoulders and his point was made when she flinched from the slight touch hissing from the pain. She'd noticed the heat of the summer sun on her shoulders, but hadn't given it much thought.

They lucked out. The bikes they rented earlier were still in the rack, so they were able to hop on and ride them back to where they'd parked. Ensconced in Kenneth's luxury SUV, Candy soaked up the cool breeze from the air conditioning. She stole glances at him as he maneuvered the vehicle from the lot.

Up to this point, the day had been great and according to him, it wasn't over. As far as dates went, this was one of the better ones she'd had. It just goes to show that extravagance wasn't always required. The simplicity of the day allowed them time to get to know each other in different ways.

Even with Kenneth keeping her sexually on edge with his random touches, kisses and innuendo laden remarks, he allowed her to see another facet to his personality at the market then again at the festival. There were so many layers to the man. She looked forward to peeling away each and every one.

Gazing out of the passenger window, she admired the well-manicured lawns of the homes on the street they'd just turned onto. Given the high temperature, she hadn't expected to see anyone outside, but there were a few people out, walking their dogs or working in their yards.

This wasn't her first time coming to Kenneth's home, but it was the first time so early in the day. Her previous visits occurred just as the sun was setting or during full darkness. Not that they were sneaking around; they were adults with work lives. Their daylight hours tended to be consumed with their jobs.

Pressing a button on the console, Kenneth slowed the vehicle and guided it into the driveway of his two-story home on a large corner lot. Parking inside the three-car garage, he shut off the engine then hopped out of the vehicle. Once he'd assisted her in getting out, he grabbed the items from the cooler in the trunk.

Since his hands were full, she snagged his keys and opened the door leading from the garage into a short hallway. Bumping the button to close the garage door, he stepped inside kicking off his shoes.

"Thanks for getting the door, Baby." Pressing a quick kiss to her forehead, he continued down the hall to the kitchen.

Closing the door behind her, Candy slipped her shoes off and followed him. Entering the large eat-in kitchen, she observed Kenneth pulling items from the various bags and inspecting them before placing them to the side. When he spotted her standing in the doorway, he immediately stopped what he was doing.

"I almost forgot."

Snapping his fingers, he pulled open a drawer retrieving a pair of scissors. At least they kind of looked like scissors to her, but not really any she'd seen before. One of the blades was slightly curved and he flicked a button forward to open them.

Striding into the next room, he was gone a few seconds before reappearing with a piece of aloe in one hand. Going back to the counter area, he grabbed a knife from the block then set it on the cutting board already on the countertop.

"Come here, Sweetheart."

Her feet started moving, obeying his directive without her consciously issuing the command to them. He bordered on bossy most days, but she apparently liked it, because she didn't push back often. *What did that say about her?*

The internal question went unanswered as she walked fully into the kitchen, not stopping until she was directly in front of him feeling the warmth wafting off his body.

Chapter Nine
WHO MADE THEM?

Kenneth sliced down the center of the aloe breaking through the skin exposing the natural healing gel inside. Candy's normally golden-brown skin had darkened under the hot sun, but the redness on her shoulders was the start of a potentially painful sunburn.

He'd worn a short-sleeved shirt covering his shoulders and biceps giving him more protection than she had with her tank top. He was also one of the fortunate people who didn't burn very easily. Candy was apparently the opposite. Even though they applied sun protection before they stepped from the car, she needed to re-apply at the suggested intervals and they hadn't done so.

He suppressed his smile at her automatic response when he directed her to come to him. She liked to think of herself as fiercely independent, which she was. But, with him, she revealed a more submissive nature. It was a declaration of trust he didn't think she even realized she was making.

He wouldn't go so far as to point it out to her. She might push back for the sake of being contrary. After their *talks* in the pantry, he knew she wouldn't allow him to run roughshod over her, but she trusted him to take care of her. Which is what he planned to do right now.

"Turn around for me, Baby."

She rotated, placing her back to him. Lifting the straps of her tank top, he carefully attempted to slide them from her shoulders. When it became obvious the material wasn't stretchy enough for him to do what he planned, he reached for the bottom edge of the garment.

"We need to take this off. Lift your arms for me." She shot him a glance over her shoulder, but complied.

He was aware of how serious and focused he appeared in the moment. Cautiously, he removed the shirt. She lowered her arms back to her sides once it cleared her fingertips.

Steeling himself against the lustful feelings invading his mind at seeing so much of her skin exposed, he focused on lowering her bra straps without scraping against the rounded tops of her shoulders. Knowing one flick of his fingers would release her bountiful breast to his view was torturous. Inhaling deeply, he wrangled his libido concentrating on the task at hand.

Scooping some of the aloe onto his fingertips, he gently rubbed the gel onto the reddened areas of her skin. The soft sighs she emitted were confirmation of the healing plant doing it's work. Taking the time to coat any spot that looked suspicious, he hyper-focused on the activity to keep his raging cock from inserting its horny intentions into the situation.

He finished administering the natural medicine and placed a kiss at the base of her exposed neck.

"All done, Baby. You can put your shirt back on if you want." As much as he loved looking at her, it was probably better if she did put her shirt on.

It was on the tip of his tongue to praise her for how well she followed instructions, but he stopped himself. He'd stumbled upon Candy's praise kink pretty early on and most of the time, he had no problem exploiting it. However, this time he restrained himself. Later though, all bets were off.

After placing the remaining piece of aloe in a plastic baggy, he crossed over to the dark wood-stained cabinet, grabbed a glass filling it with water from the refrigerator dispenser. When he turned back to Candy, she was pulling her shirt down, hiding her luscious body from him once more.

He told himself it was for the best as he passed her the water encouraging her to hydrate. Once he saw her take the glass to her lips and sip, he performed the same task for himself. Drinking the contents of his glass in two large gulps, he refilled it and checked Candy's progress.

Seeing her glass was still half full, he went back to his original chore of sorting through their purchases from the market, setting aside what he'd use for dinner. Washing what needed to be cleaned, he placed the remaining items in their designated places. Candy leaned against the other side of the counter and watched. He slipped easily into instructional mode when she observed him so intently.

Occasionally she asked a question about why he selected something or what he intended to do with it. He answered each question with the same thoroughness he would if they were in a classroom setting and not standing in his kitchen.

Just as he finished his sorting, he noticed her eyes droop a bit. She needed a nap. Georgia heat in July had a way of sapping a person's energy. They'd been going non-stop for over five hours—with the majority of that time being outside in the aforementioned heat.

Removing the now empty glass from her fingers, he placed it in the sink. Grabbing the aloe, he guided her from the kitchen with a hand at the small of her back. She didn't object when he led her up the stairs into his bedroom. He heard not a squeak of protest when he nudged her onto the bed, removed her socks and covered her with the blanket from the ottoman.

After removing his own socks, he climbed onto the bed with her. Pulling his cellphone from his pocket, he set an alarm then placed it on the nightstand.

Taking care to avoid direct contact with Candy's shoulders, he snuggled behind her wrapping one arm around her waist and nestling her ass into the cradle of his hips as they lay on their sides. In less than a minute, he heard her breathing even out indicating she was asleep.

That explained why she didn't put up a fight about being put down for a nap like a kid. She was wiped out. Tucking his other arm beneath the pillow, he cuddled close to her and joined her in dreamland.

When his phone chimed a little over an hour later, he quickly silenced it. Candy lay on her stomach with her head turned away from him, still sleeping peacefully. He couldn't resist placing a kiss on her cheek before rolling off the bed. Opting to let her sleep a bit longer, he hit the bathroom before going back downstairs to start the prep for dinner.

It was still mid-afternoon, so dinner was a few hours away, but he needed to occupy himself. If he didn't, he'd be tempted to wake her and as soundly as she was sleeping, she obviously needed the rest.

Continuing with his theme of simplicity, he'd planned for them to make pizza together. He didn't mix the dough the night before, so that's what he did while she slept. While he waited for the dough to rise, he puttered around the kitchen for a bit before going to the den and switching on the television.

He was halfway into hate-watching a show on one of the cooking channels when Candy's light footfalls drew his attention to the open doorway. Looking adorably disheveled, she entered the room. He wasn't certain she was fully awake.

Her zombie-like shuffle into the room made him think she was still half asleep. When she reached his side, she stood there looking so cute and confused, he tugged on her hand to pull her onto the sofa next to him. Sitting, she immediately curled into his side then went right back to sleep.

Curving his arm around her waist, he rested a hand on her hip, picked up his remote and went back to criticizing the celebrity chef who it seemed had never been introduced to *actual* seasonings in culinary school.

He could get used to this. Having her with him this way. As new as their relationship was, it already eclipsed those in his past. He knew without examining it too closely she fit perfectly into his life. The question was, did he fit into hers?

~

One month later

Kenneth pulled his silver SUV into position behind a lifted four by four on the side of Andrew and Bonita Frost's home. He was still feeling slightly irritated that Candy didn't accept his offer for them to ride together. They'd been seeing one another for almost two months, going out while doing all of the things couples did. All of the things except show up to family functions together apparently.

He tried, but he didn't understand her logic. They started their morning with her wrapped in his arms, but they couldn't share a car ride to the event to which they were both invited? Shaking his head, he turned off the vehicle then stepped out. Rounding the back, he pulled out the two twenty-four packs of drinks from his trunk.

Not wanting to add any anxiety to her already nervous anticipation, he didn't belabor the point, but they'd definitely talk about it later. The Labor Day Cookout would be her first time bringing a prepared food item to contribute.

Over their time together, she'd confided in him as to what drove her to sign up for the Adult Cooking class. So, he was aware of how important it was for her to not fumble the opportunity for her family to see her in a different light.

She'd settled on deviled eggs as her offering. It was a smart choice, because of the simplicity of the recipe. It was also a gamble depending on how much importance the people in attendance put on the dish.

Despite his irritation, he smiled when he recalled the look of pride on her face when she placed the last egg in the cute little carrier she purchased specifically for the cookout. The only help he'd provided was to suggest she sprinkle fresh chives over them after she dusted the eggs with paprika.

Children's squeals of laughter and the sound of adults conversing against a back drop of old school music reached his ears as he walked up the long driveway. For a change, he didn't bring a dessert, opting to purchase drinks after he spoke with Driscoll about what he could bring to the gathering.

Tugging at the brim of the ball cap shading his face, he balanced his packages, pressed the doorbell then waited. Shortly afterwards, he heard Mrs. Frost call out for him to come in. Stepping from the scorching heat into the cool interior, he greeted those standing in the kitchen.

He'd noticed the room was somewhat of a hub during these gatherings. People tended to congregate in the kitchen, by the pool or under the deck with the men at the huge grill that Mr. Frost only allowed AJ to man when he wasn't doing it himself.

"Hey there, Kenneth!"

"Hello, Miss Bonita. How are you?"

"Oh, I'm doing fine. I can't complain."

He noticed her eyes traveling between the drinks in his hands and his face. She'd probably never admit it, but she looked forward to the various cakes or pies he normally brought with him.

"Where should I put these?" He looked around the space for a cooler or a free surface area to place the items.

"You can put them over there by the door." She waved to the empty space beside the glass doors leading out onto the deck.

Per usual, McKenna was in the kitchen with her mother. An addition to the group were AJ's wife Safara and their twin daughters, Aminata and Aida. The twins were actually in the lounge area to the right, but their giggles carried over into the kitchen space.

Savory smells filled the air making Kenneth's stomach grumble. Once he deposited the drinks, McKenna got his attention.

"Thank you for bringing more drinks, Kenneth, but where's my cake?" McKenna asked with one hand pressed to her barely perceptible baby bump.

Smiling at her frankness, he replied. "Blame your husband. When I asked what I should bring, he suggested drinks. He said between you, Miss Bonita, and the other aunties dessert was covered."

Lifting a single eyebrow, McKenna nodded. "Mhmm. Okay. I'll just have a little talk with my darling husband. I had my mouth all set for another Sock It To Me cake."

Raising his hands in surrender, Kenneth smiled, then apologized once more before turning to join the men outside. As he reached for the handle, the other door opened stopping him in his tracks. Accompanied by two young children and her sister, Candy walked in beaming.

"Hey y'all!" She called out brightly holding the two trays of deviled eggs as if they were precious cargo.

The children uttered their excited greetings and zipped past Kenneth to join the twins. Safara drifted over behind them. His eyes raked over Candy's form appreciating the way the calf length sundress accentuated her curves. The large red flowers against the white background gave her skin a glowing quality.

The dress was not what she was wearing when he left her house earlier. If it had been, there was a good possibility they would've arrived much later—if at all.

"Are those deviled eggs, Candy?" McKenna asked, smiling encouragingly.

"Yes!" Candy's smile was so big, Kenneth couldn't help but to smile as well.

Despite his irritation, her joy was contagious and he was extremely proud of her. Her confidence in her cooking abilities had grown so much in the past two months. Bringing anything, that she made herself, to one of their family gatherings was a big deal for her.

"Who made them?"

Candy's smile dimmed slightly with her aunt's question, but she held it when she responded. "I made them, Auntie."

Placing the trays on the countertop she lifted the lid. McKenna and Candy's sister, Cherry, peered into the container.

"Ooo…They look so pretty." Cherry said bringing Candy's smile back to full mega-watt status.

"Thank you."

"Since when do you cook, Candy?"

"Mama!"

"What? I'm just asking."

"Mama…" McKenna gave her mother a warning look.

Kenneth stiffened, but didn't intervene. As much as he wanted to come to her defense, this was her family. Besides, he knew Candy could and would speak up for herself when she'd had enough.

"I can do stuff besides apply cosmetics and order take-out, Auntie." She said with a wiggle of her shoulders.

"Mmhmm." Was the only response from the older woman.

McKenna shot her another warning look before engaging Candy again comparing notes on recipes. She attempted to be subtle, but Kenneth knew what she was doing. She was allowing Candy to show her aunt her capabilities.

Inserting himself into their conversation, he strolled over. "I love a good deviled egg. Mind if I have one? I know it's not time to eat yet, but everything smells so good it's making my stomach rumble."

On cue, a loud growl emanated from his belly. Rounding the counter, he stood slightly behind Candy leaning one hand on the surface. When he reached toward the container, a sharp tap struck the back of his hand.

"Aht! You know better. Wash your hands first."

Miss Bonita's reprimand catapulted him back to the early days when he and his uncle lived with his Aunt Toni. She had done the exact same thing when he'd reached for food without washing first.

Grinning ruefully, he went to the sink to wash his hands. Drying them, he noticed Candy had shifted to allow him more space, but he stood exactly where he stood before slightly behind her on her left side. He didn't get a chance to reach inside the container because someone had already made him a sample plate.

He noted there was just the one egg removed from the container. Everyone's attention was glued to him as he lifted it popping the whole thing in his mouth. Closing his eyes, he savored the creamy texture of the filling, and the zing the Dijon mustard added.

"Mmmm... Perfect." Lifting his lids, he glimpsed the lustful look on Candy's face before she cleared it off.

Uncaring of their audience, he gave her a smoldering glance of his own. Blushing, she turned away from his gaze.

"Thank you." She murmured.

Snagging two more eggs from the tray, he pressed a kiss to her cheek, declared his intentions to find the guys and walked out onto the deck eating his pre-meal snack.

Chapter Ten

YOU OWE ME AN APOLOGY

Heat crept up Candy's neck and settled in her cheeks. She couldn't believe what he'd just done. It's not like they were seeing each other secretly, but they also weren't family official. *What was he thinking?*

Cherry leaned against the bar-top side of the counter with her chin propped on her hands. "So... Are we just going to pretend that didn't happen?"

Placing the top back on the container, Candy took the trays to the refrigerator. "Cherry, don't start."

"Don't start what? I'm just asking a question." Hopping up onto one of the tall stools, she looked to the other two women for back-up.

"Inquiring minds wanna know and he just put y'all business in the street. So, spill it. I've been with children for the past seventy-two hours. I need some adult conversation."

"You're not looking for conversation. You wanna gossip."

Placing a hand against her chest, Cherry sat up straight. "I do not. It's not gossip. Gossip is when you talk behind a person's back. I'm going straight to the source." She smiled cheekily, nodding in agreement with her own statement.

Before Candy could acknowledge her sister's statement, the children's laughter got louder and closer as Safara shooed them outside. Stepping partway onto the deck, she called down to AJ and the others below to inform them they were now on duty.

Closing the door behind her, she sauntered over to their group then slid into the seat next to Cherry. The other women watched her with curious expressions.

"What?" She hunched her shoulders. "You didn't think I was gonna sit over there with the children and miss out on the juicy stuff did you?" Her Kenyan accent coming through more strongly than usual with her question.

Everyone but Candy chuckled in response to Safara's statement. When their laughter died down, the four women pinned Candy with expectant looks. Kenneth had bumped a hornets nest, then walked away leaving her with the fallout.

"Spill it." Cherry prodded when Candy didn't start talking quickly enough.

"Spill what? There's nothing to spill. Kenneth and I are dating." She tried to play it off as no big deal, but they weren't buying it.

Candy really didn't like being the center of attention or focus of conversation. Unlike many middle children, she didn't do things for recognition to remind people she was more than someone's older or younger sister. The scrutiny made her uncomfortable.

It's not that she hadn't dated before Kenneth. However, the extended family had never met any of the guys she'd dated previously. A couple of the guys met her parents, but that's about it. Cassandra's track record made Candy gun shy when it came to bringing guys around.

Her older sister picked one criminal after another. Even if two of them were the white-collar type, a crook is a crook. The last one talked her into helping him hold McKenna hostage in her own home, which landed Cassi in prison.

"Don't act all shy now, Candy. We like Kenneth around here. If we didn't he wouldn't have made it past one visit." Her aunt chided.

"I'm not, Auntie. I just wasn't expecting him to do that."

"Why not? How long have y'all been seeing each other?"

"Close to two months."

"What?! And you didn't say anything?" Cherry screeched.

"Why would I? Do you know how many guys I've dated for a couple of months prior to now?"

"Other guys don't count." Cherry pouted. "Besides, I bet you told Kari."

"Cher, please don't start about me telling Kari things I don't tell you. I don't complain when you tell Kim things you don't tell me."

"Whatever." Cherry huffed. "Don't try to change the subject. We were talking about you and Mr. Perfect."

"Why do you call him that?" Safara's brow wrinkled with her question.

"You've seen him. He's handsome, tall, as well as muscular without being bulky. Straight, white teeth. Dresses nice. Still has all of his hair. You get the picture." Cherry flipped her hand palm up in the universal 'duh' gesture.

"You've been looking mighty close."

"Not like that, Auntie." Cherry said quickly. "I have eyes though and he's a good-looking guy. But, Mr. Perfect is what some of the other cousins call him."

Candy perked up at that statement. "Other cousins like who?"

She wasn't jealous. She was simply curious as to who was scoping Kenneth out. That's all. Pure curiosity.

Waving a hand, McKenna pulled Candy's attention.

"Ahh... Forget all that noise Cherry's talking. You said two months. You two have been seeing each other for two months. Which means all summer.

This ain't cuffing season, so I suspect this is more than a hook-up situation—especially with him openly showing affection in front of all of us. I'm not trying to tell you what to do, but I'd suggest you have a chat with him before Aunt Sherilyn gets here."

"OOhh!... Mama doesn't know?" Cherry covered her mouth in shock.

Pushing Cherry's shoulder McKenna shushed her. "Stop it. You're being messy. Leave her alone." Turning back to Candy with a serious expression she advised, "You do need to go talk to your man though, because it seems like today is coming out day for y'all."

A chorus of agreeing sentiments came from the other women. Realizing she had to roll with the situation or get run over, Candy left the kitchen in search of Kenneth. She seriously hadn't planned for this, especially not the whole possibility of dealing with her parents.

The heat immediately hit her in the face when she stepped out onto the deck. Happy her dress had pockets, she reached inside and retrieved the hand fan she'd stashed there earlier. The habit of carrying a fan in the summer was a holdover from their Nana Hortense. She gifted many of the girls with pretty decorated fans when they were younger.

Following the sound of male voices, she located Kenneth below the deck with Driscoll, AJ, her Uncle Drew and Papa Earl. Not wanting to interrupt, but knowing her parents would probably show up any minute, she stepped into the shaded area.

Greeting everyone, she hugged her grandfather and uncle before politely asking Kenneth if she could speak to him. His ready response of "Sure, Babe" caused some raised eyebrows, but she studiously ignored them as they walked around the corner.

Since the pool area was too crowded for her tastes, she led him inside to one of the basement bedrooms. Once they were alone, she wasn't sure how to begin. They'd had a tense conversation earlier when he brought up the subject of them riding together, and she didn't want this to turn into a full-blown argument.

The room was relatively sparse containing only a bed with one night stand and a mirrored dresser. Kenneth leaned against the dresser. He watched her pace for a few moments before breaking the silence.

"What's going on, Candy?"

"Why did you do that?" She hadn't meant to blurt it out, and she definitely didn't mean for it to come out so harshly. But, she couldn't take it back.

"Why did I do what?" Snagging her wrist, he tugged her between his spread legs, wrapped his arms around her, resting his hands on her lower back. When he'd positioned her where he wanted her, he asked again.

"Why did I do what?"

"Kiss me. In front of them. Then you called me Babe. In front of my grandpa."

A line appeared in his brow as he regarded her. "I kiss you all the time. Every time I see you. Whether it's hello, goodbye or see you in a bit. I kiss you quite often. Am I not supposed to kiss you just because your family is around?

It's not like I shoved my tongue down your throat. It was a little peck on the cheek. What's the big deal?"

"When you kissed me, they started asking me all these questions about us." She picked at the design on the front of his shirt to avoid looking directly at him.

"Okay..." He dipped his head to capture her eyes.

"I wasn't ready."

"Ready for what? For your family to know we're together?"

Lifting her head, she bravely met his gaze. "Well... Yeah."

Kenneth's expression darkened causing her stomach to clench with trepidation. She wanted to take her statement back, but it was too late. Besides, it was true. She wasn't ready to be under the microscope. They were too new and if things didn't work out, it could get awkward.

After a brief, but intense silence, Kenneth spoke again. "Tell me something. Is your issue with your family knowing we're together or knowing it right now?"

"Both." Her voice was barely above a whisper, but he heard her. His brow knitted with his building frustration which her next statement turned into to a full scowl.

"We haven't discussed any of this. For all I know, you could be seeing me and someone else at the same time. We haven't made any promises to one another."

Kenneth's head jerked back as if she'd slapped him. His jaw clenched so hard she saw the muscle rippling under his skin. Gasping when his arms tightened around her, she braced her hands against his chest. She couldn't help but to notice the granite like feel of his pecs beneath her fingers. His entire body was poised for battle.

"I'm going to give you a chance to fix what you just said, because I'm certain you didn't mean for it to come out the way you said it. There's no way you think everything we've done for the past two months means nothing."

Pleading eyes met his molten grey orbs and her stomach flipped from the intensity of his stare.

"I didn't say it meant nothing, but I don't do the whole '*meet the family'* thing unless we've agreed to be exclusive. Even then, it's after a longer period of time. Two months is too soon."

"You're really hung up on this whole two months thing, but you're starting to piss me off right now." His left hand latched into her hair disturbing the curls she'd neatly pinned up to keep them off of her neck. "Do you think I'm some little fuck boy who goes around sticking his dick in whoever will let him?"

His fingers tightened causing stinging at her scalp. Her traitor of a pussy slickened with arousal in complete conflict with the way she thought she should respond to the twinge of pain. A muted cry pushed through her lips only to be silenced by Kenneth's mouth taking hers in a fierce kiss.

Pulling back, he seared her with his penetrating gaze. "Answer me, Sweetheart. Is that what you think I am? Hm? Do you think I fuck every woman I'm with raw? Do you think I fill them to the brim with my hot cum the same way I do to your sweet pussy? Is that what you think?"

"No." Her breathy response was met with a devious chuckle.

"You're damn right I don't. I'm a grown ass man. I'm not playing games with you and I'm not going to be hidden away like some dirty little secret."

The gruffness of his voice when he said those last words struck a chord with Candy and she finally realized what she'd done with her hesitancy. She'd given him the impression she was somehow ashamed of the important people in her life knowing about their relationship.

Nothing could be further from the truth. From the first time she'd glimpsed him at the wedding, she'd felt drawn to him. She'd fought it because she didn't think the attraction was mutual. When he'd disabused her of that thought, she was apprehensive about falling too fast. But, she knew how it felt to have someone try to hide her. She couldn't allow him to think it was her intention.

Cupping his face, she searched his eyes, seeing the anger tinged with hurt. "I'm not trying to hide you. You aren't a secret. *We* aren't a secret."

"Then what's all this about?"

"It's..." She trailed off, unsure of how to articulate the swell of emotions and thoughts swirling in her head. Despite the tension she still felt when she rested her hands on his shoulders, he didn't rush her.

"Things are really good between us, but they're also really new. I was just hoping for a little more time before my family poked their noses into things. You've been around enough now to see they have boundary issues."

"Sweetheart...Do you understand that I'm not playing around with you?" He searched her face for understanding.

"This isn't some experiment. You're my woman and I'm your man. Period. Whether it's been two minutes, two months, two years or two decades, it won't change the fact that you're mine. And, I won't dial it back or pretend it's not the case. Not for anyone."

Punctuating his statement with a blistering kiss, he closed the miniscule distance between them aligning her body flush with his. She felt his length thickening despite the layers of clothing separating them. When he released her lips, he probed her with a stern expression.

"You owe me an apology."

Pulling back, she searched his face to determine if he was serious. "What? Why?"

"You hurt my feelings. You owe me an apology and something to make amends for your transgression."

The hand he still had in her hair tightened on the tresses while the one at her waist moved to cup one ass cheek giving it a generous squeeze.

"I apologize for hurting your feelings, Kenneth." She said sweetly. Stroking his chest, she leaned in placing a lingering kiss on his lips. "Forgive me?"

He focused his eyes on her lips for a brief moment before shaking his head. "Not good enough. I'm severely wounded." Licking his bottom lip, he pinned her with his smoldering gaze.

"If the actual words aren't enough, what else can I do?" The question was innocent enough, but the second the words left her mouth she knew she'd made a mistake. One look at the seductive smirk he wore was confirmation. "No, Kenneth. We can't. Not here."

Looking around as though someone could see them behind the closed door of the bedroom, she whispered, "This is my aunt and uncle's house. My *grandfather* is right outside. We can't."

Every word she spoke fell on deaf ears as Kenneth stood to his full height, then reached out a hand, flicking the lock on the door. Using his hold on her body, he guided her backwards towards the bed, silencing her protests with a brain addling kiss.

When the backs of her thighs made contact with the bed, he released her from the kiss, grasped her ass in both hands and placed her on the bed with her legs hanging over the edge. Pressing her back, he leaned over her, but didn't place his full weight on her body.

Ripping the ball cap from his head, he flung it across the room and kissed a trail from her lips, down her neck, to her almost bare shoulders before ending the trek at her cleavage. Gliding her fingers into his hair she tugged at the strands. He'd let it grow out, so she was able to grab more than a little bit of it.

At the tugging, he lifted his head to look at her. "I'm serious." She said in a breathy moan. "We can't..."

"Sh...I know, Baby, but you want to make it up to me don't you?" Kissing the swell of her breast, he slid one hand beneath her dress.

"You know what will make everything better don't you? Hmm?" His digits found the edge of her panties and tugged.

"I just need a little taste. You wouldn't deny me one little sample of my sweet candy now would you?"

As he asked, he pressed against her clit with his thumb moving it in a slow circle the way he knew drove her wild. Squirming under his touch, her words got lost on the way from her brain to her vocal cords. All she could do was whimper and moan her pleasure from his touch.

"What's that, Sweetheart? I can't hear you. Do you want to make it up to me? You know pleasing you makes me happy. So, can I eat your sweet pussy? It would make me so very happy if you said yes."

Candy's core clenched and gushed with anticipation as his words along with the smooth sound of his voice caressed her as much as his physical contact with her honeyed center. In lieu of waiting for her reply, he dropped to his knees. Stripping her panties down her legs, he parted her thighs and took one long swipe between the folds of her sex.

A gasp tore from her lips, but her moan was captured by the hand he quickly placed over her mouth. "Careful, Baby. You know I don't like to be interrupted while I'm eating."

Those were his last words for a while as he went back to enjoying using his fingers and tongue to drive her to the brink repeatedly before finally allowing her to fall over the edge. Breathing heavily, she lay on her back staring at the ceiling as her consciousness drifted back into her body.

Kenneth's handsome face blocked her view when he hovered above her wearing a broad grin. His lips held the sheen of her essence. Her core spasmed in remembrance of what he'd just done with those lips and that tongue.

Swooping down, he shared her taste with her in another drugging kiss. Her body started gearing up for more when he pulled away.

"That'll do for now. I'll collect the rest of my apology later." Dropping one more kiss to her semi parted lips, he hopped up from the bed. Walking across the room, he picked his hat up from the floor and strode to the door.

"Kenneth?" She stopped him before he opened it.

"My panties?" She held out a hand for the garment.

Patting his pocket, he smiled showing two rows of straight white teeth. "Those stay with me." Winking, he unlocked the door then left the room.

"Kenneth! Kenneth, you can't be serious!" she whisper-yelled as she sprung off the bed to go after him. Catching her reflection in the mirror, she stopped short and gasped. What she saw made her close the door instead.

She looked like she'd been thoroughly fucked. There's no way she could follow him looking like that. Everyone would take one glance at her and think the worst.

Cursing Kenneth as well as his entirely too talented tongue, she set about putting herself back together before straightening the bed then leaving the room. She made a quick stop in the bathroom before taking the back stairs leading up to the main floor. It was impossible for her to walk back outside and look into her grandfather's face after what they'd just done.

Entering the lounge area beside the kitchen, she saw the group had lost Safara but gained a replacement in her mother, Sherilyn. They were all sitting around the table in the breakfast nook on the far side of the room. Stepping around the dividing wall, Candy joined them making a bee-line for her mother.

"Hey, Mama. When did you get here? Where's Daddy?" Candy asked as she gave her a quick hug.

"You know your daddy. As soon as we got here, he went looking for his partners. He's out there with Drew and the rest of the guys." Her mother flipped her hand toward the deck doors.

"Oh, ok."

Candy slid into the empty seat at the table, doing as she normally would. She tried her best not to concentrate on the orgasm Kenneth delivered before he abandoned her, taking her underwear with him. Thankful for the coverage of the calf-length dress, she shifted in the chair, internally cursing Kenneth for his shenanigans.

Noticing that the conversational flow hadn't resumed when she joined the group, Candy's gaze traveled around the table.

"What?" She asked, while simultaneously praying for a reprieve.

"Nothing. I was just asking about you." Her mother dragged out the last word with a knowing grin.

"Asking about me for what? We talked on the phone yesterday. Has something happened since then?"

"No. Nothing's happened. Your sister said the two of you rode together, so I asked where you were. I saw Kenneth's vehicle outside and assumed the two of you arrived together. I was surprised when Cherry said she picked you up on her way here."

Candy's jaw dropped at her mother casually mentioning Kenneth's name as if it were a foregone conclusion that the two of them were together. They were, but when did Sherilyn Hampton find out about it? One look at Cherry's face and she was certain she hadn't said anything.

Her little sister was a terrible liar. She tended to blurt out truth bombs. Had she said anything, Candy wouldn't have to ask her. Cherry would tell on herself.

"Mama, why would you assume Kenneth and I would come here

together?" Candy asked the question slowly as if she were speaking to a person with low comprehension skills.

"Because y'all are together." She said the words with such certainty, Candy was shocked into silence. Mistaking her silence for denial, her mother asked. "Y'all are together aren't you?"

Dumbfounded, Candy responded, "We are, but how did you know?"

"It's not like it's a secret. Y'all have been all over Atlanta and Logan City hugged up on each other. When Robert and I took the kids to the Ice Cream thing at Piedmont Park last month, we saw the two of you. We were wrangling Neveah and Bryson, so we didn't come over to say anything."

Unsure of how to respond to her mother's nonchalant acceptance of a situation she thought might get tense, Candy simply sat there. Internally, she breathed a sigh of relief. If her mother's statement was the extent of their discussion about her and Kenneth's relationship, Candy would take that gift and run with it.

McKenna stood from the table, but came back soon after. She placed a bottle of water in front of Candy. "You look like you could use this." Her expression gave nothing away, so Candy took the offered beverage.

"Thank you. I am a bit thirsty." Briefly reliving the reason why her throat was dry, she closed her eyes. Attempting to mask her feelings, she took a deep swallow of the cooling liquid.

AJ entered from the deck carrying a large metal pan covered in foil. His appearance brought everyone's attention back to the other reason for the gathering. Food.

"This is the last of it, Mama." He announced, placing the pan on the stovetop.

The ladies popped up from the table as Aunt Bee gave out assignments to get the buffet set up for people to eat. When Candy went to stand, McKenna leaned over and whispered in her ear.

"The next time you and your man go off to 'talk', don't forget to fix your face after. You did good with your hair, but you were wearing gloss earlier. Now you're not."

Candy's hand flew to her bare lips. She was so concerned with her hair, she didn't give a thought to her once shiny lips now lacking the color she'd carefully applied at home. McKenna winked, patted Candy on the shoulder then walked away. The women in her family were pieces of work. Shaking her head, Candy jumped into the fray.

Chapter Eleven
ARE YOU GONNA FEED HER TOO?

Kenneth sat in the cushioned metal chair at one of the long folding tables he'd help set up earlier. His plate was filled to capacity with delicious food that he would soon devour. Driscoll sat at the other end of the table with his son between he and McKenna in a high chair.

Candy sat to his left. Across from them her cousin, Kari, sat with her husband Daisuke. He was pleased with the change in Candy's demeanor after their earlier conversation, she seemed much more relaxed. He wasn't sure if it could be attributed to her talk with her parents going well, the orgasm, or him returning her panties so she didn't have to walk around bare assed.

Kenneth smiled when DJ reached out a pudgy little hand snagging the fry McKenna offered him after ripping the sharp ends off. Seeing his friend with his family tugged at something inside Kenneth. The whole vibe of love and acceptance he received when he was around the Frost family touched a place in him he didn't often get to experience.

After his parent's death, and his uncle's estrangement from the rest of their small family, they'd began sharing holidays with his surrogate Aunt Toni's family or with just the two of them. Summer cookout's with the Frost family reminded him of when he and Uncle Ray had attended Mississippi Day in Central Park with Aunt Toni.

Digging into the food in his plate, he allowed his mind to drift to memories of when Aunt Toni first invited them to participate in Mississippi Day. It was during the first summer they lived with her. Her family was originally from a place called Guntown in Mississippi. It was a small, mostly rural, town in the northeastern portion of the state. She reflected fondly on her time visiting her Nana in the summers learning the recipes she later used as the staples in her restaurant.

Unfortunately, the event was cancelled in response to the anti-gay legislation passed in Mississippi in twenty-sixteen. As disappointed as he was to no longer share that time with Aunt Toni and Uncle Ray, he understood the stance the group took to support gay rights.

He'd probably never understand how anyone could decide that their own belief systems should determine who other people could love. As long as they were consenting adults, Kenneth was a live and let live kind of person.

The concept hadn't always meshed well with his previous dating life. It seemed some women assumed his classically handsome looks and style of dress implied he shared their homophobic ideologies. By some women, he really meant Annalise. She was the last person he'd dated exclusively until Candy. Their relationship fell apart when it became obvious she had an issue with what she called his uncle's *lifestyle choices*.

She'd never been anything but polite to his Uncle Ray when she saw him, but Kenneth recognized the methods she used to try to separate him from his uncle. That could never happen. His Uncle Ray was the one person who always supported him no matter what. When it came to a head, she revealed her true bigoted nature. At which point, he quickly showed her and her holier than thou upbringing to the door.

Thinking of Annalise put a bad taste in his mouth, but it reminded him that he and Candy needed to have a more in-depth discussion about their relationship. It seemed she was under the impression they were free agents and could see whomever they wanted. He'd have to nip that idea in the bud as soon as they were alone—not just locked behind a door with her family right outside.

"Are these seats taken?"

Kenneth looked up from his plate to see two of the Ripley cousins standing behind the chairs to Daisuke's left. He'd been introduced to them earlier, but hadn't said more than a few words to either of them.

Both young ladies were looking at him waiting for a response. Why were they asking him? Despite the warm way he was treated, he wasn't a family member.

He didn't dictate who could sit where. From the few times he'd attended these cookouts there didn't seem to be any real seating order other than making sure the kids were near their parents and the older people were in shaded areas or inside.

Directing his gaze to Daisuke and Kari, Kenneth replied, "I don't think so, but you should ask them." He nodded toward the couple seated across from he and Candy.

Daisuke did nothing more than look over his shoulder at them, then looked at Kari before turning his attention back to the grilled meat on his plate. Shaking her head, Kari waved the two women to sit.

"Girl, y'all know we sit wherever a chair is available. Go on and sit down. Quit playing crazy."

Had he not been paying attention, Kenneth would have missed the brief, but silent, conversation between Kari and Candy. He wondered what it was all about, but didn't dwell on it as he returned to his meal as well.

Other than DJ's babbling and occasional responses from McKenna or Driscoll, there wasn't much talking taking place at their table. Not until their visitors arrived.

"So, Ken. What is it that you do?"

"Kenneth." His clipped reply came immediately in response to her shortening his name.

"I'm sorry. What?" Her surprise at the correction left her flustered.

"I prefer to be called, Kenneth. Not Ken."

"Oh... I apologize. I didn't know."

"No worries."

He softened the correction with a slight smile and went back to eating. Even if he was okay with the nickname, he didn't know her well enough for her to take such liberties. For the life of him, Kenneth couldn't remember her name even though they'd met less than an hour ago.

"Why do you prefer being called Kenneth? Is it because you just met us and we aren't friends yet?" The younger of the two asked.

"No. It's simply my preference."

"One he doesn't have to explain." Candy supplied giving her cousins a pointed look.

Kenneth ignored the barely contained snickers coming from his so-called friend at the other end of the table. Driscoll knew why he didn't like the nickname. Kenneth's sandy blond hair, light eyes and physique bore a striking resemblance to Barbie's boyfriend of over forty years. It didn't take long for the correlation to be made when someone decided to call him, Ken.

The remaining seats at the long table filled up with a few more of their relatives. To his relief, the focus of the conversation shifted away from him and his name. His parents never shortened his name. Neither had his uncle. They either called him Kenneth or used his initials, KG.

His resemblance to the toy hadn't really been a consideration until he hit puberty and he started getting attention from girls. One of them, he couldn't even remember who, made an off-hand comment about his features being as perfect as the doll. That was all it took for boys to run with it and do what teenage boys seemed compelled to do—try to use it against him.

At his current age, it wasn't the childhood memories which drove him to dislike the name, it was the comparison to perfection that got under his skin. No person was perfect. Who decided features like his were the pinnacle of male beauty standards? He found it tiresome and irritating.

Did he appreciate when the women he was attracted to also found him physically appealing? Absolutely. However, in his opinion, society's beauty standards were far too narrow and entirely too Euro-centric. If he were to subscribe to them, he would've overlooked more than half of the women he'd dated. Including Candy.

Stealing a glimpse at her smiling and talking with her family, she completely captivated him. How anyone could see her and think she was anything but desirable was insane. His eyes traced the outline of her collarbone exposed by the strappy top of her sun dress.

Admiring the soft glow of her skin, his eyebrows drew together in concern. They weren't sitting in direct sunlight, but he noticed a slight reddening along the tops of her shoulders.

Wiping his hands with a wet wipe from the container on the table, he ran his fingers along the area. His touch drew her attention. She faced him with a questioning expression.

"Baby, did you put on sunscreen before you came out here?" His frowned deepened with her look of chagrin. "You didn't. Did you?"

"I forgot..."

"Babe, we've talked about this." His jaw hardened in frustration as he dug into the side pocket of his cargo shorts and pulled out a small tube of sun screen.

"Turn." He bit out.

"I can to it." She held out her hand for the cream.

Quirking an eyebrow, he twirled his finger in silent instruction for her to do as he said. Releasing a frustrated huff, she repositioned herself so her back was to him.

Squirting the lotion into one hand, he leaned forward and whispered in her ear, "I'll add this little display to your apology list. You can make it up to me later."

"Excuse me?" Looking over her shoulder at him, her voice was barely above a whisper, but the table had gone completely quiet. All eyes were trained on the two of them. Kenneth didn't allow that to deter him.

"We'll discuss it later." He tapped his temple. "I have the list locked in. I won't forget."

Spreading the protectant along the tops of her shoulders, the exposed parts of her back then down her arms; he left no visible skin untouched. Except for her chest and legs. Knowing she would balk completely at the slightest hint of him applying sunscreen there, he handed her the tube motioning for her to do her legs and chest area.

Giving Candy a pointed look, he waited expectantly for her to open the tube and spread the cream on her sensitive skin.

"Are you gonna feed her too?" Driscoll's voice cut across the silence.

"Mind your business." Kenneth grumbled then resumed his stare down while Candy pouted but complied with his request.

He released a satisfied chuckle when McKenna reached around DJ's high chair to poke Driscoll in the arm reminding him of his own overly protective ways. Kenneth swore if McKenna so much as stubbed her toe, Driscoll was ready to pick her up and carry her around the rest of the day. So, he had no room to poke fun at Kenneth's actions.

"Wait...You two are together?"

Since he couldn't remember their names and wasn't compelled to ask again, Kenneth began referring to the two cousins as Red and Blue in his mind. Based on the color of the t-shirts they wore. He had no intention of answering Blue's question.

Apparently, Candy was of a different mind. "Yes. We are. You sound surprised."

Her voice was deceptively calm, but Kenneth picked up on the tension in her body language. She'd stopped applying the sun block and placed the cap back on the tube. She'd skipped doing her legs, but he thought better of mentioning it.

"Oh, no. I didn't mean it like that. I didn't know you had a boyfriend, Candy. That's all." Blue quickly backpedaled.

"Mhmm," Candy responded. She handed him the tube of lotion to put back in his pocket.

Kenneth wasn't dumb. He'd patently ignored their flirtations earlier. The last thing he wanted to do was to cause a rift between Candy and her family, so a change of scenery was in order. He was done eating anyway.

"Hey, Babe. Do you think there's still some peach cobbler left inside?" He pulled Candy's plate over to him and stacked hers on top of his empty one.

"Possibly. It normally goes fast though."

"I'm in the mood for a little dessert. Join me." It wasn't a request. He didn't pretend it was.

Standing, he put a hand on the back of her chair. One glance at his determined expression and Candy rose nebulously promising to catch up with everyone later. Despite knowing it wasn't likely, Kenneth didn't say a word to contradict her.

As they walked away, he overheard one of the late comers lighting into Blue and Red about their behavior. He didn't spare them a backwards glance. Maybe it would teach them to read the room a bit better.

Once they made it inside the house, Candy turned to him placing a hand on his chest. "Don't think I don't know what you're doing."

"I never said you didn't."

"Good. I had it under control by the way."

"Of course you did, Baby." Pressing a kiss to her forehead, he nudged her toward the dessert table. "Let's get some cobbler."

Candy unbuckled her seat belt and placed her hand on the door handle. "Thank you for bringing me home."

Chuckling, Kenneth shook his head at her attempt to duck out on him like he was a car service and not her man. Instead of correcting her assumption that he was dropping her off and driving away, he shut off the car. In a few seconds he was standing at the passenger door extending his hand to her.

Accepting his offer of assistance, she stepped down from the vehicle. The sun was just dipping below the treetops dropping them partially in shadow as they traversed the curved walkway to her front door in silence. The slightest hint of nervous energy wafted from her as she unlocked the door. He'd address that soon enough.

Following her inside, he closed then locked the door while she disarmed the alarm system. Slipping her sandals off, she placed them on the rack next to the door and slid her feet into a pair of flip flops.

At the snick of the lock, she turned to look at him with a raised eyebrow. Responding in kind, he maintained eye contact while he removed his sneakers placing them on the rack as well. He held out his arm in the direction of the living room as if it were his home and he was inviting her in. Her pursed lips in response drew a deep chortle from him.

"You're looking at me like a woman angling to have her ass spanked for being contrary." Delivering a light pat to the aforementioned area, he gave it a squeeze for emphasis.

"Excuse you!" Candy jumped before dancing away. Taking careful steps, she walked backwards into the living room eyeing him warily.

"You should turn around and watch where you're going. Trust me, anything I do to you, you'll see coming." Smiling at her lasciviously, he winked.

Slowly, she turned keeping her eyes focused on him until the very last moment. Due to the last strains of daylight coming in from the large windows and the lamp glowing on a side table, the room wasn't completely cloaked in darkness.

Her living room wasn't over the top frilly, but it held many soft, feminine touches. Unlike his dark leather furnishings, hers were lighter and made of a fabric which invited people to sit and get cozy.

"I take it since you locked the door, you intend to stay for a while." Candy made the statement as she walked through the room to reach the kitchen area.

"You say it like you don't want me to stay."

"I didn't say that. I simply made an observation." Taking a glass from the cabinet, she filled it from the water dispenser on the refrigerator door.

"Well, your observation sounded kind of snarky." Neither confirming nor denying his assertion, Candy shrugged. Kenneth watched her from the doorway of the galley style kitchen.

In his opinion, it was entirely too small, but until recently, Candy didn't cook much. People who don't cook tend to overlook the kitchen when they purchase a home. He could manage in the space, but he'd complain under his breath the entire time.

Taking another glass down, she asked if he wanted something to drink as well. He wasn't in the mood for alcohol or a sweet beverage. So, he opted for water. He had more than his share of the sweet tea laced with lemon earlier.

Sweet tea was a southern treat he took to immediately when he relocated to the Logan City office six years ago. Now, when he went home to New York, he couldn't drink the iced tea they served in most restaurants.

Regarding each other watchfully, they both took hefty sips until their glasses were empty. Venturing into the space for the first time that evening, he placed his glass in the sink and walked closer to her. Setting hers down, she put her hands up as if to block his forward advance.

It didn't stop him. The way he lifted her onto the countertop was becoming somewhat of a habit for the two of them. Releasing a light gasp, Candy steadied herself with her hands on his shoulders. Tapping her knees, he created space to step into the cradle of her legs.

"We should talk."

"Okay...Why does talking require this?" She waved a hand between them emphasizing their current positions.

"It doesn't. This is merely how I want to do it."

"Do it?" Her lip twitched with a stifled smirk.

"Don't try to distract me. I'm serious." Piercing her with a stern look, he squeezed the sides of her thighs before resting his hands at her hips.

"Ok. I'll behave."

"I doubt it, but we'll see." He was certain, she'd attempted to deflect from the heavy conversational vibe he was putting off. However, he didn't call her on it.

"We need to finish our talk from earlier today." His fingertips glided along the sides of her legs before he latched his hands at her hips once more.

Her normally smooth brow scrunched with mild confusion. "Which talk? Before or after you coerced me into doing something completely inappropriate at my aunt and uncle's home."

"First of all, we're adults. Nothing we do together is inappropriate —no matter where it happens. Second, you weren't complaining while I feasted on your sweet pussy. Don't try to make me the bad guy. Stay on topic."

"What? How dare you—"

"ZZz-it!" Kenneth made a zipping motion along with the noise to end Candy's statement of fake outrage. "Stay on topic."

The command was issued along with a squeeze to her hips. "Seriously, Baby. We need to talk."

Her lips pursed, drawing his gaze to their fullness. Internally admonishing himself to stay on the subject, he lifted his eyes to hers. "What have I done or not done to give you the impression that what we have isn't a real relationship?"

Chapter Twelve

BE A GOOD GIRL

The directness of Kenneth's question combined with their physical proximity flustered Candy. She felt the heat creeping up her neck settling in her cheeks. When she attempted to drop her eyes from his penetrating stare, he cupped the side of her face demanding they maintain the connection.

"Don't do that. Don't look away. Answer me, Baby. In what way was I not clear about who we are to each other?"

This time, when she lowered her gaze, he didn't try to make her sustain eye contact. Her hands still rested on his chest. Previously immobile, her fingers began absently tracing the few buttons of his shirt. Silence stretched between them before she finally responded to his question.

"We've talked about a lot of stuff as we've spent as much time together as our schedules allow. When we're together, I know I have all of your attention. I feel your focus and commitment to being with me in those moments. What we haven't done is had a specific conversation about being together exclusively."

Kenneth had never given her a reason to fear him. Fear what he might do to someone else on her behalf? Maybe. But she'd never been truly afraid of him. Even as she watched the storm brewing, turning his irises from light grey to a darker more ominous color, she still didn't feel he'd do her physical harm. Locked beneath his thunderous glare, she wanted to snatch the words back, but it was too late.

The muscle in his jaw ticked under the pressure of his clenched teeth. Unlike the expression from earlier, he looked more pissed than hurt. His lids dropped covering the tempest. Watching him closely, she observed him as he appeared to go through a process of calming himself before he lifted his eyelids to look at her again.

His hands left her hips. Immediately, she felt the loss. It was short-lived since his fingertips slipped beneath the edge of her dress which was hiked midway up her thighs.

"You know what, Babe. You're right." His normally deep voice held an additional scratchy quality, as if swallowing his anger had damaged his vocal cords.

"I'll admit, for a few seconds I was all set to argue my point. Telling you what we are to each other was obvious. I wondered how you would be confused, but then I got it. I figured it out."

Her breathing hitched when his questing digits made contact with her inner thigh—inches from her slickening core.

Leaning forward he invaded her space even more. "You need the words. That's it isn't it?" The warmth of his breath brushed her cheek as he nipped her ear.

"You need to hear me say I'm yours and you're mine. You want me to tell you that if some other man even looks at you too long, he doesn't love life. Because, I'll have no problem fucking up his existence."

Sexual anticipation rendered Candy incapable of replying to anything he said. Tipping her head to the side to allow him better access, she closed her eyes reveling in the sensations. Pulling her back from the torment to her senses, his voice barely filtered through the haze.

"You've gone quiet on me, Baby. Use your words. Tell me the requirements for you to believe this isn't a game."

How in the world did he expect her to concentrate on what he was saying while he tortured her with searing kisses? Her breath hitched as his fingers inched closer to her now weeping core. What had he said? Her panties were shifted to the side as one long digit teased her clit before slipping inside her slickness. Holding onto anything other than the way he made her feel was a lost cause.

His lips traced a path along her jaw before ghosting across hers. "Come on, Baby. Be a good girl. I need to know you understand."

Technically, she heard his words, but she'd stopped actively listening when he started his pleasurable assault. Another finger joined the first and her walls clamped down on their guests as they found that sensitive spot applying the exact amount of pressure needed to heighten her enjoyment. Just as she teetered on the edge of release, the pleasure was abruptly snatched away.

Frowning at being jerked from the precipice, Candy's eyes fluttered open. She felt the pout forming on her lips as her gaze met Kenneth's.

"Why did you stop?"

"No orgasms for you until you give me an answer."

An answer? To what? *What the hell were they talking about again?* It took a solid minute of confused staring for the fog to lift. Mentally replaying his words, she sifted through the information. The digits he removed from her core kept her stimulated by gliding through her folds teasing the hooded bundle of nerves.

"I understand."

The words came out in a huff. Her fingers curled grasping two hands full of his shirt attempting to pull him closer. He didn't close the miniscule distance between them. Instead, he leaned back. While his hands kept her primed, he took away his kisses.

"What is it that you understand, Baby? I have to hear the words."

Although his eyes telegraphed his arousal, his expression was serious.

"We're together."

Shaking his head, he refused to let her take the easy way out. "Not good enough. It's a given that we're together. What else?"

"We're a couple." The pinch to her inner thigh made her jump then quickly add to her statement. "An exclusive couple."

"Good girl."

A shiver skated down Candy's spine at the simple praise. The area Kenneth pinched didn't sting, yet he dropped down, pushed her skirt to the side and kissed her inner thigh. Apologizing to it for the minor infraction.

A puff of warm air gusted across her sensitive panty-covered labia. He was so close to her dripping center it clenched in anticipation. Without conscious thought, she lightly gripped his hair and tipped her hips forward. The rumbling chuckle he released heightened her awareness of his current position.

Unexpected pleasure ricocheted through her senses when he nipped her through her panties. It was almost enough to tip her over into the orgasm he denied. Almost. Strong fingers pried her digits from their grip on his hair.

Standing, he fused his lips to hers, his tongue dipping inside her mouth completely commanding her compliance. Her legs naturally wrapped around his waist as he pulled her to the edge of the counter until she felt his hard length pressed to her center. Even through the barrier of clothing, she felt the pulsing of this rigid cock.

Releasing her from his drugging kiss, he placed lingering pecks on her lips. A pleasing sting accompanied the light smack to her butt cheeks.

"Let's take this show to the bedroom. You owe me restitution."

"Restitution? For what?"

"You need to make amends for the slights you've committed against me today. Actions have consequences."

Any rebuttal to his accusation was swallowed by his retaking of her lips. She should've expected it considering their position and his words, yet she still swiftly inhaled when he slid her off the counter. Her legs tightened around his torso as he carried her down the hall to her bedroom. The soft feel of her weighted blanket met her skin as he laid her on the bed. Briefly, he disentangled himself from her limbs to turn on the bedside lamp.

Quickly shucking off his own clothes, he pulled her to standing so he could do the same for her. It was an unspoken rule. When they were together, he did the undressing. Getting rid of his own clothing was always done quickly. Hers...Not so much.

Once she stood from the bed, he whipped back the blanket and top sheet then he focused on her disrobing. The simplicity of her dress didn't allow for his usual agonizingly slow game of Get Candy Naked.

He mumbled his complaint of her robbing him of his fun while simultaneously praising how good she looked.

"You know what I wanted to do to you the minute I saw this tease of a dress? Hm?'

His hands on her shoulders nudged until she rotated facing away from him. He didn't really want a reply. The sound of the zipper releasing was the only noise aside from his voice and their heavy breathing.

"You wore it just to fuck with me. Didn't you?"

The closure opened; the straps fell easily from her shoulders. A laced covered bra exposed the tops of her breasts. Deftly releasing the clasp of the pretty undergarment, he turned her around as he dragged his fingertips from the tops of her shoulders down her arms, pulling the bra straps along the way.

Candy's nipples puckered when the cool air hit them, drawing Kenneth's focus to her heavy globes. Licking his lips, he placed suckling kisses on each of the peaks before moving on to the removal of her drenched underwear. His blunt nails scraped lightly across her hips then down the sides of her legs as he rid her of the last barrier between them.

As if he couldn't control himself, he swiped his tongue at the juncture of her thighs. Groaning, he pulled away sweeping her off of her feet and back onto the bed. Crawling over her body, he hovered above her breast with his knees straddling her chest. The position placed his long, thick cock in her direct line of sight.

"Time to make those amends, Baby."

The fingers of one hand stroked his shaft while the other traced her lips. One digit slipped between them. Eagerly, she sucked it inside simulating what she would soon do to his stiff erection. The suction and movement of her tongue had him cursing softly and withdrawing.

Bracing one hand on the wall above the headboard, Kenneth brought himself closer to her lips. A pearl of pre-cum sat at the tip of his length. Licking her lips, Candy's eyes devoured his veiny shaft while her hands traced a path up his thighs toward her target.

Tapping the mushroom shaped tip against her bottom lip, Kenneth's voice was heavy with lust.

"Wrap those pillowy lips around my dick. He's feeling a little territo-rial. He wants to be sure you know every part of you belongs to us."

Not giving her a chance to reply, he guided his length between her parted lips. The moment the tip of her tongue touched the head, she brushed his hand out of her way wrapping her fingers around his velvety length. Braced above her, with both hands on the wall, audible moans reached her ears as his head dropped back on his shoulders in an expres-sion of his enjoyment.

The tangy sweetness of his essence hit her tongue and she hummed around his thickness enjoying the experience as much as he was. The fingers of the hand not wrapped around his cock migrated from his hip to grasp his firm ass pulling him deeper into her mouth.

Candy wasn't averse to giving oral, but she'd never been as eager to have a piece of man meat in her mouth as she was with Kenneth. Maybe it was because he was also such a giving lover. He genuinely relished in giving her pleasure to the point he rarely allowed her to reciprocate.

Although he moved closer at her urging, he didn't try to shove his dick down her throat. As she worked his length into her mouth, she used the fingers of one hand to stimulate the part she couldn't handle. His hips jerked reflexively in response to her efforts, but he did nothing more than offer praise and encouragement. The more he expressed how well he enjoyed it, the harder she worked to bring him to a release.

Too soon for Candy's liking, he jerked, pulling himself from the hot depths of her mouth. She grumbled in protest of being robbed of her treat only to be shushed by Kenneth's lips crashing down on hers. Breaking the kiss, he wrapped one hand around her face threading his fingers into the hair at her nape.

"Don't pout, Baby. You know the only place I put my cum is inside of you."

One strong hand latched onto her left leg behind the knee. Lifting it up and out, he made room for his trim hips between her parted thighs. Without the use of his hands, his cock pierced her dripping core.

With two smooth thrusts he was seated inside her channel to the hilt. Candy moaned at the feel of him stretching her walls so deliciously. The way he wielded pleasure was yet another thing she had no idea she liked until she met him.

Between the way he moved inside her and the nasty things he whispered in her ear, she lingered at the edge of an orgasm almost constantly. While being held at the cusp could be frustrating, it was also stimulating to get close without getting there all the way. The withholding made actually reaching nirvana that much sweeter.

Her moans and exclamations of desire joined the sounds of their lovemaking. Her enjoyment had a galvanizing effect on him. He amped up the movement of his hips; the fingers at her nape fisted in her hair just enough for her to feel it, but not enough to truly hurt.

The little tug to her tresses was an expressway to a gushing core. Her eyes slammed shut as the tingling in her pussy increased to nearly unbearable levels. Just when she thought she would get to experience release, Kenneth suddenly withdrew taking his magical dick away right before she made it to the pinnacle.

"What are you doing? No... Don't stop." The whining note in her voice hit her ears wrong, but she couldn't control it. She was so very close. She didn't care how pitiful she sounded as long as she got what she needed.

"Begging won't save you this time."

Sitting back on his knees, he crossed her leg over her body turning her to her side. A firm smack to her exposed butt cheek told her what he wanted before he uttered the words.

"On your knees, Baby. Show Daddy that ass."

Doing whatever it took to get him to put his thickness back where she wanted it, she scrambled into position—ass up. He was really on one tonight. He'd never called himself Daddy before.

Barely a second after she was in position, she felt Kenneth sinking inside her. The snap of his hips sent his length so deep within her walls, it snatched the breath from her lungs. Pitching forward she unconsciously shifted her hips away from the invasion.

His deep chuckle rumbled in her ear. Strong fingers gripped her hips, pulling her into position. The heat from his chest blanketed her back as he leaned over her.

"Get your ass back here. You can't run from restitution, Baby. You'll take this dick. Every. Single. Inch."

Punctuating his words with punishing strokes to her over-stimulated pussy, he pulled her into each thrust with one powerful hand on her shoulder. Angling his hips just so, he hit her G-spot sending her senses spinning.

All the while, he alternated between strumming her clit and pinching her nipples. Each time she showed signs of coming, he'd halt the extra effort, then only give her enough friction and touches to maintain her arousal. Time was meaningless. Candy was on the verge of tears when she started outright begging him to let her come.

"You wanna come? Hm?"

Kenneth grated right into her ear tickling the lobe with his words. While his voice was rough, mirth was evident. Without looking at him, Candy knew he was smiling as he tormented her senses.

"You know the magic words..."

She did. She knew exactly what he wanted her to say. The strong independent woman inside told her to tell him to fuck off. That bitch was crazy stubborn. On the other side, her horny inner vixen screamed at Miss Independent to shut the hell up. Candy was with the vixen. Her internal battle lasted milliseconds as she rushed to give him whatever he wanted so he would give her what she needed.

"Please! Please let me come." She had no fight left in her to pretend she didn't know precisely which phrase held the key.

"Good girl."

Adjusting his grip, he slid his hands under her shoulders lifting her until she was sitting upright on his lap while he rested on his knees. Still impaled on his turgid length, she moaned at the sensations the position allowed.

He stretched her sheath so beautifully. Pressed against her back, his hard chest shared his warmth with her. Once he had her thighs draped over his, he wrapped on arm around her, clasping her breast. He applied enough pressure to the globe to keep her constrained tightly against him.

Latching onto her shoulder with his lips, he worried the skin while simultaneously seeking her clit with the fingers of his other hand. He didn't keep her on the edge for long. Thrusting with intention into her weeping core, he strummed her little button.

Candy couldn't do anything but accept the amalgamation of carnal delights Kenneth served. Gibberish fell from her lips as her orgasm ripped through her tossing her into oblivion. She completely lost control of her limbs. Limply slumped against him, with her head lolled back onto his shoulder, she twitched with after effects of her release while he pumped into her a few more times before following her over the edge into bliss.

She was only semi-cognizant of him withdrawing his flaccid cock and lifting her off his lap. Sighs drifted from her as he arranged her wilted limbs placing a pillow under her head. Vaguely, she heard water running, but didn't bother to investigate. Occasionally, she'd shudder with the effects of mini-orgasms as her body adjusted.

Languidly lifting her lids, she watched him go through his routine of cleaning her sex knowing he'd soon force her to move. Kenneth took caring for her seriously. He left for another brief moment and she heard the water stop.

"Come on, Baby." Kenneth prodded. "Your bath is ready."

Not resisting, but not offering a great deal of help, Candy sat up and scooted to the edge of the bed. Looking at him through sex drunk eyes, she observed that he looked just as thoroughly fucked as she felt. At least she wasn't the only one. Her pussy clenched like it was foolish enough to want to go again.

"Stop looking at me like that. You can't handle another round. At least not right now." He chided.

He was right. She couldn't. It didn't stop her from considering it though. Shaking his head, he lifted her bridal style and walked toward the bathroom.

Chapter Thirteen

WE DIDN'T NEED THE BED AT ALL

Kenneth leaned against the island countertop watching Candy. Her face was scrunched in concentration as she looked at the ingredients assembled before her and the sauce pan on the stove. While they'd moved into a full-on relationship, he continued to help her improve her cooking skills.

It was important enough for her to sign up for a class, so he encouraged her to continue. With private lessons. From him. He hadn't signed on to teach the remaining sections of the three-part class and he'd be damned if he let another chef anywhere near his sweet Candy.

She completed the first section of the course with success. The class wasn't graded. So, technically, no one could fail. However, the honey glazed salmon she prepared for her final assignment was delicious. Their private sessions were building on where they left off with the level one class.

It was pasta night. To make things a bit easier for her, he didn't insist on making the pasta from scratch. He'd recommended one of the brands he tolerated using from a dried state. The pot was on heating the water for the penne, but it hadn't started to boil. The air fryer hummed in the background, cooking the chicken.

Pushing off the counter, he stepped behind her wrapping his arms around her waist. Smooching the sweet spot behind her ear, he looked over her shoulder at the butter melting in the sauce pan.

"You're thinking too hard. You're better at this than you believe. You don't lack skill, just confidence."

"If you say so." She sighed in resignation.

"I know so." He squeezed, hugging her to his chest.

"Why can't I just buy the pre-made Alfredo sauce from the store?"

He met her question with a smack to her butt. "Don't you ever speak such blasphemy to me. We don't do premade sauces around here. It's enough that we're using dried penne and not making it fresh. Fresh is so much better."

"Kenneth..." She stopped him before he went on a tirade about the improved taste and texture of using fresh pasta as opposed to the dried variety found in most grocery stores.

"Anyway... It's time to add your cornstarch."

Releasing her from his hold, he moved to the side to give her free range of motion. Per their agreement, he wouldn't help her unless she asked. He'd try, but it bothered him to see her upset, so at the first sign of frustration, all bets were off.

Propped against the countertop on the other side of the stove, he gave her space. As much as it pained him, he didn't offer any input. He watched in silence as she went through the steps he'd taught her.

"Why does it look like that?" Candy poked at the lumpy, but actually decent first pass at making an Alfredo sauce.

"Do you really wanna know?"

Resting the wooden spoon on the spoon rest, she gave him side eye. "Why would I ask if I didn't want to know?"

"It could've been a rhetorical question."

"Don't be a smart ass, Kenneth. You said you'd help me one on one if I didn't sign up for the second class at the school. So, help. Please."

Stepping closer to her, he lifted a whisk from the utensil carousel placing it in her hand. Standing behind her, he guided her hand to stir at the lump-filled sauce.

"First, your proportions of corn starch and butter were a little off. It wouldn't have been a problem, but you didn't blend it well when you added in your liquids."

"If you saw me messing up, why didn't you say anything?"

"We had an agreement. Remember? You've watched me make the sauce a few times and you wanted to do it by yourself. I agreed only to help if you asked."

"I know, but..."

"Don't whine, Baby. We still might be able to make this work. And, if we can't, we'll start over. We have everything we need."

Dipping a clean spoon into the sauce he brought it to her lips. "Taste." Leaning around, he tracked the motion of her tongue as it peeked out to swipe at her lips. "How's the flavor?"

Bright eyes met his. Her apple cheeks lifted with her smile. "It's not bad. It's a little salty, but it's good."

"See, part of the battle is already won. It doesn't have to look perfect if you get the flavor right. Besides, we're going to pour it over the pasta and mix it a little more. It'll be fine."

"If you say so." She took over moving the whisk around the mixture as he watched over her shoulder. "What do we do about it being salty though?"

Taking a taste of the sauce, he gauged it. It was a little salty and slightly raw. But, overall, it wasn't bad.

"We don't need to fix it. When we combine it with the pasta, it will soak up some of the sauce. The sauce has to share its flavor with the pasta. So, while it tastes salty alone, when we put the two together, it'll be fine."

While they worked to finish the dish, he talked her through things she did well, then offered suggestions on where she could improve. Impatience had driven her to start adding her liquids too early, which was why the sauce had a hint of rawness in the taste. Most people probably wouldn't notice, but he'd spent time in his Uncle Ray's kitchen working under his best Saucier while he was in culinary school. Javier would never allow anything less than perfection to exit his station. The lessons stuck with Kenneth. However, he wouldn't hold his sweet Candy to Javier's exacting standards. For her first try, she did an excellent job.

"Good job, Baby. Let's get the rest of this meal ready so we can eat."

Beaming under his praise, she moved around his kitchen with much more certainty in her motions than before. Her increased comfort and self-assurance were sexy; driving his thoughts toward the type of eating that had very little to do with the cooking on the stove.

They had an extremely active sex life, and he was certain she wouldn't turn him away if he initiated it. But, they needed time doing things outside of making love—no matter how much he wanted to live with his shaft buried inside her. Later though. Later, he wouldn't deny either of them the erotic pleasure they shared.

Persistent ringing pulled Kenneth from his dreams. Internally cursing, he unwrapped one arm from its hold on Candy's waist. Swiping at the device before it could wake her as well, he answered the call from his uncle.

"Uncle Ray, it's six-thirty a.m. on a Saturday. Why are you calling me so early?" Kenneth groused while trying to keep his voice down. He should leave the room, but his sweetheart's body was curved to his so comfortably, he was reluctant to do anything more to disturb her.

"I know what time it is, KG. I've been up for two hours already. I have to make sure the prep for the lady's brunch crowd is on point."

"On point?" Kenneth questioned his uncle's attempt at using slang.

"Yeah! That's what the kids say. Isn't it? I don't have my head in the sand. I know what's going on. I keep up."

"If you say so, Uncle Ray."

Candy squirmed against his side. Not wanting to wake her, but still unwilling to leave the comfort of the position, he grabbed his wireless earpiece placing it in his ear. His uncle was still talking, catching him up on things in his life and the restaurants.

Sunday was normally their day to talk, because it was the only day the restaurants weren't open. Not for religious reasons. The church of his uncle's youth hadn't looked kindly on his 'lifestyle', so he'd long ago walked away from organized religion.

No, all RKH locations were closed on Sundays because Uncle Ray was a die-hard football fan who usually had season tickets. It was one of his few indulgences. It was also one of the things Kenneth missed about being in New York. Attending those games was the one activity where it was typically just the two of them.

When his uncle turned the subject to his plans for the upcoming holiday season, Kenneth tensed. For the first time in a long time, whether he'd fly home for the holidays was in question and it had nothing to do with his job. It was because he wanted to spend that time with Candy, but he wasn't one hundred percent certain she'd agree to go with him.

"I'm not sure about the holidays yet, Uncle Ray."

"You're not? Do you have a case? Why wouldn't you be able to come up. I'd love to see you and you know Toni loves to spoil you when you visit."

"It's...complicated."

"Oh...So, you're still seeing your Sweet Thing, huh?" His Uncle teased. "I see you, Nephew. Get a new woman on your face and you just forget all about your poor, single old uncle spending the holiday season all by his lonesome."

Laughter burst out before Kenneth could control it. The thought of his uncle being by himself wasn't funny, but his normal irreverent way of speaking made most things humorous. The sound startled Candy awake.

Wide, sleep-fogged, eyes sought his face. Kenneth quickly offered apologies and did what he should've done when the call first came in. He left the bed to keep from disturbing her further.

Taking the call into his ensuite bathroom, he closed the door to continue their conversation while he went through his morning routine. It was unlikely he'd get back to sleep after speaking with his uncle. Besides, him awake next to a sleeping Candy was a recipe for him disturbing her sleep far more than his phone conversation with his uncle ever could.

"Uncle Ray, we both know with or without me for the holidays, you won't be alone or lonely. You might not have anyone steady, but don't pretend you don't have at least a couple of somebody's on standby."

"You don't know my life." His uncle shot back.

Chuckles ensued at the quick response. "Uncle Ray, we're going to have to get you out around more people your age. You sound like some of the kids on that clock app."

"You don't have to do anything of the sort. Don't hate because I'm keeping up with the times and you still talk like Ward Cleaver."

If his uncle knew half of the things he said to Candy, he wouldn't ever compare him to the father on the sitcom from the nineteen fifties. Managing to suppress his amusement at his uncle's statement, he tried to get the conversation back on topic.

"Back to the subject of the holidays, I might be able to swing Thanksgiving, but I was hoping you could come down here for Christmas this year."

"You might? Is your *might* contingent on if a certain someone agrees to come with you?" His uncle shifted into total 'get in Kenneth's business' mode.

Scrubbing his hand across the stubble on his face, Kenneth regarded his reflection in the mirror. Candy wasn't a secret to his uncle. They'd spoken about her on previous calls. His uncle's reference to Candy as his Sweet Thing was because of Kenneth's slip-up. He'd referred to her as his Sweet Candy during a call and Uncle Ray hadn't let it go since.

Changing it to suit his narrative, he never referred to her as anything other than Sweet Thing. Thankfully, he never said it to her face. Kenneth couldn't take comfort in that knowledge since the two had never met face to face.

"I'm going to ask her to come with me. Actually, I was planning to speak to her about it today. If we're coming, I'd need to get the tickets and put in for some additional time off at work. I should be able to let you know something soon either way."

His uncle's whoop of joy brought a smile to his face, but also left him with a tinge of guilt. He hadn't seen him in months. Since Kenneth moved to the Logan City office, his visits with his uncle had gone from bi-weekly to semi-annual—quarterly at best. It was a difficult adjustment for both of them.

After being in Georgia more than five years, it was still an adjustment. They'd only had each other for so long, their bond was stronger than the usual Uncle-Nephew relationship. Even though Aunt Toni and her family were welcoming, it wasn't the same as when they were able to be there together.

Kenneth hoped Candy was open to the idea. He wanted her to meet the people he called family. Her family had been amazing to him. Her dad didn't give him as much guff as he expected, but Kenneth figured that was mostly due to them already having a friendly relationship before he and Candy started seeing each other.

Aside from the customary warning to treat his daughter with respect, Mr. Hampton had been far more accepting than Kenneth anticipated. He'd been told more than once he had a way with parents. It's possible the trend held true with Candy's.

With a promise to speak to him again on Sunday, Kenneth wrapped up the call with his uncle. Just as he was finishing his routine, two short taps preceded the door opening. A tousled Candy entered the bathroom.

Stepping back, he watched her zombie-like trudge to the water closet closing the door behind her. She'd fallen asleep without her bonnet the night before and her hair was sticking up at odd angles similar to a Troll doll. It was fucking adorable.

When she exited the private toilet, her eyes were open a little more as she stood at the second sink to wash her hands. Kenneth watched. Waiting. Any second, she'd catch her reflection and see the state of her normally tamed tresses. The urge to set the timer on his watch was only squelched by knowing she wouldn't appreciate the humor in his gesture.

Almost on cue, her eyes finally opened enough to see herself in the large mirror above the sinks. The realization settled on her in stages. First, the vigorous handwashing slowed. Then she leaned closer as if to make sure her eyes weren't deceiving her. This was quickly followed by the rinsing of her hands and grabbing the towel to dry them.

Once her hands were dry, she began rubbing and tugging at her hair while searching the vanity presumably for a brush or a comb. During her search, her gaze met his in the mirror. Seeing the barely contained laughter, her eyes narrowed.

"This is your fault!" She huffed. "Fooling with you, I forgot to wrap my hair last night. Now look at it! I don't have half the things I need to get it looking like something."

Tentatively moving behind her, he wrapped his arms around her dropping a kiss on her shoulder. One kiss led to two which led to him sliding his hands inside the loosely tied robe she wore. She was naked beneath the covering simplifying his mission. He loved the weight of her breast in his hands. The generous globes drew his touch like they contained homing beacons.

"Nope." Candy latched onto his wrists attempting to halt his playtime with the girls. "This is why I'm looking crazy about the head right now. We aren't falling back into bed."

Tugging his wrists from her grasp, he released the tie of the robe. "Who said anything about a bed?"

Nuzzling the side of her neck, he orchestrated a dual attack with one hand seeking a breast while the other slipped between her legs to fondle her folds.

"I'm serious..." Her words tumbled from her lips with very little conviction. Her actions contradicted them when she leaned into his embrace widening her legs to give him better access.

"That's my good girl." He crooned before nibbling on her earlobe while tweaking her nipple. His morning wood thumped eagerly against his thigh.

She had no idea how sexy he found everything about her. To him, her mussed hair was a testament to a well-satisfied woman. It assured him he did his job last night. Watching the rise and fall of her chest beneath his talented touch, he planned to do it again. Maybe more quickly, but still just as thoroughly.

Eager digits delved between her folds finding her hot center already leaking with desire. Groaning at the feel of her slickness, he dipped two fingers into her channel moving them in an undulating motion seeking that special spot. Her responding gasp was his fuel as he ramped up his caressing of her breasts and exploration of her silky walls.

Her breathing picked up signaling her pending orgasm. Amid mumbles of protest, he removed his fingers from her pussy bringing them to his mouth to lick off her essence. *Damn she was sweet.* As much as he enjoyed feasting at her temple, his dick was threatening a strike if he didn't get inside her immediately.

With one hand at the center of her back he pressed her forward until her chest was resting on the countertop. Stripping the robe off completely, he lined up behind her sinking his rigid length into her depths. Every time with Candy was like new. He absorbed the sensation of being surrounded by the satiny feel of her delicious pussy as her channel pulsed around him.

Her sounds of pleasure rang out into the bathroom in testament to her gratification in their coupling. Knowing he was pleasing her took his enjoyment up a notch. Soon they were catapulting toward release together.

Her cries and screaming announcement that she was cumming was all he could take. With both hands full of her ample ass, he drove his throbbing cock into her dripping core. Not even air separated them as his length pulsed inside her—his seed jetting out in copious spurts.

Leaning over her back, he swept her even more disheveled hair from her face.

"See, Baby. We didn't need the bed at all."

Chapter Fourteen
THIS WAS A BAD IDEA.

"You don't think it's too revealing?" Candy stood in front of her full-length mirror eyeing the form-fitting red dress trimmed in black around the neckline. The gold emblem rested on her left breast to complete the *Starfleet* look.

"This was a bad idea." Biting her bottom lip, her eyes met Kenneth's in their reflection in the mirror when he walked up behind her.

Wrapping his arms around her, he pressed a kiss to the sliver of her shoulder exposed by the asymmetrical vee at the top of the dress.

"It's not too revealing and it was an excellent idea. You look gorgeous. We don't have time for you to change, anyway. We're slightly behind. Besides..."

He touched the tips of the pointy prosthetic ears he wore. "If I have to wear these and be Spock, you have to be my sexy Uhura."

Nibbling her bottom lip nervously, she compared her outfit to his. With her thick thighs on display combined with the tall boots that were a bitch to find, she wasn't nearly as conservative as he was in his long-sleeved blue shirt and black pants.

Granted, both of their costumes hugged their bodies, the only skin showing on Kenneth was above the neck. Although the skirt of her dress was longer than typical Uhura cosplay costumes, there was still more than a couple of inches between the bottom of it and the top black knee-high boots.

"I don't want to embarrass the kids. Maybe I should wear something else to take them to their thing, then change for the adult party later."

Turning her to face him, he placed his hands on her hips tugging her close. "We talked about this already, Baby. Our schedule is too tight for extra trips."

His lips were cool as he placed a reassuring kiss on the tip of her nose. "I promise. Everything will be fine. We've gotta get going. We told your parents we'd be there no later than seven to get the kids. They'll only get an hour and a half at the event as it is."

Normally, Candy had no issues rocking her curves in whatever she chose. However, she remembered the social dynamics of pre-teens and teens well. Bryson would probably be oblivious, but Neveah would be highly attuned to what her peers thought of her chaperones. Things were difficult enough with both of her parents being guests of the state.

Internally chastising herself for not coming up with a better plan, she grabbed her purse double-checking the contents. Keeping with the theme of her costume, the purse was designed to look like the infamous Tricorder from the original *Star Trek* series.

Their outfits and her purse were courtesy of the costume designer from the last movie Candy worked on. When the woman overheard her on the phone with Kenneth discussing their costume choices, she'd jumped at the chance to outfit them both. It paid to have good relations with the rest of the crew.

Sitting in the front passenger seat of Kenneth's oversized SUV, Candy tugged at the edge of her dress. Between the length of the skirt, the dark panty hose and the tall boots, she really wasn't showing very much skin. She had no explanation as to why she was suddenly so self-conscious. Kenneth's long fingers wrapped around hers stilling her movements.

"Please stop worrying. You make a stunning Uhura. Personally, I think you got the better end of this deal."

"How so?"

Releasing her fingers, he pulled at the pants clinging to his thighs. "These things hide absolutely nothing. I had to call Uncle Ray to ask him how his drag queen friends did that tuck thing to keep from traumatizing small children."

Tipping up one side of her mouth, Candy gave him side eye. "You just had to find a way to say your dick is too big for your costume didn't you?"

"I didn't say it. You did."

Playfully shoving his shoulder, she giggled. "You're a whole mess."

Smirking, he placed his free hand on her thigh, rubbing in small rhythmic circles. Thankfully, they reached her parent's house before he could slip his hand beneath the skirt to start things they couldn't finish. The stuff they said about a man's libido slowing down after forty didn't seem to apply to Kenneth. Sometimes, he was like a teenage boy. The difference being his better knowledge of the female form paired with his ability to capitalize on that expertise.

"Thank you again for agreeing to come with me to the kids event. My parents could use a break. Even if it is for just a couple of hours."

"No thanks needed, Baby. I like your niece and nephews." Taking off his seat belt, he opened the driver's side door. "Besides, it's good practice."

"Good practice for what?" Candy asked his retreating back.

He'd dropped his little verbal bomb and hopped out of the vehicle before the response left her lips. Watching him walk around the front of the car, she wondered if he meant what she thought he meant. She'd have to wait until they were alone to discuss it. The front door of her parent's home opened just as Kenneth made it to the passenger side to help her from the SUV.

Her mother stood behind the glass storm door, but Candy wasn't fooled by the distance nor the glass barrier. She was convinced her mother had bionic hearing—especially when it came to things her daughters didn't want her to overhear.

Taking Kenneth's extended hand, Candy pushed back her questions and attempted to mask her thoughts. With their fingers intertwined they walked up the stone path leading to where her mother stood watchfully. When they reached the top step, she swung the door open ushering them inside.

"Rob, Candy and Kenny are here to pick up the kids." She called out.

Candy felt more than saw Kenneth wince at the shortened version of his name. Knowing he wouldn't be rude to her mother, she spoke up.

"Mama, please don't call him that. He prefers Kenneth."

"He does?" She looked to Kenneth for confirmation.

"Yes, ma'am. I prefer Kenneth."

While he wouldn't be rude, he was quick to confirm Candy's statement. With a mildly disappointed expression, she led them from the foyer into the family room.

"I just thought it was so cute, Kenny and Candy. Candy and Kenny." She said their names in a sing-song manner as she waved her hand to an imaginary melody.

"Ok, Mama. If you say so."

Candy's eyes swept around the family room. While some of the décor had changed from her youth, the overall vibe of the room remained the same. A console had been added that looked like a docking spot for electronic devices. If her parents held true to form, the kids were only allowed certain amounts of time glued to their electronics. Her parents were big on structure and stimulating one's brain in other ways than staring at a screen.

They didn't get a chance to sit. The kids filtered in starting with the youngest, Bryson, streaking into the room in his yellow outfit trimmed in red in honor of his favorite cartoon character—the boy who flew by asteroid and breathed in space without special gear. Newton Star. Amid chastising from his grandma about running in the house, he skidded to a stop in front of Candy.

"Auntie! Auntie! Can you guess who I am?" He asked excitedly.

Of course, Candy knew exactly who the character was. She'd scoured the internet and called a few contacts to find that particular version especially for him. He, like many of his peers, was in love with the pajama wearing, mystery solving, pint sized super heroes.

If anyone spent time around the eight and under crowd, they'd watched at least one episode of PJ Masks. Her nephew's excitement was contagious. Not wanting to spoil his big reveal, she played along. Tapping a finger to her chin thoughtfully, she regarded him with an assessing gaze.

"Hmm... I'm not sure. Can you turn around?"

Bopping on the balls of his feet, Bryson gave his little body a quick turn showing her the back of the costume.

"Let me guess. You're a super hero right?"

Beaming, he nodded vigorously. "Uh-huh."

"Yes, ma'am." Her mother automatically corrected.

"Yes, ma'am." Bryson parroted.

Pulling him back to their conversation, Candy asked, "If you're a super hero, where's your cape?"

"Not all super heroes wear capes, Auntie."

His still high-pitched voice deepened slightly in typical 'duh' fashion without actually saying the word. Candy cut Kenneth side eye at his barely stifled laughter at her nephew's comeback. Bryson's little mind probably didn't have a clue the different ways that phrase was used.

"Well, I'm not sure I know any cape-less, heroes. Maybe you should just tell me."

"I'm Newton Star! You know, from my favorite cartoon." His eagerness seemed to dim a little when she didn't guess.

Guessing she overplayed her hand, Candy stopped feigning ignorance. "Of course! Why didn't I see it? He's the one who doesn't need a special suit to breathe in space right?"

Bryson's eyes lit up again; his wide smile showed the gap where he'd recently lost a tooth. He was so adorable he made her ovaries scream. *No ma'am! Stop it!* She'd never focused on the metaphorical biological clock and she wouldn't allow her nephew's cuteness to combine with Kenneth's off-hand comment to send her down a womb-filling path.

Thankfully, the older two children garnered her attention. Nevaeh walked into the room dressed in combat boots, slightly baggy denim jeans, and a dark blue fitted long sleeved shirt. Her outfit was topped with a black cap with long box braids hanging down her back. The whole thing reeked of Cherry. Her sister was a huge Janet Jackson fan. She'd turned Neveah into a mini version of her favorite entertainer—with the exception of the display of mid-drift.

"Well, hello, Miss Jackson." Candy teased the ten-year old who'd grown a recent obsession with being a full-fledged teenager. Thankfully, they still had a few years before that happened. They'd need all of them. Nevaeh had a strong personality which was bound to morph into an active rebellious stage during her teenage years.

"I'm Justice, Auntie. From an old movie Aunt Cherry won't let me watch even though she showed me pictures of the people."

Candy couldn't tell if the child's eye roll was from being called Miss Jackson or from her other aunt referencing a movie she wasn't allowed to see. Either way, Candy wasn't the one or the two. She was big on letting kids be themselves, but also on them remembering to be respectful. Exasperated, borderline condescending eyerolls were disrespectful in her book.

"Be careful who you roll your eyes at, little girl." Piercing her with a look, she waited for Nevaeh's acknowledgement. After the mumbled, 'yes ma'am', Candy continued.

"I know the movie. I was referring to the actress who played the role. Her name is Janet Jackson. She had a song saying to call her Miss Jackson. Next time you visit with Auntie Cherry, you should ask her to play it for you. I'm sure she has it in her streaming rotation."

Even though she'd set Nevaeh straight after her little show of attitude, Candy's voice held no trace of censure when she suggested asking Cherry to educate her on Miss Jackson. Just because she set boundaries, didn't mean she wanted a contentious relationship with her niece.

Moving on, Candy looked at her oldest nephew. Kaden didn't appear to be in costume at all. Wearing regular sneakers with loose fitting—not sagging jeans—and a hoodie, he looked like a regular teenaged boy.

"What's up, Kaden? You didn't want to wear a costume?" Candy asked. If he didn't she wouldn't press him. It wasn't necessary for the community event they were attending. There was a contest for the best costume, but attendees weren't required to wear a costume nor participate as contestants.

"This is my costume, Auntie."

Confusion wrinkled Candy's brow. "I don't get it."

"I do." Kenneth remained silent through the costume reveals until

Kaden's declaration. "If he has the black framed glasses and a controller, he's A Typical Gamer."

Kaden's face transformed. Instead of looking bored, he wore a similar expression to his little brother's when Kenneth validated his wardrobe choice. "That's right!"

Candy still didn't get it, but she wanted to be supportive. "So, you're dressed as a gamer?"

"Not 'A' gamer. The Typical Gamer." Kaden answered.

"That's what I said. Isn't it?" Candy was genuinely confused.

Chuckling, Kenneth brushed her shoulder and gently patted her back. "It's a whole brand, babe. There's a pro gamer who goes by the name, Typical Gamer. He has an entire line of merch." Pointing to the hoodie Kaden wore, he indicated the 'T' logo on the front.

Realization dawned on Candy when she inspected the design more carefully. It was the letter T at the center of a upside down triangle with the word 'typical' in typewriter script below it. Lightly tapping her forehead with her palm, she voiced her own, 'duh'.

"I'm sorry, K. I guess I should have looked more closely. In my defense, I don't know much about gamer culture."

"That's ok, Auntie. Most older people don't."

"Excuse you, little boy? Who are you calling old?" Not really offended, but unwilling to let her fifteen-year-old nephew throw shade, she raised one eyebrow giving him an affronted expression.

Dipping his head, Kaden gave her an embarrassed smile. "I didn't mean it in a bad way. Mainly hard-core gamers know about him. Not many people your age keep up with stuff like that."

"You know you didn't clean that up at all right?" Candy continued the banter at which point the young man, who topped her five-foot ten-inch height by two inches, came closer giving her a hug.

"Come on, Auntie. You know I wouldn't call you old. I know you're just messing with me."

"You're lucky my feelings aren't easily hurt."

Candy hugged him back before prompting the children to get what they were taking with them. The sooner they got to the event, the more time the kids would have to play games and interact with children their age in a safe environment.

Surprisingly, no one had questions for she and Kenneth regarding their costumes. Other than raking her eyes over the two of them and smirking, even her mother offered no comments. Refusing to look a gift horse in the mouth, she hugged her mother, called out a goodbye to her father who was somewhere in the back of the house then ushered the children out. The kids piled into Kenneth's vehicle. He drove them to the nearby community center for the Halloween extravaganza.

It took less than thirty minutes for Candy to look at Kenneth like he was her favorite make-up palette on sale for a tenth of the normal price. She was totally in love. He was amazing with the kids. Since Kaden was older, he was given a little more leeway to wander inside the building without being glued to their side.

Until the kids' varying interests forced them to separate, Kenneth threw himself into playing whatever game they wanted to play. When they wanted to do it alone, he offered encouragement or help when asked. Even when they were on separate sides of the building, they kept in constant contact with each other and checked in with Kaden. It was one of the smoothest outings she'd had with the kids in ages.

The time flew by. Soon, it was time for them to gather the kids to take back to her parent's house. Candy was sure had it not been for the obvious closing down of the activities, she and Kenneth would've had more trouble dealing with Bryson's potential meltdown.

Of the three of them, he enjoyed himself the most. With the large age gap between he and Kaden, they didn't have enough in common to enjoy the activities Bryson liked. Nevaeh was in the 'Ew boys' stage when it came to interacting with her brothers for long periods of time. Naturally, the little guy didn't want to give up the opportunity to have someone's undivided attention.

By the time they made it to her parent's, Bryson was fast asleep clutching his bag of prizes. Kenneth lifted him from the car while Candy grabbed the booster seat. Holding on to their own bags of goodies, Kaden and Nevaeh exited the vehicle walking slowly up the walkway to the front door.

This time, her father met them. Giving hugs and kisses to the older kids before they ventured off to their rooms, she gave her dad the rundown on the evening's events. Taking the sleeping Bryson from Kenneth's arms, her father thanked them.

"No thanks necessary, sir. We enjoyed spending time with them." Kenneth's response to her dad's thanks echoed her sentiments, but her fiercely independent streak made her feel some type of way about him speaking for the both of them.

However, the more reasonable side of her nature kept her mouth firmly sealed. They felt the same way. He simply beat her to the punch. Reason won out. She kissed the sleeping child's cheek, then bid her father goodnight.

Although it was barely nine p.m. Candy sincerely felt like going home instead of to the costume party Kari had insisted she and Kenneth attend. Settling into the smooth leather seats of Kenneth's SUV, she allowed her mind to wander while he drove.

Her bestie was an interesting mix with her love of sports, cosplay and finance. What Candy didn't have to wonder was how Kari convinced her stoic looking husband, Daisuke, to not only attend the party, but to come in costume. There were very few limits on what he would do for Kari. Candy couldn't even be mad. Her cousin deserved someone who loved her with his whole heart.

The abrupt stop of their forward motion, brought Candy out of her thoughts. While Kenneth didn't exactly slam on the brakes, the stop was sudden enough for the seatbelt to tighten across her chest.

"Sorry about that. The car in front of us smashed on their brakes." One hand left the steering wheel to pat her thigh reassuringly.

"Oh. Ok." Looking and now actually seeing their surroundings, she noticed how close they were to the venue. Traffic was heavier. Fighting the urge to ask Kenneth to deviate from the plan, she watched the people walking on the sidewalk. Some were dressed for the holiday while others were in normal Friday night out gear.

Her desire to back out was crushed by Kenneth turning into the hotel and stopping next to the valet station. Before she could wrap herself in her jacket, he was at her side waiting to help her out. *Well, here goes nothin'.*

Chapter Fifteen
DID I SAY SOMETHING WRONG?

Walking through the hotel lobby with his hand on Candy's lower back just shy of her ass, Kenneth resolved in his mind that they wouldn't stay long at this party. She probably thought she hid it well, but he knew she'd lost her desire to attend somewhere along the drive. It was fine with him, but he was certain she wanted to at least see Kari and Daisuke.

While he relished the time they spent together alone, he was actually looking forward to an adult night out. He didn't socialize much. Between their work schedules, they tended to spend time at one another's homes instead of going out on dates. He was happy for the opportunity to take her someplace where they could have a nice evening.

A costume party wasn't his first choice, but when she brought it up, he jumped at the chance. It's possible his enthusiasm was tempered by knowing she'd agreed to come to Brooklyn with him for Thanksgiving thereby missing that time with her family to be with his.

His mind wandered back to their bathroom activities following his conversation with his uncle. After their shower, while she was still mellow from their lovemaking, he broached the subject.

"Hey, Babe?" Kenneth ran a towel over his hair as he watched Candy in the mirror pulling at her tight curls with her fingers.

"Hmm?" Her eyes met his using the mirror's reflection.

"I talked to my Uncle Ray this morning. I haven't seen him in a while. I was thinking of going up for Thanksgiving."

"Oh. Ok."

Her gaze transitioned back to her own reflection, but he heard the tinge of something he didn't like in her voice. The note made him hurry up and get to the point.

"Will you come with me? Spend the holiday in Brooklyn with me, and Uncle Ray? He's been asking about you. But the truth is, I don't want to go if you can't go as well."

Dropping the towel, he wrapped his arms around her waist nuzzling the crook of her neck. Recapturing her gaze in the glass, he let his eyes convey his feelings. Was he playing fair? Absolutely not. Did he care? Nope. Not if it got him what he wanted.

Her hands dropped from her hair and rested on his forearms. Tipping her head to the right, she regarded him watchfully.

"You want me to meet your family?"

"Yeah. I do. Do you not want to?" Although it was still kind of early in their relationship, he didn't think it was an unreasonable request.

"Of course. I guess it's only fair. You've met mine... I was just surprised."

Placing a kiss on her shoulder, he rested his chin on the same spot pulling her even closer to him.

"Why are you surprised? You know we aren't a secret. He's aware I'm seeing someone and that someone is you. It's a logical next step for you to meet the person who raised me."

"I guess. Maybe since meeting your uncle means more than driving across town, I thought I probably wouldn't meet him any time soon. Unless he came down for a visit."

"Well, he's not right across town, but the airport is. We'll get on a flight. It might take a few hours longer, but it can still be done in a day. Not that I'm suggesting a single day turn around trip."

"What are you suggesting?"

This was the part he thought she'd balk at—the time. "A week? We'd fly up the Sunday before the holiday then fly back the Sunday after."

"Kenneth..."

"I know it's a long time, but you deserve a break. You've been going almost non-stop for months."

"I know, but I'm usually in high demand around the holidays."

"Are you booked now?"

"I have a commitment the weeks leading up to the holiday, but I usually leave a block of time open just in case."

"If you don't have a booking, what's the problem?"

"There isn't a problem per se, but..."

"But what?"

"I'm self-employed. Other than being professional and doing my job well, I have a reputation for my responsiveness to clients with last minute emergencies."

"Baby...I'm not trying to minimize what you do, but there are make-up emergencies?"

Huffing, she tried to pull out of his embrace. "I know it doesn't seem lifesaving the way most people view it, but there are situations where me being available to a client helped them land the role of their career. Which in a sense, saved their life."

Tightening his hold, he refused to let her pull away. He mentally smacked himself for making it sound like her career wasn't important. It really wasn't his intent. Pressing kisses to the column of her neck and shoulders, he apologized.

"I'm sorry. That came out all wrong. I haven't had much opportunity to associate with people in the entertainment business the way you have. I'm ignorant to much of their lives."

Relaxing in his hold, her eyes met his once more in the mirror. They silently assessed one another before he organized his thoughts into what he surmised might be a better approach.

"You're highly sought after in your field, right?"

"Yes."

"Then why are you leaving openings for people to interrupt your life at the last minute? It allows them to disrespect your time if they know they can call you in to save the day instead of planning ahead."

Capturing her bottom lip between her teeth, she tortured him by nibbling on it as she considered his statement.

"They may be famous or important industry people, but you're a *fucking rock star. No one gets to call up a rock star at the spur of the moment and ask them to alter their plans."*

"You sound like Kari. She's always telling me I'm too accommodating."

"You have to set boundaries, Baby."

"I do set boundaries. I have people I refuse to work with who know they can't call me. For anything."

"But those in your good graces still have too much leeway if they can call you at the last minute during the holidays you celebrate. They knew they needed someone. If they didn't plan in advance, they're treating you like a backup plan. You're too talented to be anyone's second choice."

Tears welled in her eyes; her lips trembled with emotion. Shit! Had he said the wrong thing again? Grappling with the shift, he turned her to face him swiping at the wetness on her cheeks.

"Hey, what's this? Why the tears? Did I say something wrong?"

Candy's hands cupped his face and she pressed a watery kiss to his lips. "You didn't say anything wrong." Pulling him closer, she pressed her forehead to his.

"I've never had anyone, besides my family, support me so fiercely. I'm a big baby. I just got a little emotional."

Relief flooded him at learning he hadn't hurt her. He'd probably never get the happy tears thing. Releasing a shaky breath, he stroked his fingers into the hair at her nape, his gaze locked on her.

"I'll let it be known I won't be available from...?" Her voice trailed off waiting for him to fill in the blank.

"The twentieth through the twenty-seventh." He supplied.

"The twentieth through the twenty-seventh. I'll let the booking agents, I work with, know first thing on Monday."

Peppering her face with grateful kisses, he backed her into the counter to initiate a round of celebration sex. He couldn't get enough of her and she matched his energy.

Snapping back into the moment, Kenneth swept the room of costumed/cosplaying adults. It wasn't his normal crowd, but he wasn't uncomfortable. He saw a few other men dressed as the new Spock with some Captain Pikes thrown in the mix. In his opinion, none of the Spocks came close to him.

Not because of him or his physique, but because of the effort his Candy had put into the small details of his costume and makeup. As it turned out, she did more than glamour makeup. She was also quite skilled in special effects makeup. His pointed Vulcan ears looked like he could step onto a movie set and fit right in.

"Do you wanna take pictures?" He'd spotted the area set up along one wall for photos. If they were going to do this, they might as well have the whole experience while they were there.

"Sure, if you want." Candy's words contradicted the sparkle in her eyes at his suggestion. Other than random snapshots, they hadn't taken photos together. He needed to remedy that. The way she snapped pictures of her niece and nephews spoke of the way she liked to catalogue experiences.

As they made their way toward the photo booth, he noticed the not so sly glances they garnered. Kenneth was no fool, he knew they made a striking couple in their regular clothes. In their costumes, with Candy's voluptuous curves on display, they were guaranteed to capture more than their fair share of attention.

Opting to use the photographer onsite, they stepped in front of the green screen. Taking a few normal couple hug pictures, they had a little fun using Candy's Tricorder purse as a prop before Kenneth placed his hands on her face to imitate the famous Vulcan Mind Meld. Dissolving into laughter following their impromptu photo shoot, they moved farther into the gathering.

Kenneth always had a good time when they were together. However, he really enjoyed seeing the carefree side of her. Once she was in an adult setting, she didn't once appear self-conscious about her outfit as she had before they left. Confidence oozed from every pore of her being and he basked in her glow.

They'd been there roughly thirty minutes before Candy spotted Kari and Daisuke. Pointing them out to Kenneth, she tugged on his arm leading him over to the couple.

"Oh my goodness! You guys look amazing!"

Kenneth watched as Candy gushed over her cousins. The couple was dressed as *Superman* and *Wonder Woman*. No. Not *Wonder Woman*. *Nubia*. Wonder Woman's sister.

Both athletically built, they pulled it off well. Seeing Daisuke's costume, Kenneth decided he'd gotten a better deal with Candy wanting to cosplay *Star Trek* characters instead of super heroes. While Daisuke didn't seem to mind, Kenneth knew he personally wouldn't have been comfortable in so much spandex.

"We look amazing? Y'all are the perfect Uhura and Spock. You have the classic Uhura Bobb. Kenneth even has the pointy Vulcan ears."

Blushing, Candy linked her arm in his. "Let's just agree that we're all killing it."

"I can live with that." Kari answered with a bright smile.

Having her best friend nearby appeared to rejuvenate Candy. The lethargy she'd displayed when they'd arrived was gone as she and Kari tipped their heads together chatting. The ladies didn't only talk to one another, but they did seem to feed of each other's energy.

After securing a table big enough for the four of them, he and Daisuke ventured to the beverage line to get drinks. Techno-music thumped through the venue speakers making normal conversation nearly impossible which suited him just fine. Neither he nor Daisuke were big on small talk.

After securing drinks for themselves and their significant others, they waded through the thickening crowd to find their table once more. As they sat, the music changed from Techno to a song with a Reggaeton beat. A whoop went up from the people on the crowded dance floor as their gyrations took on a different vibe.

A flash of red caught Kenneth's eye toward the center of the crowd, but he didn't give it much thought. Considering the costumes they'd seen so far, it could be someone dressed as a giant bird of prey for all he knew. The song faded out ushering in a slower tune causing the dancing crowd to thin out. With the space created, the flash of red was visible. It was some type of headdress worn by a woman standing well over six feet tall.

"Is that Nikki?" Kari's question was accompanied by taps to Candy's arm.

"Huh? Where?"

"On the dance floor. The one in the black and red bustier wearing a red hat that looks like the queen of hearts from *Alice in Wonderland*. Next to the guy dressed like Shrek."

All eyes from their table followed Kari's directions. Due to her height and colorful headgear, she was hard to miss. Turning toward them, she smiled then waved before making her way over. Kenneth had met Nikki the previous year when a friend of a friend needed help locating a kidnapped child.

The child was her godchild, so Nikki used her resources in private security to help them rescue the little girl along with others who were being trafficked. It was a tense time. He didn't ask how Candy and Kari knew Nikki, but they seemed friendly enough when Nikki approached.

Standing, the ladies hugged Nikki before starting the routine of complimenting one another's costumes again. Wisely, Kenneth and Daisuke watched without comment until they were drawn into the conversation.

"It's a good thing y'all are here with your men. Y'all are looking too cute and sexy for this crowd." Nikki smiled widely swatting at Candy and Kari as she praised them again.

"Girl, stop." Candy replied with a swat of her own. "What about you? Walking around looking like Meg's taller, sexier sister."

"You don't know who I am?" Stepping back, Nikki whipped the long black train of her outfit then struck a pose with one hand up.

"I'm the fabulous Grace Jones! She's the reason Meg gets to be Meg rapping about whatever she wants and dressing however she feels."

"How did I not know that?" Candy tapped her forehead with the heel of her hand. "I've practically studied all of the great divas looking for inspiration at some point."

Thoroughly entertained by the ladies, Kenneth was content to watch and listen. Daisuke stood next to his wife with his hand on her back watching the room as if he expected trouble at any minute. Citing sore feet, Nikki invited herself to their table and everyone once again took a seat.

The volume of the music didn't allow for much conversation, but they managed. Watching the light in Candy's eyes coupled with the broad smile on her face, he was certain this night out was exactly what she needed. Nikki was recounting a story from her adventures with her best friend Stephanie Barker when she stopped mid-sentence.

A sour expression flit across her face before she covered it with a different smile. One which didn't quite reach her eyes. Apologizing and saying she forgot something, Nikki hopped up from her seat quickly stepping away.

Not ten seconds later, a hulking blond giant walked past their table giving Kenneth the briefest of nods. While everyone else at the table looked around dumbfounded, Kenneth followed the progression of the giant he knew to be Asher Peterson, as he caught up with the retreating Nikki.

"What was that all about?" Candy asked looking from Kenneth's face to where his attention was fixed.

"I'm not quite sure, but I've got a feeling our friend Nikki has gotten herself into a bit of a pickle." Kenneth answered as he rubbed her arm affectionately.

"Who is that guy? Is she okay?"

Candy's brow creased as she looked over her shoulder to see what Kenneth saw—Ash slipping his arm around Nikki's waist and speaking directly into her ear.

"That's Asher Peterson. He won't hurt her." *At least not the way you think.* He added in his head.

If their body language was correct Asher was planning something similar to what he planned for himself and Candy before the night was through. Lucky bastard would probably get his prize before Kenneth could even convince Candy to go up to the room he'd secured when he bought their event tickets.

"Are you sure?"

"You know Nikki. She strikes me as a person who doesn't do anything she doesn't wanna do. Do you think she'd let him so close to her if she didn't want him there? Besides, if I'm reading them right, they're quite familiar with each other."

Leaning closer, Kenneth spoke directly into her ear. "As familiar as I want to get with you. As soon as you say we can split, I'm going to split those legs and have a taste of my personal Candy."

A gasp escaped Candy's lips; her shoulders wiggled in a shiver. Her eyes widened a fraction before her lashes dropped covering them from view. She didn't have to say anything for him to know her body was preparing for him to keep his promise.

Only marginally caring about being rude, he offered an obviously flimsy excuse to Daisuke and Kari before tugging her away to the coat check, barely giving her time to say a proper goodbye. Instead of going to the valet stand, he ushered her to the elevators.

"Where are we going?"

Standing behind her, he wrapped his arms around her waist pulling her back flush to his front. "To our room."

"When did we get a room?" Subtly rubbing her ass against his erection, he knew she didn't care about the answer.

Placing his hands on her hips to still her motion, he willed the elevator to hurry. He'd spent too many excruciating hours wanting to slip beneath the skirt of her dress to re-acquaint himself with her velvet center. Any additional delay was torture.

Finally, Kenneth heard the glorious ding and a set of doors slid open. Nudging Candy to enter in front of him, he was pleased they were alone in the car. Pressing the button for the fifteenth floor, he backed her into the corner beneath the camera.

"Let's discuss you teasing me just now."

Widening her eyes innocently, she stared up at him. "I have no idea what you mean."

Slipping a hand under the edge of her skirt he grabbed a handful of her delicious ass giving it a squeeze. "Let me refresh your memory."

Capturing her lips, he devoured her gasp as his fingers found her slick core. He didn't release her until the electronic ding announced they'd reached their destination.

Chapter Sixteen

LESS TALKING, MORE DOING

This couldn't be normal. That was Candy's thought as they stumbled into their room barely clearing the doorway before they began tugging at one another's clothing. Their level of sexual chemistry and the way they couldn't look at one another for too long without something popping off was unlike anything she'd ever experienced.

It couldn't be normal, but damned if she didn't love every second of it. Being treated as if she was the most desirable woman alive was intoxicating. She was literally drunk off of him. The alcohol she'd had at the party didn't pack one tenth of the punch as a single kiss from Kenneth's lips.

Tumbling onto the bed, he continued his worship of her body—scrambling her thoughts until her sole focus was the pleasure he delivered. He appeared to be on a mission to drive her insane with want.

Unzipping her boots, he placed kisses on her hose covered legs as he slid the faux leather from her limbs. Once her footwear was removed, his eager digits moved to her waist. The ripping sound informed her that her pantyhose had been rendered useless. It was fine with Candy; she rarely wore the things anyway.

Where Kenneth's hands traveled, his mouth followed while he adored every inch of her skin as he exposed it until she was bare before him. His touch set her entire body ablaze with desire. It ignited an urgency within her to join them together. Once again, she pulled at his clothing, working to remove the barrier between them.

Pulling away, his hooded grey gaze never left her as he shucked his costume with complete disregard for where it landed. He still wore the dark wig and prosthetic ears, but they didn't take away from the pure sexual energy pouring off of him. The way his eyes raked over her body was enough to make her core clench. The look promised a night filled with carnal delights.

"Give me your hands."

His words were a gruff command which prompted Candy to place her hands in front of her before her brain completely caught up. A flood of moisture gathered in her center at the domineering tone. *What the hell was that?*

"Good girl..." One of Kenneth's silk ties appeared in his hands as if by magic. Lightly binding her wrists, he kissed her palms then her lips.

"Is this okay, Baby?"

A mute nod was Candy's response. She'd never trusted anyone enough for this type of role playing, but she also had never been in a relationship with a man like Kenneth. He inspired confidence in his ability to care for all of her needs.

"If it's not, you can tell me. I won't do anything you don't want to do. Okay?"

At Candy's responding nod, he prompted. "I need the words. I have to hear you say you're okay with this." He tugged on her bound wrists to emphasize his point.

"I'm okay. I trust you." Candy's throat clogged with emotion. It was true. Kenneth had her trust. This type of play was unknown to her, but there wasn't anyone else she'd consider experiencing it with.

His lips met hers in a kiss that dragged her further into his lustful web. Pulling away, he pinned her with a serious expression.

"If you want to stop at any time, we can stop. I only want to make you feel good, Baby."

"Less talking, more doing." Candy's goal was to get rid of tentative Kenneth and get shit-talking, take-charge, Kenneth back. She appreciated him wanting her to be comfortable, but the question had been asked and answered.

Her words had the desired result. A darkness descended over his face then his grip on her bound wrists tightened.

"Are you sassing me?"

Candy's stomach flipped at the gruff timbre of his voice. It was like her words flicked a switch. His whole vibe projected his intentions before he spoke to confirm them.

"It sounds like you want me to fuck that sassy mouth, but putting your lips on my dick is a reward you haven't earned yet."

Pressing her back on the bed, he lifted her hands above her head. "Keep them there."

Her skin tingled in anticipation of his next move as he hovered over her not giving any indication of what he had planned. The expectation was more titillating than Candy had ever imagined. Alternating his method of stimulation, Kenneth worked his way down her body placing kisses, sucks and nibbles in random intervals from her neck to her stomach.

When he shouldered his way between her legs to her dripping core, she reflexively dropped her hands to the top of his head. In a move which left her spinning and disoriented, he seized her hands flipping her over onto her stomach.

"Since you can't keep your hands to yourself, we'll try it this way." His chest warmed her back as he growled into her ear. Once again placing her hands above her head, he issued another warning.

"Move them again and I'll tie you to this fucking bed."

*That should **not** be so freaking sexy.* But, it was. Her pussy was leaking in response to his rough handling. The way he moved her around like she was a lightweight was an unexpected turn-on; she loved every second of it.

Determined to wring every ounce of pleasure from the moment, Candy grasped two hands full of the bedcovers to help her obey his instructions. The smack to her ass cheek caught her off-guard. Considering his current demeanor, she should've expected it, but she didn't.

Rubbing the spot on her butt, he soothed the sting then grabbed her hips to position her on her knees. Her face was turned to the side as her upper body was pressed into the bed. At this point, she expected him to plunge his thickness into her weeping channel. That's not what happened. Instead, she felt a breeze on her rosette when Kenneth spread her cheeks then latched onto her lower lips—delving his tongue between her folds lapping at her dripping essence.

Holy fuck! She wasn't close to virginal when she met Kenneth, still no one had ever tasted her from this position before. The angle and exposure sent her flying over the chasm in seconds. Gripping the sheets, she rocked her hips into his face. With another smack to her other cheek and grumbling moan into her center, Kenneth expressed his approval of her participation.

Redoubling his efforts, he brought her to another skin sizzling orgasm in short order. Just when she thought she couldn't take anymore, he halted his oral invasion. When he released her overstimulated sex, her legs slid from under her hips, leaving her prone on the bed.

Detangling her fingers from the sheets, he untied her wrists and moved her arms behind her back. Her spaghetti noodle limbs allowed him to do whatever he pleased. Placing her hands at the small of her back, he re-tied her wrists leaving a gap between them.

"Are you tapping out on me, Baby?"

A barely audible 'no' pushed past Candy's lips, but she honestly didn't know if she could handle even one more orgasm. Her disloyal pussy didn't care, it continued to clench at nothing begging to be filled.

Nudging her back to her knees, Kenneth used the tie to pull her upper body in an arch as he plunged his length into her greedy channel. The sudden intrusion was deliciously edged with a twinge of pain as her walls fought against accommodating all of his thickness so quickly.

"That's it, my sweet Candy. Take it. Take every single inch of my cock." Withdrawing from her depths, he quickly drove back in like he couldn't stand being outside of her walls.

"Damn, Baby. You're so tight, you're gonna suck the cum right out of my balls."

Pulling her up until his chest met her back, he bit her earlobe before drawing it into his mouth giving it a soothing suck.

"Is that what you want? Do you want me to pump you full of my seed? You want me to fill you so full it drips down your leg? Hm? Tell Daddy what you want. You know I'll give it to you."

Kenneth's questions served to heighten Candy's arousal. He was hitting all the buttons she didn't know she wanted pushed tonight. *Who is this man?* The query floated across her mind, but he answered as if she'd spoken it aloud.

"I'm *your* man. I'm the only one who sees to your pleasure, Baby. Even when you don't know how to say it. I'll be here to give it to you. Every. Single. Time."

His last words were punctuated with sharp thrusts of his hips sending his shaft deeper than he'd been before, triggering an earth-shattering explosion inside her. Tears cascaded down her cheeks as she gave herself over to the feelings he evoked.

Kenneth's moans and grunts reached her ears through a fog of bliss. With one hand on her throat, the other sought her clit as he made one final snap of his hips locking them together while he kept his promise—flooding her channel with his cum.

The external encouragement combined with the feel of his length jerking inside her tossed her into an orgasm she hadn't thought was possible. It was too much. Over-stimulated and exhausted, Candy slumped against Kenneth's sturdy frame before slipping into darkness.

Awakening in Kenneth's arms had become an indulgence Candy never wanted to give up. Waking to him sliding his very thick, very stiff dick into her silky walls was even more decadent. Despite him fucking her to sleep the night before, she tipped her hips to allow him better access.

Kissing her shoulder, he plucked at her nipples with one hand while using the other to guide her on and off his dick.

"That's my good girl. Wake up and take this dick." Quickening his pace, he pushed them to the precipice in a matter of minutes. Holding her hip to keep himself completely embedded inside her, he placed kisses on her shoulder, neck and the side of her face.

"Fuck... I can't seem to get enough of you. You feel so good wrapped around me." Despite his deflating erection, he gently rocked his hips to keep his length inside her channel.

"Mmm...Kenneth..." Candy moaned.

It's a good thing she had an IUD. The way they enjoyed condom free sex, she'd be surprised they hadn't created a life with the way they couldn't keep their hands off each other. Well...Their hands weren't really the problem. It was her inability to say no to any chance to ride or be ridden by that weapon he called a cock.

Finally releasing her from his hold, he flopped onto his back emitting an exhausted sigh. Turning, she propped her head on her fist looking at him. At some point during the night, he'd rid himself of the rest of his costume, so the wig and pointy ears lay in parts unknown somewhere inside the room.

A quick feel of her own head found her wig was missing as well. However, she still wore the wig cap she'd pulled over her corn rows. A look in the mirror would confirm it, but she was certain she didn't look remotely sexy in her wig cap with likely smeared makeup on her face.

No matter how good the product, not much could stand up to the level of sweat and activity they got up to the previous night and this morning. Despite Candy looking what she considered far from her best, he'd awakened hard—ready to be inside her. Not for one second did she feel anything less than desirable while they made love.

That's when it hit her. She was utterly and irrevocably in love with Kenneth Holmes. In the past, there was no way she would have allowed a man to see her the way Kenneth had seen her too many times to count. She certainly wouldn't let them see her in corn rows and a wig cap.

Yet, he'd seen her that way. Not only had he not cared, he'd held her then made love to her like her hair was perfect and she'd worn her sexiest lingerie. It filled her heart near to bursting.

Mumbling about needing to clean up, she scrambled from the bed making a beeline for the ensuite bathroom. She needed a few minutes alone to deal with her revelation.

Chapter Seventeen
IT DON'T TAKE A WHOLE DAY TO RECOGNIZE
SUNSHINE

Kenneth waited patiently for Candy to get settled in her seat. Once she was done situating herself, he clasped her hand in his. He'd sprung for First Class seats to keep them from having anyone included in their bubble as they traveled to New York. Her fingers gripped his and her smile was one of relief.

Regardless of how many times he'd told her over the past few weeks that his uncle was already smitten with her, she was still nervous. Kissing the back of her hand, he encouraged her to take a nap. Their early flight meant they'd awakened at the crack of dawn. Considering he had to force her into bed at two a.m., they were working on less than five hours of sleep.

On a normal day, it wouldn't matter. However, Kenneth was sure his Uncle Ray had a day full of visits and activities planned. So, there wouldn't be a moment for them to take a break until it was time for bed. If he guessed correctly, bedtime was in a very distant future. So, they had to take rest when they could get it.

As the wheels of the plane left the runway, Candy's head tipped onto his shoulder and her eyes slid shut. *She was so fucking beautiful.* She wasn't just physically appealing, she was smart, talented and an amazingly loving individual.

On top of all of that, she matched him sexually. He had no idea how he'd gotten so lucky, but he didn't plan on messing it up. Anyone looking to split them apart would be in for the fight of their lives. Candy was his. Forever. She just didn't know it yet.

Placing a kiss to the top of her head, Kenneth decided to take his own advice by grabbing some shut eye. The flight would last a little over two hours. It was plenty of time to get in a quick doze.

When the plane touched down at JFK airport, they were both refreshed. Candy's eyes were bright and he was pleased she didn't appear as anxious as she was before. He was smart enough not to mention his observation, although he wondered what brought on the change.

Their disembarking and retrieval of their luggage was uneventful. He even managed not to make another quip about the size of her largest piece of luggage. The death glare she'd given him the first time he mentioned it was enough to keep his lips firmly sealed.

His normally agreeable woman looked ready to detach his head from his body when he kept joking that they were only going for a week, not *moving* to Brooklyn. Knowing it was nerves and her desire to be ready for any eventuality, he tried not to take it personally.

Wheeling their luggage while she rolled her small carry-on, they finally made it to the designated pick-up spot. Uncle Ray insisted on coming to get them. He'd said it was wasteful for Kenneth to rent a car when he had options for them to choose from. That's what Uncle Ray said, but Kenneth thought he was simply too eager to finally meet Candy.

While his Uncle was perpetually single, he constantly encouraged Kenneth to find a nice woman and settle down. There hadn't been anything more than short lived dalliances in Kenneth's life since he called it quits with Annalise six years ago.

Spotting his uncle's electric blue BMW X5, he nudged Candy to the curb. They'd have very little time to get loaded then pull away. The airport was pretty strict in regards to not parking in the loading and unloading areas. Anyone taking too long to do either, risked being ticketed.

"KG! It's so good to see you, son!" Despite the time crunch, his uncle pulled him into a hug. "And this beautiful lady must be Candace."

His exuberant smile reached his bright blue eyes as he stretched out both arms to Candy before he thought better and extended one hand to shake hers.

"It's okay if you want to hug, Mr. Holmes." She said with a hint of mirth in her voice.

The words had barely hit the air before she was swept into Uncle Ray's arms. Honking horns pulled them back into awareness and his uncle lifted the rear door. Between the two of them, they stowed the luggage quickly.

When Candy attempted to get into the backseat, Kenneth hurriedly corrected her course buckling her into the front passenger seat before securing his own seat behind her. Concerned about his long legs, Candy went to move her seat forward until he stopped her.

"Did you forget about your own long legs? I'll be fine. There's plenty of space to spread out back here."

"Don't worry about him." His uncle joined in. "As long as you're fine, he'll be fine. He likes taking care of you."

He said it with such certainty, Kenneth felt his uncle had been listening to his inner thoughts. Wracking his brain, he tried to recall if he'd spoken those words aloud. They talked so much; he really couldn't remember.

A flush crept up Candy's cheeks. She didn't like being the center of attention. Even in small groups. As his uncle maneuvered the vehicle into traffic, Kenneth changed the subject.

"So, what's on the agenda for today, Uncle Ray?" That one question was enough to get his uncle to focus on something else.

"First, we'll stop by my place to drop your things off, then I told Toni we'd come over."

"How is Aunt Toni doing?" It had been over a month since he'd last spoken to his honorary godmother.

"She's fine. She said not to expect anything special for dinner since she's prepping for Thanksgiving, but you know her."

"Yep. Nothing special still means she got up before the sun this morning to start cooking."

"You know it." His uncle agreed with a laugh. They continued their banter with he and his uncle sharing stories of Uncle Ray's best friend Toni Martin, including a few from when they were crashing in her living room.

After a brief lull in conversation, his uncle started in on a topic Kenneth wasn't expecting.

"So, Candace. How did you and my nephew meet? Of all the things he's told me about you, I don't remember him mentioning how the two of you met."

"We officially met at one of my family's cookouts. His friend, Driscoll, is married to my cousin. I can't remember the occasion, but he showed up with a Sock it To Me cake. It was a big hit."

Uncle Ray caught Kenneth's eye in the rearview mirror. "You used Toni's recipe?"

"Of course."

"That's my boy. Hit 'em with the good stuff first."

Candy's eyes bounced between the two of them while she smiled at their exchange.

"So, you two met at the cookout and hit it off?" His uncle prompted Candy to continue.

"I wouldn't say that...Come to think of it, I don't even think we were formally introduced. I saw him at my cousin's wedding the year before. At the cookout, it was just one of those things. Someone told me Driscoll brought his friend Kenneth then pointed him out and we kind of fell into a polite acquaintance type deal."

"Polite acquaintance? When was this cookout?"

"Mmm... I think last year." Candy looked back at Kenneth to confirm.

"Yes. It was an End of School thing they put on for the kids at your aunt and uncle's house."

"So...you two have been together for over a year?"

Kenneth recognized the tone and prayed his uncle was able to find the filter he so often lacked in conversation.

"Oh, no." Candy laughed, ignorant to the undercurrent. "We've only been seeing each other for about five months."

"KG? You mean to tell me all the time I put into trying to teach you how to recognize a treasure and you let a whole year pass before you made a move? What happened? I know you're not blind."

"Nothing happened, Uncle Ray. Everything happens when it's supposed to. It wasn't our time then. It is now." Reaching over the seat, his fingers brushed Candy's shoulder. Hers tangled with his giving them a reassuring squeeze.

"If you're scared, just say that."

"Uncle Ray—"

"What did Common say? It don't take a year to recognize sunshine?"

"First of all, the lyric is, 'It don't take a whole day to recognize sunshine.' Secondly, when did you start quoting rappers? Have you been hanging with the Sous-chefs again?"

Uncle Ray brushed off Kenneth's correction of his misquoted lyric. "I told you; they keep me hip. Anyway, a day, a year, it means the same thing. Don't sleep on a good thing."

Thankfully, his uncle turned into the parking garage of his building. Cutting the conversation short he pulled into his designated space and opened the lift gate. Hopping out, Kenneth helped Candy from the car before unloading their luggage.

They stayed at the apartment long enough to drop their bags, and give Candy a quick tour of his uncle's two story, four-bedroom home. The property was the first thing his uncle purchased after his first restaurant was successful enough to move out of the cramped two-bedroom flat above the establishment.

By then, Kenneth was in high school. In addition, he was already working his way up the ranks in the kitchen. The place hadn't changed much other than the addition of various pieces of art and remodeling of a few of the rooms.

The trip from the condo to his Aunt Toni's three-story brownstone probably would have been shorter if they'd taken the train, but Uncle Ray liked to drive. Because of his love of controlling his own transportation, they had to circle the block a few times before he located a parking spot.

They had a short walk before they reached the stairs leading up to the 1940's era brownstone. Kenneth recalled when she'd purchased the building. Instead of dividing it into apartments, and living on one level, she remodeled the place one level at a time until she created her own oasis in the big city.

Standing on the landing, Kenneth smelled the rich scent of Aunt Toni's version of southern delights. Even after living in the south for more than half a decade and being a dedicated foodie, he ranked her cooking as the best in down-home southern cuisine.

The door swung open. Finally, he was able to lay eyes on the woman who helped his uncle shape him into the man he was today.

"There's my Baby Boy! Come on in here and give me a hug!"

With her arms stretched wide, her smile took over her lean face showing straight white teeth. Stepping over the threshold, Kenneth hugged his Aunt Toni with as much enthusiasm as she hugged him. *Now* he felt like he was home. Something about being at Aunt Toni's filled in the missing piece to make his homecoming complete.

Releasing her from his embrace, he stepped back and snaked an arm around Candy's waist pulling her to his side. Aunt Toni's eyes pinged between them; the smile on her face grew even brighter.

"What's this, Baby Boy? So, Ray wasn't pulling my leg. You really did go and get yourself a lady-friend. He said you were bringing a young lady home, but he didn't properly prepare me for this beauty."

Squeezing a blushing Candy closer to his side, Kenneth made the introductions. "Aunt Toni, this is Candace Hampton. Candy, this is my aunt Toni Martin."

"Nice to meet you, Miss Toni." Candy said politely.

She extended her hand only to be pulled into a hug. "Come on now, honey. Give me a hug. I heard that southern twang in your voice. You know how we do."

Pulling back, holding both of her hands, Aunt Toni beamed at Candy like she'd won the best of prizes. "You are absolutely stunning."

Tossing Kenneth a wink, she moved back down the hallway pulling Candy behind her. "Y'all know where everything is, I'm taking Miss Candace with me. Dinner will be ready in fifteen minutes."

"Well...I guess we don't exist." His uncle's dry comment was accompanied by a pat to Kenneth's shoulder. "We might as well go on into the dining room and finish setting the table, if she hasn't done it already."

Stupefied, Kenneth followed mutely behind the older man. The last woman he'd brought a to meet his Aunt Toni was Annalise. To say the older woman wasn't a fan was putting it nicely. She was polite, but cold in their interaction and later told Kenneth not to bother bringing her back.

It wasn't long after that when Annalise unveiled her rigid belief system. Aunt Toni had known within ten seconds, what it had taken Kenneth more than six months to uncover. He knew Candy was nothing like Annalise, but it flabbergasted him how instantly his aunt warmed to her.

While they were pulling the plates and silverware from the large China cabinet with the ornate hand-carved mahogany features, Kenneth asked his uncle what he'd told her about Candy. Considering she was Uncle Ray's best friend, it was likely he'd told her everything Kenneth told him.

"Believe it or not, I didn't tell her much. I mean...I told her you'd met a nice lady who had your nose wide open."

"Seriously, Uncle Ray. Who have you been hanging around? Since when do you use terms like, 'nose wide open'? What does that even mean?"

Slapping at his arm with a cloth napkin, as Kenneth side stepped him, his uncle responded in a huff. "You know what it means. You know exactly where I got it from. As much time as you spent with Toni growing up, there's no way you didn't hear her say that among a slew of other southern colloquialisms."

"Okay. Fine. So, what do you make of her running off with my woman like that?"

"Your woman, huh?"

"Absolutely." Grey clashed with blue as Kenneth held his uncle's stare across the table.

"Well, alright then." Clearing his throat, Uncle Ray continued folding the napkins and placing them beside the plates. "I don't know what's up with Toni other than she doesn't get to talk to many women from home. Maybe your lady's accent made her homesick."

Kenneth didn't believe it for a second, but he'd caught on that he wouldn't get any answers from Raymond Holmes. He wasn't foolish enough to barge into his Aunt Toni's kitchen to see what she was up to. So, it appeared he'd have to wait it out.

Turning his attention back to their task, he worked alongside his uncle to finish setting the table. Switching the topic to his uncle's favorite football team, Kenneth drew him into another discussion. Other than food, football was Uncle Ray's favorite subject of conversation.

Time passed quickly. They'd barely sat on the sofa in the den before they were being called back into the dining room. Immediately moving to Candy's side, Kenneth checked her face for any indication of upset or distress.

Her fingers slid against his and she gripped them reassuringly before she accepted his help with her chair at the table. Murmuring a soft 'thank you', she graced him with a sweet smile. Seeing her smile allowed him to relax fully.

Taking the seat to her left, he lifted his eyes to see Aunt Toni staring at him with a slight grin on her face. Giving him the smallest of nods, she held out her hands. Once everyone's hands were joined, she blessed the food and they began to eat the small feast she'd prepared for them.

Chapter Eighteen

NO, I CAN'T. IT'S DISRESPECTFUL

Candy wasn't sure what she expected when Kenneth introduced her to Toni Martin, but it was fair to say being pulled into the woman's culinary sanctuary wasn't on the list.

In all the times Kenneth mentioned his Aunt Toni, he'd never said she was the well-known soul food chef and restauranteur. Only knowing he wasn't the type of person who bragged about such things kept Candy from being upset with him. Even though Candy met celebrities regularly, her insides did a little flip when she realized Kenneth's Aunt Toni was *the* Miss Toni.

Her gaze flit around the spacious area admiring the combination of modernism with traditionalism in one place. The antique white cabinetry merged with granite countertops and dark hardwood floors which gave a striking contrast. The industrial sized refrigerator somehow didn't look out of place. Neither did the large gas range with the double oven.

When Kenneth wasn't immersed in the latest tech gadget that caught his eye, he was heavily into kitchens and cooking. Being with him had given Candy more insight into such things since he loved to watch kitchen renovations in addition to his hate-watching of cooking shows.

He frequently commented about the tools and appliances the fake chefs used. Fake was his term not hers. He refused to believe all of them had actually been to culinary school or worked their way through the kitchen hierarchy the way he had.

"So, are you from Atlanta originally?" Miss Toni asked Candy as she moved to stand behind a butcher block island containing veggies in various states of preparation.

"Yes, ma'am. Most of my family is still there." Candy supplied. "Is there something I can do to help? With the meal?"

Her culinary confidence had grown by leaps and bounds. In the past, she would've never had the nerve to ask a trained chef let alone restaurant owner if she could assist them. While she didn't expect Miss Toni to allow her to do anything critical, Candy still offered.

"Aren't you sweet? You can wash your hands in the sink over there and help me finish making this salad. Everything else is pretty much done."

Following directions, Candy went to the double garden sink to wash her hands. Along the way, she noted the crockpots and pressure cookers currently in use, in addition to the steaming cookware on the stove. *Was this woman expecting an army?*

Spying her staring, Miss Toni caught Candy's expression. She seemed to read it accurately.

"Don't worry, baby. This isn't all for today. I'm getting a jump on some of my holiday dishes. I do the main part of the meal and I encourage other family members to bring the sides.

But, since everyone doesn't have the same skills and there tend to be unexpected guests, I always have a few sides tucked away to fill in the gap."

"Oh." Candy blushed slightly with embarrassment.

Picking up the knife Miss Toni pointed to when she made it back to the island, Candy pulled the decorative glass bowl closer to her to begin her assignment.

"Miss Toni, do you want a rough chop or smaller pieces?"

"Smaller pieces please. Not too small though." Using her own knife, she demonstrated for Candy. "By the way, you can just call me, Toni."

Stopping with the knife poised over the sweet red pepper, Candy's gaze landed on the older woman. "No, I can't. It's disrespectful."

"Sweetheart, it's really not necessary. We're both adults." Miss Toni flipped her hand between them.

"Yes ma'am we are. I still can't call you by your first name though."

Candy wasn't trying to be offensive or make Miss Toni feel old. But, her mother would twist her ear if she heard her refer to an elder adult by their first name—especially an elder black woman. Despite being well into her thirties, she'd never shed that aspect of her upbringing.

A sly smile crept over Miss Toni's features and Candy considered the possibility she'd been given some type of test.

"If you insist, I won't try to change your mind." The other woman said as she went to the refrigerator returning with three bunches of lettuce. Each was a different variety.

"How did you and Baby Boy meet?" Was the first in a series of questions Candy was peppered with as they worked to finish putting the salad together.

She didn't mind. Miss Toni was extremely easy to talk to. It didn't take much for her to understand why Kenneth held the woman is such high esteem. Her entire vibe was warm, open and caring. Hearing her call Kenneth, Baby Boy, was as amusing as it was intriguing.

Finally, she had to ask. "Why do you call Kenneth, Baby Boy? If you don't mind my asking?"

Halting in her food prep, Miss Toni pierced Candy with a probing stare. "How much did he tell you about his childhood?"

"We talked about him being raised by his uncle after his parents' deaths and how they lived with you for a period of time. I could tell it was tough for him to discuss, so I didn't push. He'll tell me more when he's ready."

"He told you about his parents?" The hint of surprise in her voice made Candy wonder if his doing so was unusual.

Although Candy wondered what the questions had to do with how Kenneth got one of the only two nicknames he actually consented to being called, she answered in the hope to receive the same.

"Yes, ma'am. Like I said, I think it's hard for him to talk about. So, I didn't press after he told me they were both in law enforcement and were killed in the line of duty."

"Well...It was a really rough time, so I understand if he has trouble talking about it. When I saw him and Ray that day lugging everything they owned, I looked into his sweet little face; my heart broke for him.

I invited Ray over to my tiny ass apartment for dinner. We ate. Then, while we cleaned the kitchen and talked, I sent Kenneth to the couch to watch television. By the time we were finished, that sweet boy was curled up on my hand-me-down sofa fast asleep.

My apartment was a literal shoe box. I was working as a line cook at the time, but I couldn't send them back out on the streets. Ray and I worked out an agreement to help each other. I got him on at the restaurant, and we did the co-parenting thing.

Even after he was financially stable enough to move them into their own place and I'd met then married my late husband, I was still involved. I might've met him for the first time, when he was ten, but he's been my Baby Boy since the night I covered him with my granny's quilt as he slept on my couch."

Ok...That was entirely too sweet. Candy's throat tightened with emotion, thinking about Kenneth as a young boy losing his mother, then being transient before being embraced by someone who filled the role for him. No wonder he spoke her name with such reverence.

"Wow...So, you're more like family."

"Not like family. We are family. Ray's my best friend, my little brother." Miss Toni continued.

Hearing her reassurance helped Candy understand why Kenneth referred to her as his Aunt Toni despite their lack of biological connection.

All done with the salad, they chatted about not so deep topics such as the flight and difference in the weather coming from so far south.

Candy's eyes roamed the surfaces looking for additional ways to be helpful when she noticed two large mason jars filled with creamy looking liquid. Next to the jars were a couple of whole onions, a box of chicken stock and dried seasonings. The ingredients were set off to the side on the counter adjacent to the stove.

Pointing, Candy asked, "Do we need to do something with those?"

Glancing over her shoulder, Miss Toni appraised the items, then responded. "Not right now. That's for the giblet gravy. We don't need it today."

"You make giblet gravy?"

Candy's voice revealed wistful awe. At every Thanksgiving and Christmas dinner, someone would lament at how much they missed Grandma Hortense's giblet gravy. Only Aunt Bonita attempted to make the sauce, but even she couldn't come close to her Nana's recipe.

"Sure do. I take it Kenneth hasn't brought it up in his lessons yet?"

Candy shook her head as she tried to figure out what the jars held. She couldn't read the labels from her position.

"I'll have to get on him. He knows that's a holiday staple in southern cooking."

"He's taught me a lot. I've explored more since I took the class at the school."

Candy couldn't let Miss Toni think Kenneth was being negligent in his teaching duties—even if their lessons lately led to more sex than cooking.

"Mhmm...I tell you what, I'll teach you how to make my recipe tomorrow if you and Baby Boy don't already have plans."

"You will? I don't know what to say. Thank you so much!"

Candy's smile was so big her cheeks ached. It didn't matter what plans they had; she was certain they could adjust. She was going to learn how to make a traditional southern holiday staple from *the* Miss Toni herself. The owner and namesake of the infamous *Miss Toni's* soul food restaurant. *This is so cool!* Kari's gonna flip out.

"You're welcome, honey. I was planning to make it earlier, but realized I didn't want to freeze it. So, I was going to put all that stuff back and it slipped my mind."

Washing her hands, Miss Toni pulled serving dishes from the cabinets. She began transferring items to them from one of the crock pots then stovetop. Everything smelled amazing. If Kenneth learned at her side, it explained his damn near snobbery when it came to using herbs and spices.

Once the food was transferred, they were ready to move. Following instructions, Candy trailed her hostess into the dining room holding the salad bowl while Miss Toni carried a covered dish. Inside was the most succulent pot roast Candy had ever smelled—which was saying something considering the skill her aunts had in the kitchen.

Once they'd set out all the food, Miss Toni called Kenneth and his uncle in to eat. The atmosphere was light, but Candy felt Kenneth silently probing her to make sure she was ok. Squeezing his fingers reassuringly, she sat in the chair he pulled out for her.

Conversation over dinner was easy and unforced. Candy listened avidly as both elders told stories about her man from his boyhood to teen years even his early days working his way up in restaurant kitchens.

"No, no, no. Wait!" Miss Toni's eyes filled with mirth. "Ray, do you remember when he took those specialty classes under that obnoxious pastry chef who claimed he was from France, but was really from DesArc, Arkansas?"

Laughing along, Uncle Ray wiped his face not bothering to disguise his amusement. "Oh yeah, I remember him. He didn't actually say he was from France. He simply pronounced the name of his home town with a haughty French accent."

"Whatever. Same thing. He spoke with a fake French inflection to fool people into thinking he was from somewhere other than a tiny town in no-where Arkansas with a population less than two thousand people. Hell, my little town is barely over that amount, but I'm not shame to tell folks where I come from."

"Uncle Ray, Auntie…I'm sure Candy doesn't want to hear all these stories in one sitting. We're here until next Sunday. Pace yourselves."

The shells of Kenneth's ears were red with embarrassment. Candy thought it was cute the way they doted on him and tried to relay happy, but hilarious memories from his youth.

"Aht, aht! Don't *auntie* me." Miss Toni said with a wry grin. "You only pull out *auntie* when you want to tug at my heart strings. I'm on to you young'un."

Tapping Candy on the arm, she went back to her story. "Anyway, despite trying to make himself seem more important than he was, Caliban was a very talented pastry chef. But, he really had it in for Kenneth.

Caliban tried his best to make him tap out. Ray thought it was because he had a crush on Kenneth and was mad he wasn't getting any play, but that wasn't it."

Intrigued, Candy scooted closer to the table resting her chin on her fist. "What was it?"

"He was so jealous he couldn't see straight. It had taken Caliban years to master the skills Baby Boy had naturally. Now, that's not to say he wasn't peeved he couldn't get a taste of the living Ken doll parading around in his face every day. But, it was primarily jealousy."

"I wasn't parading around." Kenneth interjected with a huff.

"Who's telling this story, me or you?" Miss Toni pinned him with a look only a seasoned auntie could pull off.

"As I was saying...He kept adding onto the assignments because *this one,*" she said pointing at Kenneth. "was mastering them like they were child's play. He decided to do one of those competition style bake-offs. It was like the show *Cake Wars,* but this was way before the show existed."

"He *really* shouldn't have done that." Kenneth's uncle interjected with barely contained chuckles.

"Ray, stop. I'm telling this." Miss Toni swatted at her friend. "Anyway, Caliban never missed an opportunity to show off, so he sent invites to several of the top chefs around the boroughs to the event he was touting as *Who Can Top the Top Chef—Villains edition.*

Their assignment was to create a scene or image of the villain of their choice. The kicker was the cake, icing and all decorative pieces had to be edible. The judges were chefs from a different culinary academy to avoid bias."

Candy was on the edge of her seat anxious to hear what Kenneth had done which made those events stick out in their memory. Her man had transformed from the dominant person she'd become accustomed to into a bashful twenty-year-old before her very eyes. *Adorable.*

"Everyone was going all out. Naturally, most went with traditional villains from their favorite princess movies, but not our boy. No. You'll never guess who his villain was."

Candy was like a kid standing at the ice cream truck waiting for her scoop. The buildup was killing her.

"Who?"

"Caliban." Miss Toni stated smugly.

"The pastry chef?!" Candy gasped. "That took some nerve!" She looked at Kenneth in a combination of shock and admiration for his level of petty. Her facial expression set Miss Toni and Uncle Ray off into another round of giggles lasting a few minutes before they got themselves under control.

When their giggles calmed down, Kenneth spoke. "Technically, it was the character, Caliban, from the Shakespearean play, *The Tempest*."

Recognizing the play, Candy connected the dots and dissolved into a puddle of laughter at just how deep Kenneth's petty streak ran. As a fine arts major, she'd learned the tools to perfecting her craft by working on theatre productions in college. She was familiar with the play.

"The horribly grotesque son of the sea hag? That Caliban?"

"One in the same!" Miss Toni practically cackled. "You should have seen Caliban's face when he figured it out. Then, to add insult to injury, not only did Caliban lose to a student, two other people besides Kenneth kicked his ass. Of course, my baby won, but Caliban wasn't even in the top three."

Still laughing amongst themselves, Miss Toni and Uncle Ray stood from the table. They began clearing the dishes. When Candy and Kenneth rose to help, they were shooed away as the friends moved around the table in a well-established routine.

With her hand clasped in Kenneth's, Candy was led across the expansive hallway into the den. Bold artwork hung on the walls. Coordinating throw pillows were tossed on neutral colored plush furnishing. The room was as eclectic and vibrant as the woman of the house.

Grabbing the remote from the coffee table, Kenneth changed the channel, most likely looking for another football game. Sitting next to him on the comfy sofa, Candy stared at his profile with what she was certain was a grinch level grin on her face. Possibly feeling the heat of her scrutiny, he peeked at her from the corner of his eyes.

"What?"

"I knew you had a petty streak. But you're petty-petty." Giggling, she nudged him in the side until his lips cracked allowing a smile to take over his face.

"He deserved it. He was an asshole and unnecessarily mean. Some of those kids were working two jobs to afford that class, but he treated them like shit. He had them thinking they should quit culinary school."

"You say it like you weren't essentially a kid yourself."

"I know, but I had the benefit of Uncle Ray and Aunt Toni helping me learn so much before I even started classes. She's known for her soul food, but Aunt Toni is a highly rated pastry chef.

Most of the techniques Caliban tried to teach, I'd already learned from her to some degree. He pissed me off to the point that I set up a study group to help the other students."

"Let me guess. The other two students he lost the contest to were the ones you helped."

At his responding nod, she cupped his face stroking the stubble along his jaw.

"You play at being a hard ass, but you're all gooey in the center. Aren't you?"

"Lies...I'm a mean, vengeful, hard-ass." Slipping his fingers into her hair then forming a fist, he tugged. "It would be in your best interest not to go around spreading those falsehoods, ma'am."

"I call it like I see it, sir." As soon as the last word left her mouth, she wanted to call it back.

The fist in her hair tightened. The scruff from Kenneth's short beard scraped her neck and cheek as he grumbled into her ear. "Are you trying to cut this visit short, my sweet Candy?"

She was well aware of the rules, *sir* and *daddy* weren't words she could throw around all willy-nilly. If anyone had told her she'd find the use of either titillating, she would've laughed in their face. However, with Kenneth, even the most mundane became sexy.

His gruff question was followed by a mixture of kisses combined with nibbles delivered to the erogenous zones on her neck and behind her ear. The hand she hadn't noticed on her leg, moved to the apex of her thighs locating her sensitive button through the barrier of her clothing. He zeroed in with such precision the loud clang from the kitchen barely penetrated the fog.

The noise served to douse the flames of their arousal before they got carried away on Miss Toni's couch. Candy would be mortified if the older woman or his uncle had walked in on Kenneth's hand shoved down her pants as that was surely its destination.

Grumbling under his breath that she would pay for teasing him later, Kenneth lifted his head and called out toward the kitchen to make certain everything was okay. His uncle's quick reply was enough to smooth the crease in his brow. Yet, he still seemed unsure if he should believe it.

Mouthing the word, "later", to her, he stood from the couch then walked back across the hallway into the kitchen.

Chapter Nineteen

YOU DON'T REMEMBER ME?

The next day, Kenneth and Candy were greeted at his Aunt Toni's door by her oldest daughter, Emery. Although she was an adult with a husband and children of her own, Kenneth still saw the chubby faced cherub his aunt brought home from the hospital instead of the beauty he'd punched a former friend in the face over.

"Heeey, KG! Mama didn't tell me you were coming over today." Grinning broadly, Emery nearly jumped into this arms hugging him before giving him a kiss on the cheek.

Pulling away, she turned her bright smile onto Candy who stood quietly at his side. Thank God his woman wasn't the jealous type. She looked more inclined to laugh than throw a fit about Emery tossing her petite body at his much larger frame. Extending her hand, Emery introduced herself before Kenneth had the chance.

"Hi! I'm Emery, Toni's daughter."

"Hello, Emery. I'm Candace."

"Oh, I know who you are."

"You do?" Candy and Kenneth said together.

Stepping back, Emery ushered them into the foyer. "Of course. Any black woman, serious about her skincare regimen and make-up, watches your YouTube channel."

Kenneth turned surprised eyes to Candy. "You have a YouTube channel?"

"Yes. I do make-up tutorials for different looks for people who might not have the money to hire a professional or purchase high end products."

Slipping an arm around her waist, he pulled her to his side. "You never said anything."

"Why would I? You aren't interested in make-up."

"I'm interested in you. I want to support you."

"Awww...That's so sweet! You two are the cutest." Emery's sing-song voice cut into their conversation causing Candy to blush. Kenneth shot her a big brother worthy death stare.

"Where's your husband?" Kenneth asked, trying to get the focus off of him and Candy.

"Mama sent him to the store."

When Kenneth looked over her head toward the den, she quickly informed him Titus took the kids with him. Kenneth had only seen them in pictures on social media since the prior Christmas.

"Don't look so sad. They'll be here climbing all over you before you know it." Emery patted his arm before encouraging them to remove their outerwear.

After they hung their coats on the rack next to the door, Emery told them her mom was in the kitchen as usual. Crossing the threshold from the foyer into the space, she called out, "Mama! Why didn't you tell me Kenneth was home?"

"Hold on, Ray." Aunt Toni transferred her gaze from the phone in its holder on the countertop to three of them entering the room. "Little girl, don't start with me. KG is here for the holiday and he brought his lady friend with him. There. You've been told."

"Mama!" Her voiced laced with exasperated amusement, Emery swatted playfully at her mother.

"Girl, move." Aunt Toni's actions didn't match her tone as she used one hand to shift Emery to the side while she dispensed hugs to Kenneth and Candy as if she hadn't just seen them the day before.

"You two are just in time. I was getting ready to drain this broth off the chicken and pull the meat from the bone."

Kenneth smiled at Candy eagerly moving to the sink to wash her hands before tying on the apron Aunt Toni passed her. He'd planned to take her to more places today, but rearranged their schedule when he saw how excited she was to learn a holiday recipe from *the* Miss Toni personally.

While Candy prepared for her lesson, his adopted aunt went back to her phone. The screen displayed his uncle dressed in his Chef whites with his chin propped on his fist. Certain he couldn't see much from the angle of the device, Kenneth called out a hello as he sat on one of the stools at the far side of the large island with the butcher block.

"Ray, I'm just asking for a little help here. The guy I normally use had an emergency and everyone else is booked."

"Tone, how many times do I have to tell you? Just because we both like penis doesn't make me one of your girlfriends."

"Duh, Ray. I know you aren't my girlfriend, but you are my gay bestie. You mean to tell me none of those femmes who throw themselves at you knows how to beat a face?"

"What's wrong with the face you already have?"

Pausing in the act of removing a spice container from the cabinet, Aunt Toni glared at the phone.

"This is *the* event of the year. I can't show up with my everyday face wearing my Sunday school make-up."

"Why not? Your everyday face is ten times prettier than those plastic princesses that'll be there."

"Flattery is *not* what I need right now."

Listening to their conversation, it didn't take much deduction for Kenneth to understand his aunt needed the kind of help Candy could provide. Making eye contact with his woman, they held a silent conversation which ended with her walking to stand beside him. Wrapping an arm around her waist, Kenneth whispered in her ear. Her whispered reply didn't surprise him. Of course, she would help.

Wondering why his uncle hadn't brought up the idea of Candy previously, he looked for an opening in their conversation to interject. He didn't get a chance.

"Mama, why don't you just ask Candace?" Emery interrupted the banter between her mother and his uncle.

The confused look on Aunt Toni's face matched her daughter's but each had a different reason.

"Mama, Candace is *the* Candace Hampton." At her mother's blank stare, she pulled her phone from her pocket then tapped the screen before passing it over. "This woman, the award-winning make-up artist, is standing in your kitchen and you're over here arguing with your bestie over him not helping you find someone to beat your face."

Candy's cheerful voice floated from the device as the video version of herself informed her subscribers of the technique she'd teach them in the episode Emery queued up. Looking from the phone to Candy, then back at the phone, Aunt Toni's face stretched into a smile. All of the southern she'd scrubbed from her voice in her years in New York came back in the next words she spoke.

"Well, I'll be."

Shooting her friend on the video chat a squint-eyed glare, she muttered letting him know she didn't appreciate him keeping secrets. Passing Emery the phone, she approached the island. Quickly, she gave them the rundown of her situation with the artist her stylist hired and their inability to find someone suitable to fill in at the last minute. As Kenneth expected, Candy readily agreed to help her.

"Are you sure it's no problem? It's the night before the holiday. This is your vacation. I know you kids probably had plans."

"I'd be honored." Candy assured her. "Kenneth and I came here to visit with his family and friends. From what I can tell, you're both. Besides, instead of taking care of your business, you're carving out time from your day to teach me something. It wouldn't feel right to not do what I can to help."

Snatching her from Kenneth's side, Aunt Toni engulfed Candy in a big hug. "Thank you so much! Of course, I'll pay you whatever your normal fee is."

"You absolutely will not. I'm happy to help. I won't accept a penny of your money." With a stubborn tilt of her jaw, Candy leveled her with a look which brooked no argument.

"Now...if you want to slide me a couple of recipes that'll knock my family's socks off, I'll accept them in exchange." Candy answered—the dimple in her cheek winking with her smile.

Grinning like a child on Christmas morning, the older woman rubbed Candy's arms. "Honey, I will teach you any recipe you want." She gushed then hugged Candy again.

"What do we need to do to make this happen?"

"I'll need to look at the products you have and see what we may need to supplement."

"Prepare to supplement a lot. Mama has the bare minimum when it comes to make-up." Emery offered.

"She's right. That's why I usually depend on my stylist when I have to attend events. I never really caught on to the whole thing, so I have lipstick, gloss and eyeliner pencils. That's about it."

"Don't worry about it. We have time for me to color match you. I'll need to get a look at the plan your stylist has for the evening. If I could speak with them, it would be better. Once I see what we're working with, we can go from there."

"Oh my gosh, this is awesome! Wait until I tell Sydney. She's going to be so jealous." Emery gushed as she referred to her longtime friend.

Kenneth had seen the plaques and awards in Candy's home office, but Emery's reaction brought home the reality that his woman wasn't simply *a* rock star as he'd touted to her. She was *the* fucking rock star in her field. They definitely needed to talk about the way she undervalued herself. It rubbed him the wrong way to think of her underselling herself or those around her taking advantage of her kind nature.

"Okay, okay. I know we have stuff to do for Wednesday, but it's Monday and I promised this nice young lady a lesson. So, a lesson is what is happening." Aunt Toni clapped her hands then pointed to Kenneth and Emery. "You two. Out of my kitchen."

Amid mumbles of protest, Kenneth and Emery shuffled from the kitchen—not before Kenneth snagged a kiss from Candy though. As they left, Emery peppered him with questions about his life in Logan City including how he'd met Candy. Firing them in rapid succession, she barely paused to give him time to answer.

He'd known pursuing Candy was the right move, but having it validated by those he loved relieved a pressure inside that he hadn't realized was there. Settling into the den, he grabbed the remote and tried to answer Emery's endless questions when she left gaps for him to respond.

"Me next, Unca Kaybee! It's my turn!" Destiny's toddler voice squeaked her request as her little hands tugged at Kenneth's pant leg.

Above his head was her giggling two-year-old brother, Yusuf. He'd spent the better part of the time at his Aunt Toni's being a human playground for both of them. When Titus returned from his errand, Kenneth and Emery were still in the den. Once the children saw him, all conversation with adults ceased. Playtime immediately ensued.

"Hold on, DJ. I didn't forget you." Kenneth assured the three-year-old going on thirty.

Her normal much-too-serious countenance was stretched into the wide grin. Still rounded and cherubic, her cheeks were flushed with enjoyment under her burnt umber skin. Holding onto his leg while bouncing on the balls of her feet, she anxiously awaited her turn to be a super hero flying through the air courtesy of Uncle KG.

Placing the squirming, squealing, Yusuf on his feet, Kenneth scooped Destiny up in his arms hefting her over his head. He began the trek around the playroom humming the theme song from their favorite TV show, PJ Masks. Kenneth had Candy to thank for him actually knowing the melody. The kids' excitement went up astronomically once they recognized it.

Emery's voice cut through the laughter and shrieks of delight. "Okay kids, it's time for lunch, then a nap."

Identical crestfallen looks took over Destiny and Yusuf's faces. "Don't give me those faces. Come on, let's get washed up."

Holding out her hands, she waited. Kenneth lowered Destiny, placing her on her feet. Before walking to her mother, she looked up at him.

"We'll play again later, Unca Kaybee." Patting his leg as if to console him, she walked over to her mother.

Smiling ruefully, Kenneth shook his head as he followed the trio from the room. After a quick stop in the washroom to clean up, he met everyone in the dining room for lunch. During which, he was informed that he was taking Candy and his aunt to meet her stylist.

While donning his coat, he assured Yusuf and Destiny they would continue their game when he returned. Brushing off Emery's claims of him spoiling them, he helped Candy into her coat then opened the door.

The drive to the boutique lasted roughly half an hour due to traffic, not distance. Thankfully, there was a parking deck nearby. He was able to secure a space after dropping the ladies off at the door of the boutique. By the time he made it inside, they were deep in conversation with a petite man wearing flowing garments, which draped his slender frame immaculately.

Taking his position next to the accessory display quietly, Kenneth stood to Candy's right slightly off to the side. Close enough for her to know he was there, but not so close as to crowd her. Perusing the shop, he listened to their conversation with half an ear as they discussed the stylist's vision for Aunt Toni's look for the Winter gala. Apparently, the owner of the boutique made custom alterations to the gown and the final fitting would take place today.

From his limited knowledge of lady's apparel, the boutique catered to clientele within a certain tax bracket. As his aunt, the stylist, and boutique owner moved toward the back of the store, Kenneth over-heard the stylist admonishing Aunt Toni for holding out and not telling him she knew Candace Hampton personally.

Smiling to himself, Kenneth watched Candy as she tapped through various screens on her tablet. She'd taken notes on the device while the stylist spoke. Presently, she was reviewing images of women wearing various make up styles.

"Kenneth? Kenneth Holmes? Is that really you?"

The sultry voice which used to kickstart his libido scraped against his eardrums. Looking around, his gaze landed on Annalise Abernathy. Slightly older, but no less beautiful, she stood just inside the entrance to the boutique with a shocked expression on her face.

Striding with a runway model's gait she moved closer. Stepping back when she attempted to invade his space, he lifted Candy's free hand from the display—twining their fingers together. Annalise's eyes followed the movement and her pageant ready façade slipped slightly before repairing itself.

"Oh my goodness! What a surprise. If you'd asked me who I

thought I'd run into while out doing my last-minute gala errands, I wouldn't have ever guessed it."

She was really laying it on thick. As if the last time they'd spoken she hadn't issued an ultimatum for him to turn his back on his uncle to keep her in his life.

"Annalise."

Candy's fingers tightened around his. From his periphery, he saw her blacken the screen of the tablet then lift her head. She knew about his former girlfriend who he almost made the mistake of proposing to.

The door to the shop opened again and two more women walked in. He immediately recognized her mother in the pair. Had he not known them, it was obvious from the smooth dark brown skin Annalise carried, they were related. They exuded the same presence with identical bone structure. Though striking on the outside, history had proven their beauty didn't extend inwards.

"Annalise? I thought you made an appointment? I don't see Madame LaPierre. Why isn't she here to greet us?"

Her mother's tone projected her distaste at the thought of having to wait for service. Her mother and younger sister closed the space between them and where Kenneth, Candy and Annalise stood in a less than comfortable triangle. Looking at Candy, she snapped her fingers.

"You. We want to see Madame LaPierre. Go find her. Tell her the Abernathys are here."

"Excuse me?"

"Who do you think you're speaking to like that?" Both Kenneth and Candy spoke simultaneously.

Looking affronted Mrs. Abernathy's hand flew to her chest clutching at invisible pearls.

"How dare you." She huffed.

"How dare *you*." Kenneth replied. "First of all, even if she did work here, the way you addressed her was extremely rude. Secondly, your assumption reeks of classism."

"Mother, Kenneth. Please stop. Kenneth, I'm sure Mother didn't mean anything by it." Annalise tried to calm the situation.

"I'm sure she did." Kenneth bit out.

Annalise's pretense slipped with a nervous giggle. Slender fingers with manicured nails landed on his forearm and squeezed. "You were always just a little touchy, weren't you? I assure you; it was an honest mistake. Right, mother?"

"Of course, it was."

Bronwyn Abernathy's voice didn't hold a trace of repentance. To anyone with ears, it was obvious she only said something to placate her daughter. To what end, Kenneth wasn't quite sure. While he and Annalise were together, she'd treated him with barely concealed disdain. Mostly because his family name didn't hold the same stature as the Abernathy name did in some circles.

Looking down at where Annalise's hand rested on his forearm, his gaze pivoted to her face as he tensed his limb beneath her touch. Although blocked from skin-to-skin contact by his outer layers, he made it clear he didn't desire a physical connection with her.

Eyes widening in a look of surprise, she pulled her digits back clasping her hands together in front of her.

"So, what brings you to Madame LaPierre's? You and your...friend?"

"I don't see how that's any concern of yours." Kenneth replied bluntly.

"Oh! Well, I was just trying to be friendly. It's been years since we saw each other. I was hoping we could catch up."

Candy's fingers wiggled within his hold. He broke his suspicious scrutiny of Annalise to look at his woman. Her stare held not a trace of malice or jealousy. She attempted to detangle their fingers and he mouthed, "Stop it." When she settled, he turned back to their unwanted companions.

"We don't have anything to catch up on, Annalise. We said everything we need to say to one another six years ago. Excuse us."

Bringing his and Candy's joined hands to his lips, he kissed the back of her hand never breaking eye contact with Annalise. Tugging Candy away from the Abernathys, he walked in the direction Madame LaPierre had disappeared with Aunt Toni and her stylist.

Whispered hisses reached his ears as they moved farther away. Before he and Candy closed the distance, the trio appeared from behind the heavy dark curtains which separated the front of the boutique from the private consultation area.

"Bonaventure?!" Mrs. Abernathy's normally cultured voice shrieked the stylist's name at nearly concert volume.

Bonaventure, to his credit, didn't falter in his gait as his dark gaze swept over the new occupants of the boutique. "Yes...and you are...?"

"You don't remember me?" In what Kenneth perceived as genuine shock, Mrs. Abernathy approached their group with her daughters trailing behind her.

"Bronwyn Abernathy. These are my daughters, Annalise and Tinsley."

Bonaventure's assessing gaze swept over the three women quickly before dismissing them with a swish of his long twists when he turned to Aunt Toni.

"I do believe we have everything set. I'll see you tomorrow in the suite at four p.m. sharp." Tipping his head, he pierced her with a look of warning.

Putting her hands up in surrender, she assured him. "I promise, I'll be there all scrubbed and ready."

"Good! And you, ma'am." His dark bronze face split into a huge smile as he spoke to Candy. "It has been an honor. I'm very much looking forward to working with you."

Whipping a business card from his crossbody satchel, he presented it to her. "Give me a call and we can finalize the look. You do beautiful work, so I'm sure whatever you dream up will be fabulous."

"I won't have to do much. Between her stunning looks and the vision of a gown you selected, she's going to steal the evening."

"I'm with you when you're right." Bonaventure chuckled. Extending his goodbyes to everyone—excluding the Abernathys—he exited the boutique with a flourish.

Chapter Twenty

SHE'S NO ONE SPECIAL

"Antonia."

Mrs. Abernathy's dry tone cut through the silence left in Bonaventure's wake. As she had done during the exchange between Kenneth and the woman earlier, Candy quietly watched the scene unfold.

"Bronwyn." Miss Toni responded just as dryly. It was obvious there was no love lost between the two women.

"Annalise, Tinsley, it's...interesting to see you here." Miss Toni added although the two younger women hadn't said anything.

Standing to their mother's side, only Tinsley acknowledged Miss Toni's greeting. Her hazel eyes stretched wide in an expression Candy recognized but steadfastly ignored. The sour expression on Annalise's face didn't escape Candy's attention, but she didn't acknowledge her presence nor her disdain.

Madame LaPierre broke the tension, apologizing for keeping the Abernathy's waiting. Proffering the pale pink garment bag toward Miss Toni, she wished her a great evening. Kenneth intercepted the bag, tossing it over his shoulder while maintaining his hold on Candy's hand.

Apparently, when Madame LaPierre focused her attention on Candy, expressing her pleasure in meeting her, that was the last straw for Annalise.

"Why is everyone fawning over her? She's no one special."

She snapped, sounding like a petulant child. Kenneth tensed further at Candy's side. Annalise's button nose scrunched as she regarded Candy in a way she was familiar with as a woman of a certain size in the company of a fit man. Annalise wasn't the first and probably wouldn't be the last judgmental person to look at she and Kenneth with unseeing eyes.

It was obvious to Candy that the beauty pageant queen wasn't used to *not* being the center of attention when she was in the room. Candy had never met Annalise, but she could spot a pageant girl a mile away. In her early days, she'd worked in with quite a few beauty queens. They all had a particular look about them—no matter the race.

But she knew Annalise in particular, not by name, but reputation on the pageant circuit. She was one of the first people Candy refused to work with, without ever having her in the chair. Her ill treatment of service staff was enough for Candy to put her on the never-ever-not-even-if-I'm-about-to-be-homeless list.

"Annalise! Stop it." Tinsley whisper-screamed at her sister.

"What? They're acting like she's some kind of star. But that's not possible. If she were, I'd know her. I know everyone who's worth knowing."

"No. You wouldn't." Candy said evenly. She had no intention of getting into a cat fight with Kenneth's ex, but the spoiled brat was raking her nerves.

"Not if they reviewed your information and told the people who reached out on your behalf they wouldn't work with you. Not if they told those same people no amount of money could tempt them to get on a plane to touch even one brush to your face."

Annalise's mouth dropped open. After she stopped competing, she worked in the pageant industry. Candy could only blame lack of interest in hearing too many details about her man's ex for her not putting the name Kenneth gave her to the face she knew.

"Annalise...That's Candace Hampton." Tinsley snipped.

The younger woman, who'd remained mostly silent during the Abernathy's time in the boutique spoke up. Shyly, she extended her hand to Candy. "Tinsley Abernathy. It's very nice to meet you."

Accepting the handshake from possibly the only member of the threesome with manners, Candy murmured a perfunctory response. She couldn't be sure if the younger Abernathy could be trusted completely.

At the mention of Candy's full name, Annalise's facial expression morphed once again. Even her mother's dour expression lifted slightly.

Candy really, really hated being the topic of conversation. She was comfortable being a behind the scenes person. She especially didn't like dealing with people who only put on the façade of kindness when they thought they could gain something from her. Although she never threw it around, she knew her name carried weight in certain circles.

Annalise was so transparent Candy could practically see the wheels in her head turning as she tried to figure out how to back track out of her rudeness. Nothing she could say would make an impact.

Thankfully, Madame LaPierre cut through the tension escorting Miss Toni, Kenneth and Candy to the door all the while assuring the Abernathys she would be right with them. Why the woman didn't have an additional attendant in the shop was beyond Candy, but that wasn't her business.

With Kenneth bringing up the rear, they left the shop, stepping out into the cold winter wind which had Candy adjusting her knit scarf to cover her head and ears.

Not giving the Abernathys another thought, Candy put her mind on the best locations to find the cosmetics she needed. Her goal was to secure something inexpensive, but of good quality. Since Miss Toni wasn't a regular makeup wearer, it didn't make sense to go to one of the high-end places to purchase products which would probably go bad before she had an opportunity to use them again.

Candy never traveled without the basic tools, so she wasn't concerned about those. Although she wished she'd packed her airbrush system, she knew she could work without it. Her focus was to procure foundation, powders and fixative which would work under the glaring lights of the red carpet as well as the softer lighting in the actual venue.

Kenneth was a trooper throughout the process. Not one word of complaint as they lingered over displays, nor as they went to more than one store to secure the perfect shades for the color palette Candy had in mind. It took more than a couple of hours, but she was satisfied with their purchases. Dropping Miss Toni off at her house, they continued on to meet his uncle for dinner.

When Kenneth said he'd take her to the hotel where the Winter Gala was being held, Candy didn't think he'd stay in the suite watching her work. They arrived slightly before six p.m. Miss Toni, Bonaventure, his assistant, and a hair stylist were already there.

They'd spent the past couple of days with Kenneth squiring her around Brooklyn showing her some of his old hangouts. Partially doing the touristy thing, he drove her into New York City to Times Square then to Harlem to see the famed Apollo Theater. It wasn't Candy's first time in the New York City area, but her previous visits were work related and left little time for sightseeing.

Candy thought it a little odd he'd valeted the car just to help her to the suite, but hadn't mentioned it. It wasn't until he settled into a chair propping his right ankle on his left knee that she realized he intended to stay.

Bonaventure had turned the room from a single bedroom suite into a small-scale salon including a styling chair and mirrors. It was a familiar arrangement. Although she'd heard of the Winter Gala prior to Miss Toni, Candy hadn't attended or had a client request her services.

She had no idea the magnitude of the event until she glimpsed the opulence of the decorations in just the lobby of the hotel. The entire area had been transformed leading up to the roped off red carpet which led to the main ballroom. She didn't need to see inside the room to know no expense had been spared.

By the time she had her impromptu station all set up, Miss Toni was in a robe, seated in the swivel chair waiting for the hair stylist to begin. She wore her hair in natural corkscrew curls tapered at the sides and in the back. In order to complete Bonaventure's vision, the hairstylist would work her magic to make those curls shine and pop.

Working together in synchronicity, they took Miss Toni from simply stunning to absolutely breathtaking. When all that was left was for her to slip her feet into the sparkling peep-toe heels, there was a knock on the door of the suite.

"That must be Leonardo." The girlish smile on Miss Toni's face spoke to the possible relationship between her and the previously unmentioned Leonardo.

Being the only unoccupied person in the room, Kenneth answered it. After a brief exchange with the person on the other side, he opened the door wider allowing an older man into the room. Kenneth's lips were pressed into a grim line while Leonardo wore an expression of complete awe. *Mission accomplished.*

If no one else mentioned how beautiful she looked, Miss Toni's date found her completely enthralling. His dark mahogany skin shone in striking contrast to the brightness of his tuxedo shirt. The suit was cut to perfection across his broad shoulders tapering down to his slender midsection.

His bald head gleamed under the extra lighting in the suite. Standing almost the same height as Kenneth's six-foot-three-inch frame, Leonardo was the very definition of a silver fox with his perfectly groomed beard shot through with gray and white.

"You look magnificent, Sweetheart." Leonardo's baritone was reminiscent of the crooners Candy's mother loved to listen to from the nineteen seventies and eighties.

"Stop it, Leonardo!" Miss Toni simultaneously preened and blushed under his appraisal.

"I can't stop. I have to say what's on my heart. You know I only speak the truth." He smiled displaying straight white teeth. "I'm wondering if I'm dressed for the fighting I'll have to do to keep some man from trying to steal you away."

While Miss Toni basked under the adoration of her date, Kenneth stood beside him glaring a hole into the side of Leonardo's head. It took everything in Candy not to laugh. It was hilarious to watch him behave like an overprotective kid whose mom is dating for the first time in years.

Given the time she spent with Miss Toni, Candy was positive Leonardo wasn't her first beau since her husband passed away. She was still a very vibrant woman. Of course, she'd have male companionship whenever she desired it.

"Aw hush. You're gonna have my head so big, I won't be able to fit it through the door." Miss Toni swatted at the air between herself and her date as she stepped into her heels. Leonardo was well within his right to be awestruck.

Walking around her, Bonaventure gave her one last check before passing her the glittering purse to complete the look. The gown was a fitted cream-colored creation with pearl sequins swirled in patterns of crisscrossing organized chaos from the bodice to the hem. It left one arm completely bare while the other was covered from shoulder to wrist. Depending on which way she turned, the sequins caught the light—glittering iridescently. The waist was cinched with a wide belt which attached a flowing train.

Auntie was working it. From the look she tossed over her shoulder on the way out of the suite, she knew it. Although he'd air kissed her cheek encouraging her to have a good evening, Kenneth's eyes continued to shoot daggers at her date.

Bonaventure had set up and removal down to a science. Not ten seconds after Miss Toni and Leonardo exited the room did four people show up. They began removing the salon chair, mirrors and other implements. They even packed Miss Toni's leather valise, placing it on the rolling cart with the other items. There was a sewing machine Candy hadn't noticed until it was being packed away.

Having already cleaned her brushes, and repacked her things, Candy watched the crew work. Bonaventure declined help from Kenneth and herself stating his team had it covered. Inside of thirty minutes, she and Kenneth were in the suite alone.

Grabbing the handle of the small rolling case, Candy moved to vacate the suite as well when Kenneth grabbed her around the waist.

"Where do you think you're going?" His voice held a gruff quality as the stubble of his beard scraped the curve of her shoulder.

"Aren't we leaving?" Candy attempted to keep the zing she experienced with the contact from showing in her voice.

"We could...or...we could make use of this perfectly good suite."

Prying at his hold, Candy valiantly held on to her resolve. "No, sir. We are not having sex in your aunt's hotel room"

The hold around her waist tightened pressing her body to his allowing her to feel his length thickening against her ass. Only their thin layers of clothing prevented her from being impaled by his burgeoning cock.

"Tsk, tsk, tsk...You know not to throw that word around my sweet Candy. It's almost like you want me to overrule your inhibitions. Is that it?"

Candy's eyes slammed closed at the rough, growling, quality of his speech. She had to stay strong. This wasn't their hotel room. She couldn't allow Kenneth to have her acting like a horny teen in a bed which wasn't theirs to use.

"We can't...Miss Toni and her date will probably come back here after the gala."

"Grrr! Why did you have to bring up Mr. Too-Smooth?" He grumbled in her ear. "As much as I don't want you mentioning another man while I'm working my seduction magic, I especially don't want *him* being the man you bring up."

"Why? He seems really into her. She deserves to have someone who thinks the world of her."

"He's too handsome. Too polished. Says all the right things. I don't like him."

Kenneth released her from his hold running one hand through his hair. It was slightly longer on top, so his fingers disturbed the neat tresses giving him a rakish look making him even more attractive. At least he was put off from sexing her up for the time being.

Candy would be mortified for Miss Toni to return to her suite to find evidence of their lovemaking inside. She'd never be able to look the woman in the eye after that. Shuddering at the thought, she grabbed the handle of her rolling case.

"Come on, *Baby Boy*. I'll buy you a drink and maybe an appetizer at the bar in the hotel next door. If you're good, I might spring for dinner too."

Kenneth's long fingers latched around her wrist, halting her in her tracks. Separating her from the case, he pressed her hand to the bulge in his slacks.

"Ah, ah, ah, my sweet Candy. Not so fast."

His words sent a shiver down her spine as he crowded against her back trailing kisses along her neck. Her hair was styled in an up do leaving the sensitive skin open to his assault. Her lids drooped and her head tilted to the side of its own accord. Candy's core grew heavy in anticipation despite her inner admonitions.

"You thought you'd distract me by bringing up that gigolo?"

"You don't know he's a gigolo." Candy's words pushed out barely above a whisper as she tried to maintain control of her traitorous body.

Kenneth's fingers were busy tugging her blouse from her pants. Her hand remained exactly where he'd placed it, on his steadily hardening shaft. The screams of her inner good girl were nothing but butterfly whispers as she lost the battle against her hormones.

It's not that they hadn't had sex during their trip. The knowledge of them being in his uncle's home wasn't enough to completely kill her drive, but it kept her responses decidedly more reserved.

"You have some making up to do, Baby." Kenneth growled into her ear as he walked them toward the adjoining bedroom while tweaking her breasts through the barrier of her bra.

"Mmm...what?" Candy's foggy brain was only capable of filtering so much information.

"You haven't denied me your sweet pussy, but you've been holding back. I don't like it. It hurts my feelings and I require...restitution."

The way he said the word *restitution* catapulted Candy's senses to the last such time he felt she'd slighted him, requiring her to make amends. Her visible shudder of erotic anticipation garnered a chuckle from her sexy tormentor.

Continuing to walk her forward, he didn't stop until they were in the generously sized bathroom. Her blouse had been discarded on the walk through the bedroom. Nimble fingers flicked open the button of her slacks and tugged down the zipper.

Candy was certain her initial goal when laying her left hand on his forearm was to stop him from his quest to undress her, but somehow, she simply ended up stroking him feeling the veins she knew crisscrossed the limb. The heat from his body combined with the rock-hard length beneath her right palm, had her primed for any and everything Kenneth asked of her.

He wasted no time in stripping them both bare, but made no moves toward the large shower enclosure. Instead, he led her to the plush chaise lounge adjacent to the huge soaking tub. Taking her mouth in a scorching kiss, he coaxed her to first sit, then lie back with one leg dangling from the side.

Spreading her legs, he hungrily eyed her pussy like he hadn't eaten in months and was just presented with the most scrumptious of meals. Licking his lips, he dragged his grey gaze from her moistening folds to her face where she watchfully returned his stare.

Strong fingers gripped her inner thighs while his voice took on a gravelly quality. "You owe me orgasms. I intend to collect."

Running his nose up the side of one thigh, he placed kisses in his wake until he reached her throbbing core. Capturing her labial folds between his lips, he began his oral campaign. When he latched on to her clit, Candy's eyes slammed shut, her head tipped back, and a strangled moan burst from her lips.

A sharp pinch brought her focus back to the man nestled between her legs. "Na-uh. No trying to keep quiet. You've denied me my screams all week. Not this time. I want to hear your pleasure."

Dropping a kiss onto the nipple he pinched, he pulled the puckered peak into his mouth, lashing it with his tongue before dropping back to the apex of her thighs. He traced her lower lips with two fingers before dipping them into her leaking channel.

"Do you understand me, Baby? Hm?" His expectation of a coherent response was apparent, but Candy couldn't focus enough to give him one. A nod and a mumbled "Yes" were all she could muster.

"Not good enough." He grumbled.

Curving his fingers in a come-hither motion inside her slick walls, he captured her pearl between his lips suckling deeply. The force of the action rolled over her, snatching a startled squeak from her throat.

"Better...but not quite there yet." Kenneth murmured.

Encouraged by her more vocal response, he redoubled his efforts. Nothing, aside from the overwhelming sensations Kenneth elicited throughout her body, mattered to Candy. He knew just where and how to touch her to garner the greatest response. He used his knowledge with ruthless precision driving her over the edge into a leg shaking, scream inducing orgasm.

"That's one."

His nearly menacing tone when he spoke those two words should *not* have been so sexy, but Candy felt her overheated body revving up for more of his special brand of torture. As she watched him through a lustful haze, he sat up on his knees, lifted her legs onto his shoulders and filled her channel with every inch of his deliciously thick shaft.

Babbling words tumbled from her lips as he worked her pussy until her entire body felt like one big nerve ending. Her expressions of pleasure bounced off the walls of the room fueling Kenneth's quest. He didn't tease by taking her to the edge, but not allowing her to reach her peak.

No. What he did was far more devastating. He showed her how quickly he could use his mouth, fingers and cock to toss her from one orgasm right into the next. There was no cool down period. No catching her breath. No gearing up for the next round.

As non-sensical words were ripped from her throat, he ground out the latest count as she reached peak after peak. When she whimpered about not being able to come anymore, he took it as a personal challenge to wring yet another back-arching, screaming orgasm from her overstimulated body.

When he finally released into her pulsing channel, tears leaked from Candy's eyes as she trembled from the overwhelming emotions. Kissing away her tears, Kenneth murmured words of praise wrapped in warnings not to try holding back on him again.

Hearing him, but not hearing him, Candy would've promised him anything. Kenneth had taken her to heights and depths she'd never dreamed of experiencing. He could have whatever the fuck he wanted.

Chapter Twenty-One

DON'T JUMP TO CONCLUSIONS

Kenneth stood in front of the dresser in his bedroom looking at his reflection and straightening his tie in the mirror above it. To his right, he heard the sounds of water splashing in the shower. Simply thinking about Candy standing under the spray while water cascaded over her voluptuous curves made his dick hard.

Opening the drawer on his left, he selected a watch slipping it onto his wrist. Although he heard the shower running, he looked over his shoulder before lifting the insert out and shifting the items in the drawer. His eyes landed on the neatly wrapped package containing the items he'd purchased for Candy while they were in New York.

They'd been home for over a week. He still hadn't found the right time to give it to her. It wasn't a Christmas present, and there were barely three weeks left before the holiday. He was running out of time. Stroking his fingers over the elegant bow he considered his options.

He wasn't dragging his feet. They'd both been really busy with work and social activities. The weekend after they returned from New York, McKenna invited them to what she called Cousin's Night at their new home. While it cut into their alone time, it did give his sweet Candy an opportunity to showcase her growing culinary skills.

The abrupt cut off of the shower, had Kenneth hastily returning the insert to the drawer then closing it. He fully expected the door to open releasing a billowing cloud of steam, but it didn't. Instead, he heard the flushing of the toilet then the shower started up again.

Not giving the sequence of events much thought, he grabbed his shoes from the rack in the closet and picked up his suit jacket. Knocking on the bathroom door, he poked his head inside to let Candy know he would start breakfast. Her murmured reply was enough for him to close the door and leave the room. Just the few seconds his head was inside the bathroom was enough to put a sheen of moisture on his forehead. How the hell she could stand the water that hot was a mystery to him.

They'd developed somewhat of a routine which he had to admit he mostly enjoyed. The part he didn't like was not having a clear idea of which bed he'd sleep in some nights. Whether it was her place or his, it appeared he was no longer able to sleep without curling his long frame around her lush curves.

Humming while chopping veggies for a quick omelet, Kenneth's ears perked up when he heard Candy's light footfalls on the stairs. He looked up to see her framed in the doorway staring at him warily.

She wasn't dressed. Instead of the monogrammed blouse and slacks she normally wore, she sported an oversized sleep shirt with fuzzy socks. Her headwrap was still tied around her fluffy curls.

Placing the knife on the cutting board, he closed the distance between them. Lifting her chin, he searched her face.

"Hey...What's going on? You're not dressed. Are you feeling okay?"

Noting the pallor of her normally golden-brown skin, he pressed his palm to her forehead. He had no clue what he was checking for, but it's what his mom had done when he was a little boy. So, it must be the way to do it and her skin did feel warmer than usual. It also felt slightly clammy.

His eyes roved over her features noting the dots of sweat at her temples.

"I'm not feeling so hot. I think I caught the bug that's been going around the set. Thankfully, they re-arranged the scenes, so my client isn't on set today or tomorrow."

"Why don't you go back to bed, Baby? I'll fix you a light breakfast after I let Driscoll and Scott know I'm working from home today."

"You don't have to stay home. I'll be okay. I think I *will* go back to bed though."

Before she turned to leave the room, he stopped her. Cradling her face in one hand, he searched her eyes. "Hey...I'm not leaving you here to fend for yourself. That's not how we do things.

Now, you go back to bed. I'll fix you breakfast and if you aren't feeling better by lunch, we're gonna call your doctor to see if they can get you in this afternoon."

Patting his chest, he knew she was placating him when she agreed. "I'm sure it's nothing. Most people got over it in a day. There's no reason to get the doctor involved, but I'll call if it doesn't let up by lunch."

Placing a kiss on her forehead, he turned her around with a soft pat on the butt. "Go back to bed. I'll be up when I'm done with your food."

Her lack of response beyond a halfhearted wave in his direction was a better indication than any that she really wasn't feeling well. Firing off a text to Driscoll and Scott, he rethought his initial plan for breakfast. Instead, he put the kettle on for tea.

When his phone rang, he swiped it up from the counter wishing he'd remembered to put his earbuds within reach.

"Hello?"

"Hey Kenneth. I got your message. I was just calling to touch base."

"Ok. Thanks. I didn't have any face-to-face things to do today. I was planning to dig into some of those tech alerts that came across my desk, but I can do it from here. I have my secure laptop with me."

"Ok. Not a problem with me. What's going on with Candy?" Driscoll's voice held notes of concern.

"There's some kind of bug going around the movie set. She thinks she caught whatever it is. She's looking pale. I thought something was odd when it was taking her longer than usual to get ready. I should have trusted my instincts."

"Oh yeah?"

Something in Driscoll's tone made Kenneth pause in cutting slices of bread from the loaf they'd baked over the weekend.

"What? What is it?"

"Huh?"

"The way you said, *oh yeah*, didn't sound like a real question."

"No, it was a real question."

Kenneth had a niggling feeling he was missing something and Driscoll picked up on it, but refused to clue him in.

"Well, yeah. I should've trusted my instinct to ask her if everything was ok. I could've let you know my status sooner if I had."

"Uh-huh. Question. This bug that's going around. Is it a stomach bug or like the crud/cold stuff which is common this time of year?"

"She's not coughing or complaining of a sore throat. So, I'd say it's a stomach thing. Why? What are you thinking?"

As he asked the question, the thought occurred to him, but Kenneth wanted to know if Driscoll's thoughts led him to the same conclusion.

"Could she be pregnant?"

Knowing what his friend was going to say still didn't prepare Kenneth for how he'd feel when he heard the words spoken aloud. They had never used condoms. Old enough to know better, neither of them wanted to give up the feeling of having him inside her without a barrier between them.

They'd discussed birth control and her use of an IUD. While nothing is one hundred percent, those things are pretty reliable. He also made a point of not releasing inside her every time they made love. But it only took once to plant a seed.

"Kenneth?"

"Umm...It's a possibility."

Thankful he hadn't picked the knife back up, Kenneth pressed his hands against the cool granite countertops then took a deep breath. Possibilities raced through his mind. *What if Driscoll was right? Should he ask her? Should he get a test? How does any of this work?*

At forty-two years of age, Kenneth had been dating and sexually active for more than twenty years. Candy was the first woman he'd ever failed to use condoms with. He hadn't purchased one box during the entire time they'd been together. Driscoll's voice cut through the brain fog bringing Kenneth back to the conversation at hand.

"Hey...I could be wrong. It might really be a bug. I get the feeling I totally threw you for a loop. Don't let my overactive mind put you in a spiral."

"No, no. We're good. I'm just thinking. We haven't discussed it, but I wouldn't be sad if Candy and I created a life together..."

"But?" Driscoll questioned.

"I have no clue how she'll feel about it." Kenneth detested the uncertainty in his voice. He loved Candy and, while he was sure she loved him, they were still very new in their relationship. A child would bind them together permanently.

"Sounds like you two need to talk. But, hey. Like I said, I could be wrong. I just remember her shying away from certain foods at Cousin's Night because of the smell. I'd never seen her do that before. It's the only reason I asked the question."

"Thanks."

Fingers tapping against the countertop, Kenneth considered Candy's recent behavior, weighing it against the little he knew of pregnancy combined Driscoll's observations. He and Candy definitely needed to talk, but after he made sure she ate then got some rest.

The whistling of the kettle put an end to their conversation. Kenneth set the tea aside to steep while he finished making toast. Going on the possibility of her stomach being unsettled for whatever reason, he eliminated the normal add-ons of butter and jam.

When he entered the bedroom with the lap tray, Candy was curled on her side beneath the covers fast asleep. He contemplated turning around and allowing her to continue sleeping until he heard the unmistakable growling of her stomach demanding sustenance.

Easing the tray onto the nightstand, he brushed his fingers across her forehead before gently kissing her there. The clamminess from earlier was gone, but she still felt slightly warmer than usual. As carefully as he could, he coaxed her awake.

Candy wasn't normally grumpy in the mornings, but this was his first experience with her being unwell. So, he wasn't certain what to expect. Her eyebrows drew together. An irritated pout formed on her lips before her eyelids lifted. Mild confusion painted her face when she saw him leaning over her.

"Come on, Baby. Sit up for me and try to eat something. Then, you can go back to sleep."

"I'm not hungry." Her muttered response was immediately contradicted by the grumbling from beneath the cover.

"That's what your mouth says, but your stomach says different." A smile tugged at the corner of Kenneth's mouth. Her facial expressions reminded him of a kid who was told they couldn't leave the dinner table until they ate their broccoli.

"Come on, Baby. Just try a little for me."

Sliding his arms under her shoulders, he helped her sit up propping pillows behind her back. Once she was settled, he slid the tray onto the bed next to her and held the toast up for her to take a bite.

Staring at his offering warily, she bit into it chewing slowly. When she tried to take it from his hand he moved it out of her reach. Finished with the small bite, she reached for the slice again. Once again, he moved it away.

"I'm fully capable of feeding myself. You know that right?"

"I'm aware. Now, open up."

Sliding the tray out of reach as well, he held the partially eaten bread aloft until she parted her lips for her next bite. Finally, she relaxed against the pillows accepting his brand of bedside nursing. Once she finished both pieces of toast and drank the tea, he tucked her back beneath the covers. Placing her phone next to her on the nightstand, he reminded her that he would be in his office if she needed something.

Despite her assurances she wasn't an invalid, he made her promise to text or call him if she wanted anything. No matter how small. Not having the energy to put up much of a fight, she agreed before sleep took her under.

Kenneth gave serious thought to going online and ordering a baby monitor with same day delivery. He'd normally have some sort of surveillance camera he could repurpose, but he'd left his gear at the office after their last field operation. He'd picked a fine time to follow protocol.

Working turned out to be an exercise in futility. Now that the seed had been planted, he couldn't think of anything else. When his phone rang interrupting him staring blankly out of the window in his office, he snatched it up quickly. Seeing his Uncle Ray's picture on the screen brought a smile to his face.

Tapping the earbud in his ear, he connected the call. "Hey Uncle Ray. What's going on?"

"Does something have to be going on for me to call my nephew?" The hint of amusement in his uncle's voice belied the snap of his words.

"No, sir. I guess there doesn't have to be a reason."

"Well, it just so happens I do have a purpose for this call. Two actually."

"Okay..." Kenneth sat back in his chair waiting for his uncle to share what was on his mind.

"I wanted to let you know your instincts were spot on about that smooth bastard Tone took to the Winter Gala with her."

"Oh yeah?" Kenneth perked up. It didn't make him happy to know he'd been right. If anyone deserved a happily ever after it was his surrogate auntie.

"Yeah...It took a little longer than usual for him to tip his hand, but he did it. He tried to convince her to invest in some halfcocked venture he had going. When she didn't go for it, he offered to help her expand her restaurant."

"Expand? He didn't know she already has a restaurant in six major city's along the east coast? Why would she need him to help with expansion?"

"Exactly, son. He obviously didn't do his research. Like most men, he assumed her husband helped her get established and that's why she hadn't opened any new places since he passed five years ago. Anyway, he's no more. She showed him the door. I closed it."

"Uncle Ray...What did you do?"

"Who me?"

"Yes. You."

"Not much...Just dropped his name to a couple of the guys you introduced me to in the fraud division of the New York offices."

"Uncle Ray...Did you get that man arrested?"

"Of course not!"

His uncle's shocked exclamation didn't convince Kenneth. Not in the least. Holding the line, he waited for him to reveal the rest. His uncle loved a good exposition and wouldn't be rushed.

"Ok. Fine. I dropped his name in their ear. He may or may not be under investigation after they ran a background check and found out he was into some Bernie Madoff shit on top of connections to counterfeiters on the west coast."

"Damn. I knew he was too polished, but I was thinking he was a money-grubbing man-whore, not a lifelong criminal. How the hell did he get so close to her?"

"They have a mutual associate at her church. Needless to say, that woman's name is now mud as well. I told Tone those too-churchy church ladies can't be trusted."

Nodding in silent agreement with his uncle, Kenneth made a note to make a few calls to check in with the New York office. He'd worked there a few years before he transferred to Logan City. He wanted to know the extent of Leonardo's criminal activities. The idea of anyone with deep criminal ties getting so close to someone he loved didn't sit well with him.

"Anyway. Enough about them. You haven't called me but once since you left. I figured you would've touched based to share the news by now."

Frowning, Kenneth wondered how the hell his uncle knew about his potential impending fatherhood.

"You already know? How?"

"Of course I know. I went with you to Mitchell and Soderberg. Remember?"

At his uncle's mention of the high-end jewelry store, Kenneth realized they weren't talking about the same thing. His voice flattened when he responded.

"Oh. That news. Nothing to tell on that front yet."

"Wait. What news did *you* think I meant?"

"Nothing. Don't worry about it." There was no need in getting his uncle's hopes up—especially considering he hadn't even spoken to Candy about his speculation.

"No, it's not nothing. You sounded surprised I was aware. If it's not about the ring, then it must be big..."

Silence stretched between them before his uncle let out a whoop. "KG, don't hold out on me now. Am I gonna be an uncle-papa?"

"I didn't say that, Uncle Ray. Don't jump to conclusions."

"How can I not? There's only one place to jump. What else could it be?"

Cutting his eyes at his closed office door as if Candy was standing there listening, Kenneth lowered his voice.

"I don't know for sure. She's not feeling well, complaining about a stomach bug going around at work. I didn't think anything of it until Driscoll mentioned she expressed sensitivity to certain smells at dinner this past weekend."

"What did she say when you asked her?"

"I haven't asked her about it."

"Why not? Communication is important in a good relationship."

"I know, but she's been asleep most of the morning. Besides, I haven't figured out how to broach the subject without it sounding like I'm hoping she is—which might make her think I set out to knock her up."

"One, don't say knock her up. I don't like how that sounds. Two, if she is, wouldn't you be happy about it?"

"Of course. Just considering the possibility had me looking at bigger houses and cribs on the internet instead of working. It makes me even more determined to move us to the next level. The problem I see is, if she is then I ask her after we confirm it, she may think I only asked her to marry me because she's pregnant or I thought she was pregnant. Or worse that I tried to trap her."

"You're definitely between a rock and a hard place... You still have to suck it up and find out for sure. From what I saw, you two have a solid relationship. I don't believe she'd ever accuse you of trying to trap her."

Kenneth quietly considered what his uncle said. He was almost ten years older than Candy. Although he hadn't been earnestly looking to get married and start a family, he could see himself acclimating to it quickly. Candy was successful in her career, but she was still on the rise. Marriage and a child might not fit into her plan.

His uncle interrupted his thoughts. "There are a few things you haven't considered though."

"What's that?"

"That she might be happy about having your baby. That she won't think it was intentional on your part. And last but not least, that she'll know you wouldn't ask her to be your wife unless you loved her and wanted to marry her."

Unable to respond immediately, Kenneth allowed his uncle's words to wash over him. It was quite possible he was putting the cart before the horse and Candy simply had a stomach virus. However, it was just as likely their unencumbered adult activities had accomplished a task aside from their mutual pleasure—creating a life.

An electronic ping from his laptop drew his eyes to the time on the display. It had been over an hour since the last time he'd looked in on Candy. Lunchtime was upon them. They needed to discuss her calling her doctor or finding an urgent care nearby. He'd prefer her regular physician, but he'd take what he could get.

Thanking his uncle for giving him something to think about, he ended the call. When he made it to the bedroom, Candy wasn't in bed. The toilet flushing informed him of her location. The noise was immediately followed by the sound of water splashing into the bowl of the sink.

Opening the bathroom door, he found her leaning over the sink rinsing her mouth. Once she was done, he wrapped an arm around her waist and led her back into the bedroom. The warmth he'd felt on her forehead earlier was more pronounced.

"It's time to call your doctor."

Candy looked at him with watery eyes, but offered no protest when he picked up her phone then asked for the information to call the doctor's office. Amazingly, they had a cancellation and could see her within the hour.

The more assistance he had to give her to help her get dressed, the more Kenneth began to believe he and Driscoll were wrong about Candy's condition. Sure, Driscoll had first-hand experience with pregnancy via his wife, but Kenneth hadn't ever heard of it causing fever or the weakness she displayed.

The antiseptic smell of cleaning products combined with a hint of lavender hit Kenneth's nose the moment they stepped into the lobby of the doctor's office. As much as he wanted to sit Candy on one of the remarkably comfortable looking sofas, he held onto her waist leading her to the intake desk to check in.

Twenty minutes later, she was called to the back. There was no question of him going with her and the staff didn't object. They did offer a wheelchair, which Candy refused.

In the examination room, Kenneth watched anxiously as the nurse drew blood for testing while assuring them the doctor would be in shortly. The entirely too young-looking man had already taken Candy's temperature, confirming a fever of one hundred and one degrees. No wonder she was weak. Being feverish zapped the strength from the body.

Chapter Twenty-Two

I'M SORRY. WHAT?

Candy leaned against Kenneth trying to absorb his warmth while they waited for Dr. Abrams. Instead of sitting in one of the chairs, he stood next to where she sat on the examination table with one arm wrapped around her rubbing her back.

Still dressed in the business suit he'd planned to wear to work, he made it clear that she was his primary concern. It was different having someone in her life taking care of her this way. She couldn't recall anyone other than her parents looking out for her with even a fraction of the intensity Kenneth had.

Lethargy caused Candy to almost doze off cuddled against Kenneth's chest. Dr. Abrams' entry into the room brought her back from the brink. Rolling the custom cart with a laptop attached to a pedestal, the doctor came inside and closed the door behind her. Slowly lifting her lids, Candy tried to focus on what the doctor was saying.

"Good afternoon, Ms Hampton. Goderich tells me you're feeling more than a little under the weather."

Nodding mutely, Candy watched as the doctor donned rubber gloves as she approached her. Although she'd only been in her office a few times, Candy was very comfortable in Dr. Abrams' presence and confident in her abilities.

Candy was convinced the woman was some kind of prodigy because she was only thirty-five and she'd told Candy she'd been practicing medicine for fifteen years—in private practice for five. Dr. Abrams had a warm, inviting face coupled with an engaging bedside manner. Candy took to her immediately.

"Let's have a look, shall we?"

Kenneth stepped back to give the doctor room. Candy immediately missed his warmth. Taking the penlight from the pocket of her white coat, Dr. Abrams began her physical examination by looking into Candy's throat. The steps in the exam took less than ten minutes, but it felt like forever.

While she made her checks, the doctor asked Candy questions about how she'd been feeling and when she first noticed the symptoms. Candy explained about the people on set who'd been sick and her thoughts on where she could have picked up the bug.

Typing notes then clicking her mouse, Dr. Abrams grew silent. Kenneth resumed his position next to Candy and she relaxed in his embrace allowing him to hold her up. This was the point in a doctor's visit when the physician normally left the room for twenty minutes or more before coming back to consult.

One of the things Candy appreciated about Dr. Abrams is she never did that. Once she was in the room with a patient, she stayed. Her exit from the room meant the appointment was over. Candy's eyes drifted closed again as she turned her head into Kenneth's chest to get away from the sterile scent of the room.

"Okay, Ms Hampton. I have the results from your bloodwork back. Am I free to speak in front of Mr...?"

"Holmes. Kenneth Holmes." Kenneth supplied.

Candy peeled her eyes open and looked at the doctor. "It's fine."

"Are you sure?" Dr. Abrams looked at her over the top of her glasses.

The notes of concern in her voice gave Candy pause, but she re-iterated her approval. "Yes. It's fine. He's been taking care of me. I would end up trying to tell him whatever you said and possibly leaving something out."

"Okay then..." Rolling her stool and laptop closer to them, Dr. Abrams stopped when she was within arm's reach.

"Ms Hampton, your tests show you have contracted a virus. Most likely, the same one that's floating around amongst your co-workers. As you know with viruses, we can only try to keep you comfortable while they run their course.

You're also dehydrated. Not severely so, but enough to cause me concern. I won't admit you, but you need to increase your fluid intake significantly. Rest, but hydrate.

In the meantime, I'll call in prescriptions for antibiotics to help your body fight off the virus and something to help with the nausea so you can keep food down. Food is energy. You need all of that you can get."

"Thank you, Dr. Abrams. I have a busy schedule next week. I need all the help I can get to shake this thing." Candy tried to keep her eyes open, but it was so hard.

"I'm not done."

Candy's eyes snapped back open at the doctor's announcement.

"Ms Hampton. Are you aware that you're pregnant?"

"I'm sorry. What?" Sitting up straight, Candy pulled away from Kenneth's chest. "Did you say pregnant?"

"Yes. According to your bloodwork, you're approximately twelve weeks along. So, you've completed your first trimester."

"That's not possible. I have an IUD and I had my period three weeks ago."

"We can run the test again, but they are accurate in the 99.9 percentile."

"Pregnant?" Candy whispered the question.

The world around her fell away as she struggled to absorb the word. Even though she questioned the doctor, she was well aware the only guaranteed way to avoid pregnancy was abstinence. She and Kenneth had been anything but abstinent.

They'd made absolutely no attempts to use alternate forms of birth control, relying on her IUD exclusively. When she'd awakened nauseous, the thought crossed her mind, but she immediately squashed it because of the others who'd been sick on the set. And, like she'd told Dr. Abrams she had a period just before they went to New York. Granted it wasn't as heavy as she expected, nor did it last as long, but it happened.

"I recommend another appointment to have a more thorough exam.

As you know, I am a general physician and quite capable of performing it. However, if you have an OB/GYN, or would like a recommendation to a specialist, I understand."

"No...I'm more comfortable with you." Aside from her competence, one of the main reasons she'd switched to Dr. Abrams was because she was a general physician who could handle Candy's gynecological needs as well.

"Okay. Well first things first. Do you want to continue with this pregnancy?"

Her question snapped Candy into focus. Candy's hand instinctively flew to her abdomen. Planned or not, terminating her pregnancy wasn't something she'd considered. Seeking Kenneth's eyes, she tried to determine his thoughts without actually speaking.

What she saw in his gaze was confidence and support mixed with uncontainable hope. He didn't hide his desire for her to answer the doctor's question in the affirmative. Maintaining eye contact with him, she responded to Dr. Abrams.

"Yes. I want this."

Now she understood why the doctor was hesitant to give her the news in front of him. She had no way of knowing if Kenneth was the father of Candy's baby. They weren't married and Dr. Abrams hadn't met him until today.

Watching as Kenneth's face relaxed, she felt warmth wash over her, but she had no time to delve into the feeling. Dr. Abrams was already moving on to the next step.

"Alright. That means we need to remove your IUD. While the chances are small, there have been documented adverse effects to the fetus when the IUD remains in place during pregnancy.

We have everything we need to do it here in the office. Once we're done, I'll make some notes and you can arrange a follow-up appointment on your way out.

Since you weren't aware of your condition, I'd like to get you back in here as soon as possible to get eyes on our little bean. I'd offer to do it today, but let's get this virus behind us first. I don't want to over-tax you."

"Thank you, doctor."

Hearing Kenneth thank her doctor brought Candy's thoughts around to him and his reaction to the news. She'd been hesitant to look at him while she tried to wrap her mind around what she'd heard. But, after Dr. Abram's question regarding termination, she couldn't tear her eyes away from his.

Using quick mental math, she was able to determine exactly when conception occurred. Labor Day. They'd come together so passionately that night, Candy wasn't able to get out of bed the next morning. She'd slept until almost noon. It was the first time Kenneth left her alone in his house. He'd gone off to work like it was a regular day.

Now, he met her gaze with eyes filled with gratitude along with something else she couldn't quite name. Tuning back in to Dr. Abrams in time to see her press the call button for her nurse, Candy listened as she explained the quick procedure to remove the IUD.

Candy sighed in relief when the doctor mentioned using a local anesthetic for the potential pain or discomfort. She'd had to advocate for herself in order to receive something during the insertion of the device four years ago. That incident was part of the reason she found Dr. Abrams' practice. She refused to deal with a doctor who ignored her pain.

With Candy's consent, Kenneth was allowed to stay during the process. Initially, she thought it would be awkward, but when he slipped his hand into hers and brushed her hair from her forehead, she was thankful he was there with her.

The procedure was over with quickly. Thanks to the pain medication, Candy felt nothing more than a light pinch and tug. The entire time, Kenneth held her hand offering his silent support.

Once it was complete, Candy disappeared behind the changing curtain to re-dress. After she was fully clothed again, Dr. Abrams gave both of them instructions on what Candy would need to do to fight off the stomach bug while simultaneously trying to grow a human.

A *baby*. She and Kenneth were going to be parents. Unconsciously, her hand moved to her stomach bumping into Kenneth's as his palm lay on her abdomen protectively.

When Dr. Abrams finished with her instructions, she stood to leave. Kenneth latched on to Candy's hand as they followed the doctor from the room. Goderich, her nurse, met them at the door with printouts containing the doctor's notes, diagnosis and instructions, along with the prescription just in case the pharmacy didn't process the called in order correctly.

Candy went through the check-out procedure on auto-pilot. She participated in the process of arranging her next appointments feeling like she was in the midst of an out of body fugue. To her credit, she didn't flinch when Kenneth whipped out his phone to coordinate his schedule to make sure he was able to attend her appointments with her.

The drive back to Kenneth's house was done in almost complete silence. The only time either of them spoke was at the pharmacy, which was blessedly brief as they had her prescription ready for pickup when she and Kenneth arrived. Thankful for small favors, she watched the landscape as they moved through the suburban neighborhood before turning into Kenneth's driveway.

Opting for the sofa rather than traversing the stairs to get back into bed, Candy murmured her thanks as he draped a plush blanket over her.

"I'll get you some toast and warm tea so you can take your meds. That should hold you over until the soup is ready."

"Soup?" Candy wondered if her sense of smell had been affected seeing as she didn't detect anything cooking.

"I'm going to make a light soup. Hopefully, it won't bother your stomach, so you'll be able to keep it down."

"Oh. Okay. Thank you."

"You're welcome, Baby."

Pressing a kiss to her forehead, he left her alone in the room. Alone with nothing but her thoughts, Candy picked up the remote and turned on the television. Not that she watched it, but the quiet of the room was unnerving.

Was she sad about being pregnant? No. Surprised? Yes, but not sad. While she hadn't lived her adult life actively seeking either marriage or children, she'd always assumed those things would happen for her when they were supposed to. So, she tried not to get discouraged when her college friends were getting married and starting their families.

Heck, not all of them were still happy in their choices, but they were sticking with it. That kind of life wasn't something Candy wanted; so, she resolved herself to living, honing her craft, while being the best auntie she could be in the meantime.

Now, she was looking at being a mother in less than a year's time. *Holy shit.* She was going to be someone's mother. Entering the room, Kenneth interrupted her thoughts with more dry toast and warm tea. Despite her lack of appetite, Candy forced herself to eat both pieces and drink the ginger tea, after which she was able to take her medication.

Taking away the empty mug and plate, Kenneth disappeared once more into the kitchen. Although her afternoon hadn't been filled with many tasks, Candy was wiped out—physically and emotionally. So, it could have been the meds, fatigue, or a combination of both that sent her off to dreamland.

Later, she awakened from her nap. Laying on her side, she took stock of herself. She didn't feel as weak, nor was her stomach roiling as if it planned to reject the little food she'd put in it. When she went to push herself to a seated position, she realized one of her hands was being held firmly in Kenneth's.

Following the trail of his limb over the edge of the couch, she saw her crazy man lying on the floor with a pillow beneath his head. His gray gaze swept over her face like he was a robot scanning her for possible problems he needed to fix.

"Hey." She winced. Her voice sounded weird to her ears. Scratchy and slightly hoarse.

"Hey." His eyebrows drew together. "Are you okay? Does something hurt?" Lifting until he was sitting, he searched her face.

"No." She quickly reassured him. "I didn't expect my voice to sound like that. It caught me off guard."

Squeezing his fingers, she tried to convey that she was okay. "Why are you on the floor?"

Ducking his head, he smiled sheepishly. "I wanted to be nearby in case you needed me."

"I think you could've done that without stretching out below me on the hard floor. It can't be comfortable."

Shrugging, he dismissed her words. "It's no big deal."

"If you don't care about your back..." She trailed off.

"Like I said, no big deal. My back is fine."

"You know you were in prime position to get stepped on or catch my stomach contents if I didn't keep my food down. Right?"

"I considered it and decided it was worth the risk. I wasn't sleeping. I would've had a chance to move immediately if you'd shown any signs of doing either."

"If you say so."

"I do." Kissing the back of her hand, he snared her with his gaze. "Are you ready to talk now?"

He'd changed clothes, so the business suit had been replaced by joggers and a fitted Henley. His clothing was relaxed, but the expression on his face was intense.

Sitting all the way up, she nodded. It was time.

"I know this wasn't what you had planned. I'm sure neither of us was thinking of having a baby right now."

Gathering her hands in his, he squeezed her fingers. "Hey... It doesn't matter if we planned it or not. I'm not sad, angry or disappointed." Placing one hand on her stomach, he spread his long digits across the gentle swell. "We created something exceedingly special. We're going to bring a life into this world. Together. I can honestly say, I wouldn't want to do it with anyone else."

Unexpected tears welled in Candy's eyes. His calm reassurance coupled with his blatant acceptance tossed her into the deep end of her feelings. Although he'd seemed hopeful at the doctor's office, some time had passed. Time he could've used to think and come to a different conclusion.

One in which he thought she'd tried to trap him. Afterall, he was handsome, had a great career, was financially stable, and had a charisma about himself that was hard to ignore. Very few women were immune to it.

"You don't think this is too quick? Yes, we've known each other for a couple of years, but we've been together less than six months. Now, we're going to be tied to each other through this baby for the foreseeable future."

Coming to his knees, Kenneth pushed her legs apart to make room for his trim hips. Clasping her head between his hands, he captured her lips silencing anything else she had to say. His kiss was dominating, robbing her of coherent thought. It was as if he were trying to imprint his feelings on her using the connection.

Moaning beneath the onslaught, her fingers gripped the front of his shirt. Underneath them, his heart beat steady and strong. Her own pulse seemed to automatically pace itself to match. Releasing her with lingering pecks, Kenneth separated from her mouth only far enough to look into her eyes once more.

"My sweet Candy...Even if it had only been six days, I wouldn't run from being with you. Do you have any idea how much I love you?"

Candy's eyes widened at his declaration. While he'd shown her in thousands of ways, he'd never said those three words to her. She'd almost convinced herself that his attentiveness was simply a part of his nature and he wasn't treating her any differently than he had any other woman he dated.

She was so very wrong. All the signs had been there, but she'd somehow missed them completely. Love shone from his eyes, intense and all consuming. Unconsciously tracing his face with her fingertips, she took in the image before her. The face of a man unashamedly in love —with her.

"I love you, Kenneth Gregory Holmes."

The joy on his face at hearing her assertion was nothing short of beautiful. His smile was blindingly bright as he tugged her from the couch. His hands relocated to her ass while he held her close to his body, kissing her as if she was his lifeline.

In the moment, it felt as if he was hers. In less than twenty-four hours, her life's trajectory had changed. Candy had no regrets though. Not as long as Kenneth was the man taking the journey with her.

Chapter Twenty-Three

STOP HOLDING OUT ON ME

Kenneth lay on his back in bed, with Candy cuddled into this side. Confident in his normally robust immune system, he didn't fear coming down with the virus. Besides, the medication Dr. Abrams prescribed had taken away her fever almost immediately.

The only indication of her not being one hundred percent was the small portion of soup with the large amount of saltine crackers she'd eaten for dinner. It was relatively early, so they had the television going. If pressed, Kenneth wouldn't be able to repeat one word of the sitcom or relay any information about the episode.

His mind was on the events of the day. What started as a possibility was confirmed. His new reality included the child growing in Candy's womb. A child they created together. In addition to the baby, they exchanged words of love expanding his happiness exponentially.

The only thing that could make it better was for Candy to agree to be his wife—for their family to be bound together legally. Battling with uncertainty and wanting to be able to give her the grand gesture she deserved, he considered his earlier conversation with his uncle.

Uncle Ray was right. Candy never thought for a second that he'd attempted to trap her with pregnancy. She actually was concerned he'd think she was trying to trap him. The thought was ludicrous to him. Of the two of them, she was the more prominent.

Almost everyone who was a part of the entertainment or make-up artist world knew her or knew of her. She'd been nominated for a freaking Oscar for her work. She was a total badass. Her humility, kindness and generosity made it easy to forget those things because she didn't lord her achievements over people. She simply tried to be the best version of herself every day.

Suddenly, his worry about proposing to her in some grand extravagant way seemed like the dumbest idea he ever had. That wasn't his sweet Candy. While she was a force, she wasn't fond of big productions when it came to personal things.

If he did something, he was certain she'd smile, go along with it and show appreciation for his effort. However, she'd also be extremely uncomfortable being placed in the spotlight.

His heart rate picked up as he realized what he'd essentially just talked himself into doing. Candy shifted in his arms. He was certain she'd detected it as well. Dark brown eyes sought his in the dim lighting of the room—concern etched on the smooth planes of her face.

"Are you okay?"

"Yes...No...I don't know. I think so?" Now that he'd made up his mind, words were jumbling inside his head.

"Okay..." The fingers of one hand splayed on his chest above his heart as she regarded him with apprehension.

"Give me a second, Baby." Tapping her hip, he issued the unspoken command for her to shift to allow him to get up.

In long strides, he went to the dresser. Trembling digits opened the top drawer pulling out the insert. Digging through the contents, he drew out the navy box wrapped with the pretty silver bow. Taking a deep breath, he turned back to Candy.

He didn't bother to tell her to close her eyes. Had he not been a jumble of nerves, he would've sat her on the edge of the bed and covered her eyes. As it was, she was sitting with her back pressed against the tufted headboard watching him with shining eyes.

Kenneth hadn't bothered to put the box behind his back. He approached the bed with the square package held between his fingers in clear view. As he drew closer, the tears welling in her eyes overflowed, running down her face in unchecked rivulets. Her hands were clasped together pressed against her bosom.

When he reached the side of the bed, he climbed on, but remained on his knees in front of her. Detangling her hands until he held the left one in his, he flicked open the lid of the box with his thumb.

"Candace—" His emotions were so high, Kenneth's voice cracked like a teenaged boy on the cusp of the change when he said her name. Clearing his throat, he tried again.

"Candace Marie Hampton, would you do me the honor of being my wife?"

Her fingers trembled in his hold having the effect of making him more stable as he held them within his grasp. He gained strength from knowing this is exactly the perfect moment and the perfect way to ask.

Mute nodding was her answer. Shaking his head, he tsked. "Nuh-uh, Baby. I need your words. I have to hear it from your sweet lips to know it's real."

Placing her right hand on her chest, she took a deep breath clearing her throat. "Yes. Yes, I'll marry you."

"Yes?" He asked even though he'd heard her clearly.

"Yes!" Came her more enthusiastic reply.

"Yes!!" Quickly slipping the ring on her finger, he took her lips in a scorching kiss. His heart was full near to bursting. She'd said yes and she was going to have his baby. Life literally couldn't get any better than this.

Raining kisses all over her face, Kenneth thanked every deity he knew for his beautiful woman. He couldn't seem to get close enough to her as he held her in his arms. The moment was one of the most intimate they'd ever had. Yet, there was nothing sexual about it.

The outside world didn't exist, until it did. The ringing of Kenneth's cellphone penetrated their celebratory bubble snapping them both back into reality. His first thought was to ignore it, but he reconsidered after he saw his uncle's face on the display. Swiping the screen, he answered the call.

"You didn't call me back. I've been waiting." Uncle Ray didn't give Kenneth a chance to speak once the call connected.

"I'm sorry, Uncle Ray. I've been a little busy." Snuggled into his side, Candy tapped his chest and mouthed for him to tell his uncle hello for her.

"Candy says hello."

"Tell my favorite niece I said, hi."

Kenneth didn't have to see him to know his uncle was smiling. Even though he hadn't officially told him or anyone else Candy accepted his proposal, his uncle was convinced she'd said yes.

"Baby, Uncle Ray says hi."

"How's she feeling? Since you never called me back, I've been worried." His playful uncle had disappeared. The notes of concern were evident in his voice.

"She's doing better. The doctor gave her some medicine that brought down the fever, so she's been able to eat."

Candy ducked her head and pulled away. Reflexively, he clamped his arm tighter.

"Where are you going?"

"Bathroom."

"Oh. Okay." Kissing her forehead, he released his hold allowing her to ease off the bed. His eyes tracked her progress. Even though she seemed to be much better, he wasn't taking any chances.

"I don't have to see you to know you're watching her like a hawk." His uncle broke the silence. Just that quickly, Kenneth had almost forgotten he was on the phone.

"You don't know everything, old man."

"I don't have to know everything to know you. Besides, you're a man in love. It's natural—especially with her being sick and possibly expecting."

"If you say so, Uncle Ray." Watching the bathroom door like he had ex-ray vision, Kenneth waited for Candy to re-appear.

"One day you'll admit how wise I am...Anyway, I'm happy she's feeling better. So..."

"So...what?"

Kenneth knew what his uncle was hinting at. He wanted to know if the doctor confirmed more than a stomach bug. Part of Kenneth wanted to mess with him, but he knew his uncle was almost as excited about the possibility as Kenneth was about the reality.

"Look...your aren't too old for me to take you across my knee." His uncle threatened.

"Your words would hold a lot more weight if you'd actually ever disciplined me that way." Kenneth laughed at his uncle's attempt to sound tough.

"Stop holding out on me. I have stuff in my online shopping cart and I need to know if I'm proceeding to check out or cancelling it."

"Uncle Ray."

"What? I haven't bought anything. I'm just looking."

"Will it do any good to tell you not to go overboard?"

"No. I do what I want with my money and if I want to spoil my grandbaby, I'll do just that."

"Dear Lord...To think we have six more months of this ahead of us."

"Damn right you do! Wait...Did you just say six months? As in I really am gonna be an Uncle-Papa?"

"Yes, Uncle Ray, because this is all about you."

Kenneth held the phone away from his ear as his uncle let out a happy yell. It became apparent he was still in his office at the flagship restaurant when he called out his assistant's name shouting the news. All Kenneth could do was smile. Uncle Ray's joy was contagious.

The bathroom door opened and Candy reappeared. The light behind her created a silhouette of her plush body, before she turned it off. Wearing an oversized sleepshirt with her hair secured in a silk scarf, she remained the most beautiful woman in his eyes. More so now that she was ripening with his child. Was he biased? Absolutely. Didn't mean it wasn't true though.

Again, he tracked her progress while listening to his uncle with half an ear. By the time she climbed back into bed, Uncle Ray finally remembered Kenneth was on the other end of the phone line.

Now, it was Kenneth who ignored him while he checked to make sure Candy was okay. He was aware of his uncle's voice, but he couldn't focus on the words as Candy reached over him to pick up the remote control. Propping pillows behind her back, she settled herself on the other side of the bed flipping the channels.

"Uncle Ray?" Kenneth interrupted his uncle's excited chatter. "I'll call you tomorrow."

He barely heard the response as he disconnected the call placing his phone on the bedside table—his eyes on Candy the entire time. As if she felt the heat of his stare, she cut him a side glance before turning to look at him fully.

"What?"

"Why are you way over there?"

"You were on the phone."

"I don't see your point."

"I didn't want to be rude."

If he was certain of her physical health, he would have snatched her to his side where she belonged. Instead, he plucked the remote from her hand. Crooking a finger at her, he wordlessly called her to him. Rolling her eyes, she readjusted until she was snuggled next to him once more.

"Just so we're clear, in this bed or any bed we lay in together, this is where you belong—whether I'm on the phone or not. If you weren't sick, I'd spank your ass for pulling this shit."

Her non-verbal response to his grumbling declaration was to wiggle her sweet bum which he couldn't resist tapping lightly.

"Behave. You can't handle that right now."

"You're mean."

Kenneth looked into Candy's upturned face. A line marred her normally smooth brow and her lips formed a pout. Squeezing her tighter, he dipped his head speaking directly into her ear. Using explicit language, he explained all the ways he was going to pleasure her while extracting his retribution for her *little show* of attitude.

Her responding shudder tugged his lips up at the corners in a smile that surely looked sinister. He was most definitely looking forward to keeping his promise.

Three days later, Kenneth was back at work in the office. Candy was over the viral infection. Now, her occasional bouts of nausea were due to the pregnancy. As it turned out, the studio shut production down for the week to try to stem the outbreak. So, Candy took the rest of the week to get some additional rest and work on her schedule.

The day following his proposal, Kenneth broached the subject of living arrangements while they worked out when they'd like to have the wedding. That led to if they even wanted a ceremony or whether it would be best to do something small before the baby and have a reception after.

No decisions were made, but the lines of communication were open. In theory, they had time. They weren't required to be married to have a child, but he wanted them all settled under the same roof. Period.

"So...I hear you popped the question."

Kenneth looked up to see Driscoll leaning against the doorframe of his office.

"Where did you hear that?" Sitting back, Kenneth propped his elbows on the arms of his chair then linked his fingers together loosely.

"You know where. Candy told her mom, who told McKenna's mom, who told McKenna, who told me. The family grapevine is faster than Western Union."

"Are you sure? It's Thursday, I asked her on Monday. That's not exactly the speedy express."

"Monday? You asked the woman to marry you while she was sick and tossing her guts?" Shaking his head, Driscoll looked at Kenneth in disappointment.

"What? Of course not. It was much later—after we saw the doctor who prescribed meds that helped her feel better." Straightening his already straight tie, Kenneth stared at his friend and colleague. "What kind of guy do you take me for?"

Holding up his hands, Driscoll responded. "No offense, but on Monday you told me she was throwing up and generally not doing well. Now you're telling me you asked her to marry you on Monday. What am I supposed to think? Last we spoke you were wondering if she was pregnant."

"She is by the way."

"Please tell me that's not why you asked her to marry you."

"What? Of course not." Piercing Driscoll with a gray glare, Kenneth practically growled. "I'm really getting tired of you insulting me. If you must know, I bought the ring weeks ago. I had no idea she was pregnant at the time."

"No need to put bass in your voice. I was just checking. You're my friend. Candy's now my family. You both deserve better than jumping into marriage because of an unplanned pregnancy."

"I'm trying really hard not to be offended that you'd think I'd make it to forty-two years on earth and not know I don't have to marry a woman just because she's having my baby."

"Married? Baby?" Scott bumped past Driscoll stepping into Kenneth's office. "What did I miss?"

"Nothing much. Just your friend putting his foot in his mouth. Repeatedly."

Looking between Driscoll and Kenneth, Scott appeared to perform a few mental calculations.

"Nah. Not touching it. Back to my original question. I heard something about marriage and a baby? Technically the baby could be D.I. talking about his little one due any day now, but it could be you. If it is, then I have another question. Didn't you just get that woman last week?"

Kenneth couldn't hold back the laugh at Scott's question. It wasn't so much the question as it was his delivery. He sounded completely dumbfounded Kenneth had managed such a feat.

"Whatever, man. FYI, Candy and I have been together since the summer, so it's been almost six months. Thank you very much."

"Ooo... Six whole months. In that case, you're moving slower than molasses."

Driscoll didn't attempt to hide his chuckles at Scott's joke. Both of them grinned at Kenneth like it was the funniest shit they'd heard in a while.

"You know what? Both of you can get out of my office. I have work to do. I don't have time to be your source of entertainment."

"Okay, okay, okay." Holding out his fist, Scott offered him a fist bump.

"I guess congratulations are in order though, if you got that beautiful queen to marry you and carry your big head baby."

"Did you really just congratulate me and insult me in the same breath?"

Scott had the audacity to look surprised at Kenneth's question. "What? I'm happy for you, man."

Crumpling a piece of paper, Kenneth threw it at Scott who caught it immediately sending it back at him.

"Out of my office. Both of you."

Chapter Twenty-Four

I HAVE AN IDEA

Candy stood on the doorstep of McKenna's new home waiting for someone to come to the door. It wasn't long before it opened. Kari ushered Candy in and giving her a hug once she crossed the threshold.

"Hey, Candy Corn. How are you feeling?" Kari greeted Candy with her childhood nickname.

"Hey, Queenie. I'm feeling much better thanks."

Kari was one of the first calls Candy made once she got her bearings after learning she was pregnant and Kenneth proposed. Only Candy's reassurance that Kenneth had called off work to take care of her kept Kari from coming over or siccing her mother on her.

Candy wasn't worried about her own mother, who would check on her and drop off food. She was worried about Kari's mother. Aunt Tami could smother a body with caretaking affection. It was sweet at first, but it quickly got to be too much.

"You're just in time to help finish lunch. I made McKenna sit her extra pregnant butt down."

"I can hear you!" McKenna called from the other room.

"I wasn't whispering!" Kari called back.

Waving Candy to follow her, they walked farther into the house.

Candy's gaze swept over the decorations adorning the foyer and staircase as they moved through to the living room. A large pre-lit Christmas tree was placed in front of the bay window at the front of the room. A little gate surrounded the perimeter of the tree.

She was certain it was to keep DJ from tearing into the brightly wrapped packages beneath the tree. Based on what she knew about McKenna's son, she didn't see the little fence being much of a deterrent.

McKenna sat on an oversized chair with her feet propped on the coordinating ottoman. *Bless her heart.* She didn't look the least bit comfy despite sitting on what appeared to be a very comfortable piece of furniture.

Leaning over to give her as much of a hug as she could, Candy pecked McKenna's cheek as she said hello.

"I'm glad you could make it."

"I am too. We haven't gotten together in a while where it's just us girls." In spite of the tiredness hovering at the corners of McKenna's eyes, her skin glowed and she radiated happiness.

"Do you think Cherry is going to make it?" McKenna asked hopefully.

"I'm not sure. I left her a message. If she hasn't gotten some wild hair and hopped a flight, she might be here."

Rubbing the rounded fullness of her belly, McKenna nodded in understanding. "I hope she can make it. I missed her at Cousin's Night."

After what she and Cherry's older sister, Cassandra, did to McKenna, it was a wonder the three of them had been able to maintain a relationship—let alone grow closer. It was still hard for Candy to wrap her mind around how jealous Cassi was of McKenna's life.

That she would go so far as to hold McKenna hostage in her own home was beyond Candy's ability to comprehend. She herself had never had such deep-seated resentment toward anyone—especially not family. The entire situation put family ties to the test.

There were still some extended family members who thought McKenna should've asked for leniency on Cassi's behalf to lessen her prison sentence. Candy wasn't one of those people. Cassi was an adult with full control of herself and her actions.

She bought and paid for the consequences she received. Candy didn't fault McKenna for a second. Cassi held her at gunpoint in her own home. One doesn't just brush something like that off and move on.

"Candy, come help me with the food please." Kari passed Candy an apron nudging her toward the sink to wash up.

"What still needs to be done?" Candy asked as she dried her hands.

"The steak. It's been marinated, but it still needs to go on the griddle. The potatoes are in the oven. I'm almost done with the salad." Kari informed her.

After quickly getting everyone's cooking temperature, Candy turned the flame on under the griddle section of the gas range stove. She was starting to come around to Kenneth's way of thinking when it came to cooking surfaces.

While it required more active attention, the gas range offered her more temperature control such that she was able to cook each piece to everyone's exact specifications. She even cooked an extra just in case Cherry showed up.

Once she plated the steaks, she removed the baked potatoes from the oven adding them to the plates. When she turned to put them on the table, she met the amused expressions on her cousins' faces.

"What?" Walking forward slowly, she placed the plates on the table.

"You looked so confident and comfortable." McKenna's declaration washed over Candy warming her in a way she hadn't expected.

"She did, didn't she?" Kari's grin stretched across her face. "The cooking lessons really paid off."

"Cooking lessons? Is that what happened? I thought you finally got out of your head and started trusting yourself."

"I did, but the class I took at the Logan City Culinary Academy helped with the confidence."

"Are you sure it was just the classes and not the man teaching the classes?" Kari asked slyly.

Mouthing, *"Shut it!"* to her cousin, Candy feigned ignorance. "I don't know what you're talking about. I learned a lot in those classes."

"Mmhmm...I bet you did." Kari wiggled her eyebrows. "But I'm positive you learned more in the individual sessions. So much so there's now a bun in *your* oven."

Kari's hand flew to her mouth covering her giggles at the joke only she found amusing.

Frowning in confusion, McKenna looked between the two of them. "What did I miss?"

"You really don't know?" Kari asked.

"Kay, if I knew, I wouldn't ask." McKenna shot back.

"Kenneth was the instructor of the cooking class Candy signed up for in July."

Turning her back, Candy went back to the stove to retrieve her plate before grabbing the salad from the refrigerator. She and Kenneth hadn't kept their relationship a secret, but they hadn't expounded on how they got together. Everyone simply assumed it was from interacting at family functions.

"Kenneth? I thought those classes were taught by chefs."

"He is a chef. He graduated from culinary school and worked his way through college by cooking in high end restaurants." Candy quietly inserted.

"Really? I had no idea. He's never said anything, neither did Driscoll." McKenna said with a note of surprise.

"He wouldn't. If asked, he won't deny it, but he won't bring it up. I'm not sure Driscoll knows." Candy set the salad dressing on the table. "The food is ready if y'all want to eat."

McKenna held out a hand for Kari to help her from her chair grunting as she levered herself from the cushions.

"McKenna, I can get you a tray, you don't have to get up." Candy offered.

"Nope. I need to come to the table if I stand a chance of eating my food instead of wearing it."

Kari and Candy giggled until McKenna reminded Candy that similar days were in her very near future. At which point, Candy's laughter tapered off.

"Don't worry. You have at least three or four months ahead of you where you'll still be able to see whether or not you're wearing matching shoes." McKenna joked good-naturedly.

"You're joking, but I can tell you're really uncomfortable right now." Candy pulled the chair from the kitchen table for her.

"I'm in the home stretch. This time around hasn't been the easiest pregnancy for me. I'm working from home because I can't stand for any length of time. I have roughly three positions I can put my body in to sleep at night. Poor Driscoll has become a contortionist trying to accommodate my weird sleep positions, but he doesn't complain. He's also taken over dropping DJ off and picking him up from daycare since I'm not very mobile."

Finally seated at the table, they paused to bless the food before digging in to their meal. It was a little heavy for lunch, but Candy didn't mind. Since she'd kicked the stomach virus, her appetite had picked up.

The anti-nausea meds Dr. Abrams prescribed helped with keeping the morning sickness in the actual morning instead of all day long. She had no idea all day morning sickness was a thing until she talked to her mother who mentioned experiencing it while pregnant with each of her children.

For a few moments they ate in amicable silence. Kari broke the quiet to ask a question.

"So, McKenna, just out of curiosity, what does this mean for Christmas Eve dinner at your parents' house? If you can barely stand for any length of time, you can't help Auntie with the meal the way you normally do."

"You are correct. Mama and I were talking about it since Safara and AJ will be in Africa visiting her family this year. I won't be able to do much that requires standing, but I told her I'd come over early to at least sit with her.

She's thinking of going old school and calling the other Aunties over even though Christmas Eve is a much smaller gathering than the cook-outs in the summer. I don't know why she insists on cooking like she's feeding an army every year anyway."

"You know feeding people is your mama's love language. Just like mine has the market cornered on being aggressively supportive and nosey."

Kari chuckled at her assessment of Bonita and Tami Frost. Although she didn't say it out loud. Candy agreed. Aunt Bee being territorial about her kitchen was simply a bi-product of her wanting to feed her family the best. Her delivery was blunt and sometimes harsh, but deep down, she just wanted her family to feel her love with good food.

Kari put down her fork staring at Candy. "I have an idea."

Keying in quickly as to where Kari was going, Candy immediately started shaking her head. McKenna caught on quickly. Turning to Candy a huge smile stretched across her face.

"That would be awesome! It's time to shut people up. Christmas Eve dinner is a great opportunity."

"I don't think Auntie will want my help."

"Don't worry about Mama. I'll handle her. Besides, I'll be there to offer moral support, maybe peel potatoes and stuff." McKenna grinned nudging Candy's shoulder.

"Come on Candy Corn...you know you want to do it. All these years you've offered to help, I know you want a chance to strut your stuff."

Candy knew she'd give in when McKenna teased her with the rarely used moniker. "I don't strut, ma'am."

"You know what she means." Kari entered the fray to add her two cents. "You mean to tell me you learned recipes directly from *the* Miss Toni and you're gonna act like you're not itching to make them?"

"What?! No one tells me anything anymore. When did this happen?" McKenna folded her arms across her expanded midsection pouting.

"It was when I went to New York with Kenneth for Thanksgiving." Candy offered sheepishly.

"I had no idea the woman he'd told me helped raise him was *the* Miss Toni until I met her. She was really nice and offered to show me how to make a few recipes she'd learned from her grandma in Mississippi where she's from."

"I can't believe you were in the presence of soul food royalty and didn't tell anybody. Wait until I tell Driscoll that Kenneth has been holding out on us. When we went to DC earlier this year we waited over an hour to get into one of her restaurants."

"It was worth it though, wasn't it?" Kari asked with a grin.

"Every millisecond." McKenna concurred. "The food coma I had afterwards was absolute bliss."

A smile flirted at the corners of her mouth from the memory. She closed her eyes as if she could still taste the meal. Suddenly snapping her eyes open, she pierced Candy with a determined look.

"That settles it. I'm calling Mama and you're coming over to her house to help with Christmas Eve dinner." When Candy looked like she was preparing to protest, McKenna made a zipping motion across her lips. "Nope. It's settled. It's time to spread your wings little bird."

"You know...you're extra bossy right now." Candy grumbled.

"Blame the hormones." McKenna quickly responded.

Kari clapped her hands. "I'm excited like you're going to the play-offs, Candy." After a few beats, her smile faded.

"What is it? What changed in the last two seconds?" Candy asked, searching Kari's face.

"I got so caught up I forgot Daisuke and I will be at his parents' house this year because we were with the Frost family last year... I hate that I won't be there."

"So, what you're telling me is you just tossed me to the wolves and left me."

Looking contrite, Kari pushed the remains of the potato around on her plate. "I guess I can see what time we absolutely have to be at the Sano's, then I can stop by to see y'all first."

Placing her hand on Kari's to still it, Candy smiled. "I'm just messing with you. I wouldn't dream of asking you to rearrange your day. The Sano's are your family now, just as much as we are. Don't stress about it. I'll be okay."

"Of course you will." McKenna assured her. "Mama is all bark and no bite. She might grumble a little at first, but she'll be happy for the help."

A sense of togetherness enveloped Candy as she looked at her cousins. She and Kari had always been close, but she and McKenna had grown closer over the past couple of years. It was really nice to have their support.

She wasn't as confident as McKenna that it would be easy for her Aunt Bee to let someone, other than her daughter, assist with the meal. Still, she was kind of looking forward to being in the mix for a change. McKenna was right, she did want a chance to show she could do more than slap meat onto bread.

Chapter Twenty-Five
YOU TWO ARE ON BORROWED TIME

Mid-morning on December twenty-fourth, Kenneth maneuvered his SUV from his garage onto the street. Candy sat quietly in the passenger seat. The day started a little rough for her. The morning sickness had mostly tapered off, but she had occasional bouts.

He felt guilty as hell as he held a cool towel to the back of her neck while she presented the porcelain throne with last night's dinner. It was the part of expected parenthood most people didn't talk about. From the moment he learned for certain of his child's existence, he'd started researching.

He'd promised himself he would be actively involved. So, he devoured information—some of it was confusing and conflicting, but it didn't deter him. His time with his friends' children hadn't been hands on when they were small, so he needed all the help he could get.

Kenneth was determined to provide Candy and his child with whatever they needed or wanted. And, what she needed earlier was a cool towel and moral support. It no longer jarred him to think of being a father, and soon a husband. As far as he was concerned, Candy was his long before they had their first kiss.

His house was a short fifteen-minute drive from the Frost home, so their trip was relatively short. Traversing the long driveway, Kenneth noticed Driscoll's vehicle parked in the last of the three garage bays.

"It looks like the Kellys are here already." Dropping a hand on Candy's thigh, he gave it a squeeze.

"That's good. Even though McKenna told me she talked to Auntie, I feel better knowing she's already here."

Shutting off the engine, Kenneth turned to Candy. "Question. Why do you all treat your aunt like some fire-breathing dragon? She's not that bad, is she?"

Tipping her head to the side, she appeared to consider his words. "No...she's not. She has a sharp tongue, but most of the time, she's not intentionally hurtful."

"So, why are you nervous? You weren't anxious at all when we had your parent's over for dinner. I was more uptight than you were."

"Well, you were the one who had to tell my father you knocked me up before putting a ring on my finger."

The dimple Kenneth adored peeked from her cheek when she smiled at the memory of his fumbling around during dinner with her parents. The idea of looking her father in the face while admitting there'd be actual proof he'd fucked the man's daughter making an appearance in less than a year, was more than a little unnerving.

Kenneth didn't even want to think about the future of having the same discussion with some snot-nosed kid sniffing around his own daughter. The idea made him clench his fists. He quickly had to think of something else. He was getting riled up contemplating something that may never be.

For all he knew, they would only have sons. He was definitely considering more than one child, if she was onboard with it. Being an only child had been lonely at times. Hopefully, her having her sisters would make her amenable to at least two.

"We're not talking about me being tortured by your father." Kenneth shuddered at the recollection of Robert Hampton's steely gaze throughout the entire meal. "We're talking about why you're more nervous now."

"You don't get it. I know you were with Miss Toni and her family a lot, but for Southern black families, the holidays are a big deal when it comes to the meal. Reputations are made and broken around the food cooked for those particular events.

Until Labor Day, I hadn't ever been allowed to contribute more than paper goods or drinks because of an incident when I first attempted to help Auntie.

She asked me to put a pot on to boil eggs. The phone rang; so she had to step away. I went to the other room to watch TV while I waited for her to come back.

I don't remember where everyone else was at the time. I just remember her coming from the back of the house asking me what was burning. Turns out, I put the water in the pot, put the pot on the stove and turned it on. I never put the eggs in the pot, so the pot was ruined when the water boiled out leaving it just sitting there on the heat."

"How long ago was this?"

Candy looked to the side mentally calculating. "I'm thirty-four now, so it's been about fifteen years."

"In all that time, you never tried again until you took the class?"

"Oh no. I tried. I just didn't try at big family gatherings. I offered, but was shot down. Once you have a reputation for burning water, there's very little confidence in your ability to handle anything requiring the stove."

"That seems a little harsh."

"Like I said, holiday meals are a big deal down here. If you can't cook at a certain level, no one will trust your food. You can bring something, but it's likely you'll take the entire thing back home with you."

"If that's true, why do they always eat the cakes I bring?"

"Because they think you bought them from a bakery. If you'd showed up the first time and told them you baked it, it would've been a toss-up on if anyone ate it. Out of politeness, it would've been cut, but actually eaten..." Shaking her head Candy grimaced.

"That's kind of rude."

"So, you're telling me you eat food from just anyone who brings it into the office?"

"Fuck no." Kenneth nearly shuddered at the thought.

"Why not? Isn't it rude?" She replied cheekily.

He knew she was goading him, yet he walked right into it. "I don't eat food from just anyone in the office because of hygiene concerns. Cleanliness was drummed into our heads in culinary school, but before that I had Uncle Ray instilling those values in me. What I learned at the academy is everyone doesn't have the same ideas on what it means to be clean and hygienic."

"Exactly. So, unless you have someone to vouch for you, no one is going to just dig into food brought by a virtual stranger to us."

"Okay. You've made your point." Nodding he unclasped his seatbelt. "Time to go inside and restore your reputation."

Rounding the front of the vehicle, he helped her out before going to the rear to grab the box with their contribution to the meal. They'd done some of the prep at home to minimize the time needed to finish.

Although he'd attended various gatherings at the home of Driscoll's in-laws, he still rang the doorbell. Candy cut him a sideways glance before pushing the door open and stepping over the threshold. The garage opened right into the kitchen.

They were immediately engulfed by savory smells. Although no one was visible, the lights were on inside. Two large stock pots were on the stove. Kenneth heard the television from the adjoining seating area to the right of the kitchen. Closing the door behind him, he placed the box on the bar top while Candy moved farther into the house calling out to let everyone know they'd arrived.

"Aunt Bee, Uncle Drew?" Just as she walked past the raised countertop, moving toward the sitting room, her Aunt Bonita turned the corner into the kitchen.

"Oh! Goodness! Y'all scared me. I didn't hear you come in."

"Sorry, Auntie. We rang the bell and called out." Hugging her aunt then giving her a kiss on the cheek, she apologized again.

Brushing off the apology, the older woman greeted Kenneth before her gaze zeroed in on the box on the counter. He saw the questions burning behind her eyes, but a commotion drew everyone's attention to the other room.

When Kenneth saw Driscoll and Mr. Frost wrestling an overstuffed chair with the matching ottoman through the doorway from the basement, he rushed over to help, tilting the chair so he and Driscoll held it from opposite sides.

"What's going on?" Candy asked, drawing Kenneth's gaze making sure she was out of the way of the moving furniture.

They placed the chair in front of the sliding glass doors which led outside to the deck. It was positioned perfectly to view activity in the sitting room and the kitchen. The ottoman was placed in front of it leaving a small gap between them.

"Is this good, Mom?" Driscoll watched his mother-in-law waiting for a response.

"That should work, but I'm sure McKenna will let you know." Turning to Candy she answered her question. "They brought that up from Drew's lil man cave so my baby can have a comfortable seat in a good spot. The one's in the sitting room are too low to the floor."

"Oh. Where is McKenna?" Candy asked.

"Probably still in the restroom with DJ."

Walking toward the hallway, Driscoll tossed out, "I'll go check on them. DJ woke up on ten this morning. There's no telling what he's up to."

At the mention of his name, DJ's childlike shrieks and giggles reached them from somewhere down the long hallway. Picking up his pace, Driscoll went off in search of his family.

When Kenneth returned to the kitchen, Candy and her aunt were standing at the box he'd placed on the bar-top.

"What's all this?" Her aunt asked.

Kenneth was proud of the coolness in Candy's voice when she responded. Pulling the items out, starting with the cake container, Candy rattled off what was inside.

When she and McKenna discussed what Candy could contribute aside from helping her aunt with the meal itself, McKenna suggested candied yams since it was one of the recipes she'd gotten from his surrogate Aunt Toni. By the time they went to get groceries, the yams were sold out. So, she was substituting sweet potatoes.

Kenneth regarded the interaction watchfully. So far, her aunt hadn't made any comments to insinuate she didn't want Candy's help—which was a plus. By the time Candy was done showing Aunt Bonita the things she brought, McKenna walked through the sitting room with Driscoll and DJ trailing behind her.

Another round of hugs and greetings were required. Kenneth didn't mind. One of the reasons he'd kept coming around the Frosts was because they reminded him of holidays at his Aunt Toni's—down to the matriarch running people out of her kitchen. He and his uncle didn't socialize much with the Holmes family. Not after they took his Uncle Ray to court to try to overturn the terms of his parents' Will and take Kenneth away from him.

Their family was small to begin with. The way they attempted to tear Kenneth away from his Uncle Ray drove a wedge between them that not even thirty years had been able to heal. They still disapproved of Uncle Ray's *lifestyle*, so as far as Kenneth was concerned, they disapproved of him as well. He and his uncle were a package deal.

"Mama, Candy has been holding out on us." McKenna announced as she settled into the overstuffed chair.

Driscoll put DJ down to help her elevate her legs on the ottoman. The child toddled off to his grandfather, who scooped him up heading toward the door leading to the basement. Driscoll grabbed the remote and started flipping the television.

Folding her arms across her trim waist, McKenna's mother gave Candy a shrewd look while waiting for McKenna to elaborate.

"When she went to New York with Kenneth, she met *the* Miss Toni."

"What?! That woman is amazing! I'm so jealous."

"That's not all, Mama. She taught Candy a few of her family recipes."

Kenneth had to catch himself when Candy's aunt swatted at her arm. "Young lady, you have some explaining to do."

Ducking her head, Candy looked at her aunt bashfully. "Auntie, I didn't know y'all were such big fans of Miss Toni or I would've said something. She's best friends with Kenneth's Uncle Ray."

Aunt Bonita's gaze swung to Kenneth. "Is that so? So, it's really you who's been holding out?"

Putting his hands up in surrender, Kenneth tried to figure out the most graceful way to navigate the situation. Thankfully, Candy came to his rescue. Assuring her aunt they weren't withholding information on purpose, she tried to move the conversation back to the meal. Her aunt wasn't so easily deterred.

"I was excited when they were trying to get her to do a show on the cooking network. I just knew we were going to finally have some down-home cuisine on that channel for a change. So, how did you manage to get recipes when she won't even post them anywhere online?"

Candy didn't know, but Kenneth knew why his Aunt Toni took such a liking to her. He didn't interject his knowledge into the conversation; he simply smiled knowingly.

"I guess she just took a liking to me, Aunt Bee. We were talking while she was prepping for the holiday. The next thing I knew she told me to come back the next day so she could teach me her grandma's recipe for giblet gravy."

Her aunt's eyes widened with obvious joy. "Please tell me you wrote it down or committed it to memory. We haven't had any decent giblet gravy since Mama Hortense passed away. Mine is passable, but it's nothing like hers."

Taking a moment to brag on his woman, Kenneth spoke up. "Not only does she have it written down, she helped make it for our Thanksgiving meal. It was so delicious, there wasn't a drop left for leftovers."

With her gaze pinging between the two of them, her aunt assessed them before seeming to come to a conclusion. "Ok then. You can make it for us today Candy."

Kenneth saw Candy's entire body go rigid. Sliding his arm around her waist, he gave her a comforting squeeze. Murmuring in her ear, he assured her. "You've got this, Baby."

Her eyes told him what she refused to say aloud. Her confidence was wavering. Not only had her aunt given her an assignment, she'd given her an assignment she herself hadn't been able to complete to her own satisfaction. It was a tall order.

"If it makes you feel better, I'll stay with you." He whispered into her ear. A barely perceptible nod was her response. Some of the tightness in her shoulders eased, but she didn't completely release the tension.

Having dispensed her marching orders, Mrs. Frost propped her hip against the counter focusing her shrewd stare on Kenneth. "So, your uncle and Miss Toni are besties. How'd that happen?"

Although he'd never been on the receiving end of Bonita Frost's blunt scrutiny, he didn't let it bother him. Skirting some of the more unpleasant details, he explained how his uncle came to be best friends with the popular soul food restaurant owner.

When he was done, she wore a thoughtful expression. "It sounds like you had an interesting upbringing. That explains some things though."

His curiosity peaked; Kenneth didn't let the statement fall without a follow up. "Oh yeah? Such as?"

"When Driscoll first brought you here, you didn't seem uncomfortable being in an environment where you weren't in the racial majority. Drew and I have been together over forty years. With his parents' interracial marriage, it required some melding not everyone was comfortable with.

Papa Earl never seemed to have an issue when more of Mama Hortense's people showed up than his, but not all of the Frosts were as at ease with it. Over the years I learned to pick out those relatives who either wouldn't come back or would only show up once every couple of years.

Hearing about your circumstances with your uncle and his best friend helps me understand how you fit in so seamlessly. It must be like a taste of home for you."

Nodding in agreement, Kenneth added, "All that's missing are a few drag queens—with and without their stage make up."

At her quirked eyebrow, he elaborated. "Uncle Ray has an eclectic and diverse group of friends."

"Good to know." Looking at Candy, she cocked her head to the side. "Don't you have gravy to make? I should have everything you need in the pantry. There's also chicken in the refrigerator."

At her words, Candy pulled away to get to work on her assignment. He was certain she was still nervous, but as he watched her scan the shelves in the pantry, he noticed she was focused.

"Now..." The older woman put her hand atop the box containing the Sock it to Me cake McKenna loved so much. "Are you finally gonna tell me where you get these cakes? I've googled the logo and keep coming up empty."

Candy paused with a container of bouillon in her hand watching.

"I bake them." Kenneth supplied without a hint of guile.

Tipping her head to the side, Bonita Frost's honey-colored eyes regarded him skeptically. "Seriously?"

"Seriously. The cakes I bring here, I learned those recipes from my Aunt Toni. Uncle Ray isn't much of a baker. Although, I honed my skills in culinary school. I got my foundation from her."

Swatting his bicep, she turned first to McKenna who simply smirked, then to Driscoll who was studiously ignoring everything going on in the kitchen. *Smart man.*

"Why did you let me think you bought them? I was googling my little fingers to the bone when all this time, you were keeping secrets. You tricked me."

"Did I really though?" Kenneth tipped his head looking at her over his brow.

"You know good and well we didn't know the truth."

"You all made an assumption. I simply didn't correct you."

Narrowing her eyes, she leveled him a tried-and-true look used universally. "You're playing fancy with the words, but I'm gonna let it slide."

Candy skated by them placing her pantry haul on the other end of the countertop as she organized the ingredients. Pulling her into the conversation her Aunt Bonita pointed between the two of them.

"You two are on borrowed time. I expect to be introduced to my new best friend in the very near future."

Drawing his eyebrows together in confusion, Kenneth looked at Candy for guidance before switching his gaze back to the Frost family matriarch. "Ma'am?"

"Don't play. I'm not trying to replace your uncle. A person can have more than one best friend. He can still be Toni's bestie. I'll be her BFF."

With a flip of her head, she walked away issuing instructions. While Kenneth thought she'd bypassed his admission of attending culinary school, he was mistaken. He was given tasks which meant McKenna was left with nothing to do but relax and watch.

She wasn't one, but Bonita Frost ran her kitchen in a similar manner to a trained chef. For the next few hours, Kenneth was a dicing and prepping machine.

As the day progressed, more of the Frost family trickled in. While the numbers weren't as high as during the summer holidays, by the time dinner was ready to be served, there were close to twenty people in attendance. Children's laughter rang out against the background of adults catching up even though most of them probably spoke to one another daily.

Chapter Twenty-Six

MERRY CHRISTMAS, CANDY

Candy tried to still the trembling of her fingers as she prepared to de-bone the chicken she'd seasoned and boiled for the savory sauce known in the south as Giblet Gravy. From the outside looking in, some may say she was taking all of this too seriously. That assessment would come from someone who didn't know the history of black southern families when it came to food.

Being able to feed your family something sumptuous from what was essentially considered scraps was a skill not many possessed; those who did, were held in high regard. To be included in such an exclusive club was an honor.

Aunt Bonita admitting she couldn't do something and trusting Candy to do it was *huge*. No one, other than her aunt, had even attempted to make the gravy after Nana Hortense passed. It was an enormous vote of confidence.

Focusing on the task, while trying to shake off the anxiousness creeping in, Candy trained her eyes on the wings on the cutting board in front of her. Historically, every part of the chicken was used. To not do so was considered wasteful. So, the little bag in the center of the bird was removed and cooked to make the gravy. Those items were actually considered choice pieces of the bird.

While she was teaching Candy, Miss Toni said she'd long ago broken that particular tradition. Everyone wasn't a fan of eating the liver and gizzards, among the other things in the little packet. She used wings primarily because they weren't stringy. Remembering every detail of her lesson, Candy carefully separated the meat from the bone adding it to a bowl to be chopped before being put back into the pot.

Beside her, Kenneth chopped everything from onions, to celery depending on what Auntie said they needed. Since their relationship essentially began in a kitchen, they cooked together regularly. Sometimes she learned new things, others they simply enjoyed the time together unwinding. It was an intimacy she hadn't experienced prior to being with him.

At lunchtime, Aunt Bonita produced her homemade pastries filled with meat and sauce for them to have a light snack, but not spoil their appetites. Thankfully, Candy's stomach didn't reject the offering. The instances where food wasn't her friend were her reminder that she was actively growing another human in her womb.

She didn't remember the last time she had a flat stomach, so the roundness of her belly would have to get significantly bigger for her to have her body as the reminder of her new status. If it wasn't her body sending her cues, Kenneth's increased attentiveness served the same purpose.

He didn't care for her standing so much, so he used his daddy face to make her at least sit on one of the barstools whenever possible. It was completely unfair. Using that face outside of the bedroom was cruel. Although his eyes promised, *later*, her core required a solid ten minutes of talking to in order to calm down.

The whispered, "Good girl" in her ear restarted her negotiations with her greedy lady bits. Thankfully, a steady flow of relatives began to trickle in starting with her parents.

"Hey Mama, Daddy. Where are the kids?" Smiling at her parents, Candy looked around for her niece and nephews.

"Your sister has them. She wanted to get in some extra time since she's flying out tomorrow. They had Christmas at her place last night."

"Tomorrow? That's Christmas day." Candy's smile slipped in disappointment.

She hadn't seen much of Cherry the past few months, but it hadn't been due to Candy spending so much time with Kenneth. Cherry had been traveling more for work which meant she'd been unavailable for their monthly lunch or dinner dates. Candy could barely get her on the phone half of the time because she was in some international location more often than not.

So, time differences kept their schedules from syncing. Candy had to tell her own sister she was engaged via voicemail because her calls went unanswered. Kari was her best friend, but her little sister was also a confidant.

Roughly thirty minutes after her parents arrived, Cherry breezed into the house with the children in tow. The kids' cheeks were rosy and their faces stretched with wide smiles. It was obvious they enjoyed their time with their Aunt Cherry.

Accepting hugs and kisses, Candy greeted them listening to each chatter about their early Christmas with Auntie Cherry including how they got to have three Christmases—one with Cherry, then two more with their respective groups of grandparents. Their spirits didn't seem dampened by not having their parents with them, for that Candy was grateful.

Kaden, the most subdued of the three, was happy with the headphones Candy knew cost Cherry a pretty penny. Neveah held up her new tablet for Candy's inspection, loaded with books and games. Bryson thrust his Buzz Lightyear action figure up for her viewing pleasure, while explaining the interactive game which came with the toy.

Giving them each the time for her to appropriately ooh and aah over their haul, Candy walked them downstairs to the room Uncle Drew had converted into a play room when AJ's twins, Aminata and Aida were born.

Her uncle was stretched out in the middle of the floor while DJ tried to climb up the slide section of the indoor jungle gym. The flooring had been replaced with cushioned padding, so there wasn't a concern of him injuring himself. Bryson immediately went over to join him, while Kaden dropped his lanky frame into one of the gaming chairs as Nevaeh chose the bean bag chair closest to their uncle. It didn't take long for her to draw his attention to her new tablet. Knowing she'd spend as much time as he allowed explaining each new book and inter-active game, Candy stepped quietly from the room.

She met up with Cherry in the hallway just outside the entry leading to the sitting room next to the kitchen. Her sister held her phone to one ear with her other arm wrapped around her slender frame. Before she could wipe it away, Candy saw the look of frustration on her face. When she ended the call, Candy drew closer.

"Hey, Sis. Everything ok?"

Pasting a smile on her face which didn't quite reach her eyes, Cherry brushed her off. "Of course. It's all good. A quick work call with my colleague. We're flying out in the morning."

"Where to this time?"

"Portugal. First Lisbon, then a few other cities along the coast."

"How long will you be gone?"

"Two weeks."

"So, you'll ring in the new year in Portugal with your co-workers..."

"Nah..." Cherry smiled cheekily. "I'll find something way better to do. I'll have to spend enough time with them as it is."

"Okay then. Just be safe." Candy returned her grin.

"Mhmm. Enough about me. How are you? You've gone and got yourself engaged. To top it off you're already baking my next niece or nephew."

Reaching for Candy's left hand, she tugged. "Let me get a closer look at this ring."

Inspecting the square cut diamond which was set on a white gold band, surrounded by jewels in hues of red, pink, and gold, she whistled under her breath.

"This is gorgeous. Your man has good taste."

Turning Candy's hand this way and that to catch the light, she even-tually stopped staring at the ring. Looking up at Candy wistfully, she asked her next question.

"Do you know what would be really nice? If you could give me another niece—you know to even things out?"

"Cher, I'm positive I can't simply put in an order for a baby girl just to provide you with another niece."

Candy tipped her head looking down into her sister's pouting face.

Where Candy was tall and was what her mother called statuesque, Cherry was a pixie in comparison. Barely over five feet tall, her youngest sister's head didn't reach Candy's shoulder.

"Besides," she nudged Cherry in the side, "I know you only want another niece so you can dress her up like you. You've been salty ever since Neveah stopped letting you dress her like your mini-me."

Cherry's face scrunched. "She didn't have to do me like that. I didn't ask too often."

"Cher...Did you forget you were talking to me?"

"You know what? Forget you!" Cherry stomped her foot before succumbing to laughter. She knew exactly how she looked when she did that. Pointing at Candy, she issued her threat.

"Don't you dare call me Tinker Bell. I'm not above telling Kenneth every embarrassing story I can recall from our childhood."

Candy's giggles immediately dried up. "You wouldn't?!"

"I would." Cherry stated with a mischievous glint in her eyes.

Putting her hands up in surrender, Candy's lip quirked into a half smile. "Okay. Fine. You win, Tink."

Walking backwards, Cherry entered the room. "Hey Kenneth! Did Candy ever tell you about the time she mistook a bar of soap for a piece of cake?"

When Candy picked up her pace, Cherry turned and bolted away giggling maniacally. Ignoring their mother's scolding, Candy chased Cherry around the kitchen table. Their play was cut short by their Aunt Bonita threatening to withhold dinner if they didn't stop playing in her kitchen.

For a few minutes it was almost like they were kids again. The stress had receded from Cherry's face and she was fully present. Candy hadn't realized how much she missed those types of moments with her sister. Cassandra had done nothing more than tolerate them. However, Candy and Cherry had always had a tighter bond, despite the four-year age gap.

As punishment for running in the house, they had to finish setting the tables for dinner. Other than random giggles, they worked together quietly. With the exception of when Kenneth came to check on her for the millionth time that day.

Cherry couldn't resist making googly eyes and saying "aww" at his attentiveness. She didn't hear him promising to spank Candy's ass later. She probably thought Candy's shiver was from the affectionate kiss to her cheek instead of the anticipation it actually was.

When it was time for dinner, the upper floor of the house buzzed with activity to get the children situated, transferring the dishes from the kitchen to the large dining room then plating the food. It was a chaotic symphony, but Candy loved every minute of it.

Conversation was intermittent as everyone dug into the bounty before them. Deciding what to put on her plate that her little passenger wouldn't reject was like playing the weirdest game of Match Candy had ever participated in. None of the items she helped her aunt prepare had caused queasiness from the smell, so she put small portions of them on her plate.

She couldn't even have the green bean casserole her mother brought within five feet of her, so it was definitely out. That stung because she normally loved her mother's casserole. Her mom assured Candy she wasn't offended since she knew all too well what it was like to play food roulette.

"Grandma, can I have more of the orange things?" Bryson's little voice cut into the conversational hum.

"Which orange things, Bry?" There were glazed carrots along with the sweet potatoes Candy made.

"Those." Pointing to the glass container of sweet potatoes, he licked his lips.

"These...are candied sweet potatoes your Auntie Candy made." Aunt Bonita took his plate adding more of the side dish.

"Really?" Papa Earl asked.

Everyone was well aware of Candy and her sisters' lack of culinary skill—well their history. She was breaking that reputation. Hopefully.

"Yes, sir. I did."

Lifting her chin, she smiled brightly at her grandfather, who tapped his nose then pointed at her. His cornflower blue eyes twinkled at his silent message displaying his pride in her.

"She also made the giblet gravy." Her aunt supplied, although no one had asked. If Candy wasn't mistaken, there was a hint of pride in her voice.

"You don't say?" Papa Earl was practically beaming. "Good job, Candy Corn. It's as delicious as your nana used to make. God rest her soul."

"You don't have to say that, Papa." Candy's voice, thick with emotion, was barely above a whisper.

"I'm simply stating the truth as I know it. Your nana would be proud of you for carrying on her tradition."

Tears pricked Candy's eyes at such high praise. Before the wetness could drip down her cheeks, Kenneth was there swiping her tears away.

"Well, Dad, now you know who to call when you have a taste for it. I'll get her to make you some for New Year's when I make you another pan of dressing."

Candy's head whipped around at her Aunt Bonita's promise to her grandfather. She had to be in the midst of a fever dream. There was no way she'd heard what she thought she'd heard. Unfortunately for Candy, her Aunt Bonita saw the incredulous look on her face.

"What? Don't look at me like you didn't know you put your foot in this food." Lifting one eyebrow her aunt dared her to dispute her words. "Now, y'all go on and finish eating. I'm ready for a piece of the cake Kenneth made."

Her statement about Kenneth making the cake set off another round of questions and dialogue. With Kenneth's arm wrapped around her shoulder, Candy leaned into him relishing in his warmth while she watched her family banter and enjoy their meal. Logging it into her memories, she vowed to never forget this moment.

Kissing her cheek, Kenneth nuzzled her neck before tickling her eardrum with his words. "Merry Christmas, Candy."

Epilogue

One Year later

Candy looked around the table at her family enjoying their annual Christmas Eve meal. A lot had happened in the past twelve months. She and Kenneth had decided on a small, intimate wedding with just close family and friends right after the new year.

One of Kenneth's Christmas presents had been to present Candy with four options for the home he would purchase for them. She wasn't allowed to consider price, only what she could see herself living in with him. By Valentine's Day, they were all moved in to their new five bedroom, four and a half bath home.

On the 4th of July, Vesta Alexanderia Holmes came into the world changing their lives again. They were still adjusting. Candy no longer accepted last minute bookings—no matter the client. She put her family first. Which also meant nights on movie sets were kept to a minimum.

Kenneth took care of getting Vesta to and from daycare since Candy's days tended to start much earlier than his. She could pick the baby up, but he enjoyed having those father-daughter moments together. His princess had him twined around her finger before she made her appearance; afterwards, it was a wrap. He denied her very little. Thankfully, she wasn't a demanding child. What she liked most were cuddles and things that made her giggle.

Vesta was currently gumming a teething toy grinning at her Uncle-Papa who'd not been two steps away from her since he landed at the airport earlier in the week. Uncle Ray took his grandpa duties seriously, video calling regularly to talk to Vesta even though the most the baby ever did was offer him slobbery giggles.

He had regular competition from Cherry who sent presents from wherever she was in the world at almost the same frequency. Candy had no doubt at least half of the cute little outfits her sister sent had a twin in Cherry's size just waiting to be worn.

Candy had to put her foot down on the gifts. Between Cherry and Uncle Ray, it seemed like Vesta was getting something every week from the time she was born. Vesta wasn't nearly old enough for the miniature chef's kitchen Uncle Ray sent her in advance of Christmas. She couldn't even stand yet, let alone use the functioning stove and cookware.

Candy's gaze fell on her younger sister. Cherry's face was devoid of the stress she'd carried for almost two years. Candy was certain it was due to Cherry resigning from her job. While her parents were concerned about Cherry not having a steady income, Candy knew Cherry. She wouldn't walk away without a plan. Cherry wasn't as flighty as people believed her to be. Candy was sure her sister would be just fine.

Between the family members present, the festive decorations, sounds, combined with smells made the holiday complete. She felt fully immersed in the Frost family celebration while forging new traditions with Kenneth and her new family. Candy couldn't ask for anything more.

Pausing in the action of rubbing her hands together, Candy stared at Kenneth silhouetted in the doorway between the bedroom and ensuite bath. She'd just finished moisturizing her legs.

The man was butt ass naked with the exception of the Santa cap sitting on his head at a rakish angle. His semi-flaccid length hung between his thighs with what looked like red and white striped paint covering it.

Openly gawking, she pointed to the thickening rod. "What is that supposed to be?"

Kenneth's lips spread in a cocky grin. "This? It's a candy cane. Wanna lick?"

To Candy's amazement, he began swiveling his hips making his hardening shaft rotate helicopter style. The silly grin on his face coupled with his gyrations and wide-spread arms were too much. She dissolved into a fit of giggles.

One second she was wiping her mirth-filled eyes the next she was caught up in Kenneth's arms staring into his blazing grey glare.

"Are you laughing at me woman? After I went through the trouble of making tonight's lesson pleasurable, in addition to being educational, this is the thanks I get?"

Candy's laughter calmed enough for her to ask, "What lesson?"

"We've started our pastry chef series remember?" Carrying her across the room, he placed her on their California King platform bed.

Kenneth still occasionally taught adult cooking classes at the culinary academy, but he maintained his duty to give Candy her own, personal, *lessons*. She no longer needed them, but he insisted.

Untying the sash of her robe, he slid it from her shoulders before reaching for the hem of her silky nightgown and slipping it off over her head. Kneeling on the bed between her spread legs, he threaded his fingers into her thick mane pulling her closer.

Licking her lips as she stared at his red and white striped cock, she lost her train of thought when a pearlescent droplet appeared at the tip. Unconsciously, she gripped his thighs then leaned forward to swipe it off with her tongue only to be tugged back by Kenneth's grip on her hair.

"Not yet. Don't you want to hear about all the possible applications of edible body paint?"

Looking at him through the veil of her eyelashes, she shook her head. "Not really, but if you'd rather talk about it than have me lick my candy cane, go ahead."

Her words were accompanied by her fingers slipping between his legs to cradle his scrotum. Giving them a gentle squeeze, she once again leaned forward to swipe at the precum dripping from the head of his shaft. Kenneth offered no resistance as her hot mouth engulfed his turgid length.

Humming around the flavor of the body paint, combined with his natural essence, Candy pleasured her husband with a singular focus. Her channel clenched and leaked begging to be filled, but she ignored it in place of providing him with maximum enjoyment.

Soon, both of Kenneth's hands were on her head as he fucked her mouth. Aroused beyond comprehension, Candy fisted the part of him that wouldn't fit into her mouth stroking it in time with the motion of his hips.

"Fuck, Baby. You're gonna make me—"

Kenneth's choppy words cut off as his hips jerked one final time and his seed spurted into Candy's throat without warning. Pulling his spent shaft from her mouth, he pressed his forehead to hers staring into her eyes.

Smiling at his disoriented look and heavy breathing, Candy's arousal thrummed in the background of her feelings. Ever-present, but not demanding immediate satisfaction.

Once his breathing evened out, Kenneth captured her lips in a searing kiss. Sharing his taste with him, she opened her mouth to allow his tongue to duel with hers. Leaning over her, he pressed until she fell back onto the bed. Issuing one last, firm peck to her plump lips, he pulled away.

One corner of his mouth tipped up giving him a roguish expression. "Payback time."

Kissing his way down her torso, he worshipped her breast before he continued pressing loving pecks on the stretch marks on her abdomen thanking her for sheltering his child there. By the time he reached the apex of her thighs, her core was glistening with moisture.

Stilling the writhing of her legs by hooking his arms around her thighs, he ran his nose up her slit, nuzzling her folds. Before she could complain of him teasing her, he parted her labia with his tongue and sucked her pearl into his mouth.

Stars burst behind Candy's eyelids as she slammed them shut. Her pleasure had ridden just beneath the surface while she pleased him so it took virtually no effort for him to bring her to her peak. With her chest heaving, she tried to keep a grasp on reality.

When she was able to lift her eyelids, she looked down to see Kenneth lying on his stomach with her thighs thrown over his shoulders; his grey gaze focused completely on her.

"That's one." He growled then dove back into her velvet walls with his tongue.

Candy lost track of the number of orgasms she experienced before Kenneth allowed her a short reprieve. She almost wished Vesta would do her a solid and cry out for attention, but she knew it was a lost cause. Uncle Ray had set himself up in the room right next to hers so that he would hear her if she so much as breathed too hard.

Following her last back-arching toe-curling release, her torturer kissed his way back up her body ending at her lips with a lingering peck. With her eyelids still closed, Candy felt the bed dip as Kenneth rose. A few seconds later, the sound of running water hit her ears.

She'd almost drifted off to the splashing sounds when Kenneth scooped her from the bed. Her body hadn't released all of the weight she'd gained while pregnant with Vesta, but it didn't stop him from carrying her at his whim.

Stopping next to the sunken jacuzzi tub, he guided her into the water before climbing in behind her. Her hungry gaze devoured his muscular frame as he stepped in. He'd showered as he ran her bath, removing any remnants of the body paint.

They didn't need words as he soaped her washcloth and cleansed her body. With a small child, their lovemaking sessions weren't the marathons they'd had pre-Vesta, but they were no less satisfying. Candy lethargically allowed Kenneth to pamper her knowing the next time she experienced such treatment could be at least a month away.

Dropping the towel, Kenneth's hands dropped below the surface of the water seeking her slick core. Regardless of the number of times she'd reached her pinnacle, her pussy longed to be filled with his thickness— to be stretched by his girth in all the best ways.

Always willing to oblige her needs, he strummed her pearl as he dipped two fingers inside her grasping walls. It wasn't enough. She may have said as much aloud since she soon found herself looking into her husband's handsome face as he lowered her onto his straining cock.

Bliss rolled across Candy's body in waves as she sank onto Kenneth's thick length. He filled her so perfectly; it was hard to imagine anything being more perfect than having him inside her.

The sound of his palm smacking her ass rang out into the room. The sting snapped her eyes open.

"You know the rules. Eyes on me." He growled. Adding another stinging smack to the other cheek before pumping his hips up he issued his orders. "Now ride this cock like you mean it."

With his hands on her cheeks assisting, Candy rocked her hips gliding on and off his turgid shaft. Gaining her second wind, she shook her ass, bouncing on his dick hurtling them both toward orgasm with the strength of a hurricane tossing a tug boat around in the ocean.

Reaching their peak together, Kenneth tugged her down. Her breasts pressed into his chest as he hugged her to him while his hips jerked, punching his cock as deep as he could inside her as he spilled his seed. Candy could do nothing more than rest against his hard chest and accept the pleasurable assault on her senses.

Later, as they lay beneath the covers, Candy cuddled into Kenneth's side listening to his steady breathing thinking of everything that had come to pass over the last year and a half.

Their passing meeting at McKenna and Driscoll's wedding gave her no indication of the man who would step into her life and give her the purest love she'd ever experienced. He'd encouraged and inspired her to stretch herself which was a tremendous boost to her confidence in other areas of her life.

Although parenthood came into the equation more quickly than she would've liked, she wouldn't change a thing. Uncle Ray's favorite line from Common's song, *The Light,* immediately came to mind. *It don't take a whole day to recognize sunshine.*

"Hey!" Candy cried out when the hold Kenneth had on her tightened and one hand traveled to her ass giving one plush cheek a hearty squeeze.

"I must not have done my job well enough. You're thinking so loud, it's keeping me awake."

Flipping her onto her back, then tossing the covers aside, he had his head buried between her thighs before she could catch a breath.

"Wait, wait, wait! It was good stuff. I promise." Candy really wasn't sure her body could handle even one more orgasm.

"Shhh...Baby. I got you. Now be quiet and let me have one more taste of my Christmas Candy."

With those words, her husband set about devouring his favorite treat. Her.

The End

Acknowledgments

The life of an independent author isn't all sunshine and rainbows, but there are people who make the work and effort worth every minute. I've been fortunate to have some amazing people supporting me throughout this process. I have the absolute best writing partners in Brianna Q. Price and Niccoyan Zheng. They're the first to read anything I write and are always supportive while keeping it real. Having other, more established authors, willing to step in to Beta read and help me be a better author is invaluable. Thank you Dahlia Rose and Michel Prince. My team of Beta Readers is small, but they are always ready and willing to lend their eyes and expertise to any story that I present them with. I sincerely appreciate all of you. Last but not least, the readers who continue to buy, review, support and reach out on social media. I wouldn't be able to continue to do this without you. My sincere thanks.

About the Author

Darie McCoy is an independent author of contemporary, interracial and paranormal/shifter romance books. A reader first, she enjoys reading books across many genres although romance holds a special place in her heart. Her experience working in a STEM field offers her a unique perspective which she uses in each story she pens.

Her first novel, *For Real,* began as a short story written for a reader competition during an Authors and Readers conference. It was published in November of 2021. To date, she's published three novels, a novella and has an active serial on Kindle Vella.

Born and raised in the south, Darie stands by the staunchly held southern sentiments that the best tea is sweet tea and college football is life.

Also by Darie McCoy

For Real

Sano's Queen

Chosen

Involuntary

Draft Pick (Kindle Vella Series)